Ghostwriters In The Sky

The Camilla Randall Mysteries

#1

a comedy

Anne R. Allen

Published by Kotu Beach Press

ISBN: 978-1502704863

Snarky, delicious fun! A laugh-out-loud mashup of romantic comedy, crime fiction, and satire: Dorothy Parker meets Dorothy L. Sayers.

Perennially down-and-out socialite Camilla Randall a.k.a. "The Manners Doctor" is a magnet for murder, mayhem and Mr. Wrong, but she always solves the mystery in her quirky, but oh-so-polite way.

Usually with more than a little help from her gay best friend, Plantagenet Smith.

Ghostwiters In The Sky is the second in this humorous mystery series, but it can be read as a stand-alone.

"Twisted chick-lit noir with a side of funny!"

"This book is hysterically funny AND accurately depicts the Santa Ynez Valley. Anne Allen gets it right, down to the dollar bills stuck on the ceiling of the Maverick Saloon. It was so fun to read as she called out one Valley landmark after another. Allen got the local denizens right, too"

"This feisty tale trips along like an A-list hooker in high heels, street-wise and chic."

Chapter 1— Girl of the Golden West

THE SUBWAY CAR WAS SO crowded I couldn't tell which one of the sweaty men pressing against me was attached to the hand now creeping up my thigh.

I should have known better than to wear a dress on a day I had to take the subway, but in the middle of a New York heat wave, I couldn't face another day in a pants suit.

I tried to lurch away from the large man in shirtsleeves who looked to be the most likely owner of the hand. One of his beefy paws clutched the pole just above me, but the other was invisible in the crush of bodies. Getting away from him meant I had to press closer to a besuited Wall Street type, who was engrossed in reading a newspaper over the shoulder of a woman in the seat nearest us.

I managed to move a few inches, but the hand continued its relentless journey northward.

Maybe it was the pimply kid in the Marilyn Manson tee shirt who had insinuated himself into the already overflowing car at Columbus Circle. He'd pressed in to join the three of us who had already staked claims on the center pole.

I jabbed the boy in the ribs with an elbow. He grunted an obscenity.

But the hand continued to creep.

The man in the suit turned away from his reading and whispered in my ear.

"Dr. Manners, I've been a bad, bad boy."

My throat closed. The guy wasn't just grabbing an anonymous feel. This was personal. He knew I wrote the *Manners Doctor* column. Did he imagine my good manners would keep me from protecting myself?

I reached behind me and slid my hand in between our pressed-together bodies. Grasping his wrist, I tried to pull his hand from between my legs. But he dug his fingers into my thigh and hung on.

As the train mercifully jolted to a stop, I stepped back and brought my stiletto heel down on the pervert's foot. As he yelped in pain, I pushed through the crowd and made it to the doors. A stop too soon, but I'd certainly rather walk up to West 69th Street, even in this sticky heat, than be molested for one more minute. How did millions of women ride the subway, day after day?

Life without money was turning out to be way harder than I'd ever imagined.

I hoped my lawyer was going to make my husband's lawyers to see reason soon. Jonathan was being so cruel about the divorce. I had no idea why. It's not as if I was the one who had been filmed by a paparazzo while receiving the ministrations of a street hooker on Sunset Boulevard.

I ran through the turnstile and was halfway up the escalator before it occurred to me I could simply have waited for a less crowded train. No point now. I'd have to swipe my MetroCard again, and these days I needed to pinch every penny.

I walked out into a wall of hot air. This had to be the hottest May on record. If the rest of the summer was like this, I'd actually be glad I'd had to give up my midtown office. It felt like defeat to give up the keys to the landlord this afternoon, but maybe everything would turn out for the best.

But it looked like I wasn't going to get relief from harassment anytime soon. The heat seemed to bring out the creep in everybody. A taxi driver who was stopped at the light leered as he called out to me.

"Hey, Dr. Manners, I've been bad. Wanna give me a spanking?"

What was it with these people? Had they all turned into raving sado-masochists?

I crossed Broadway as quick as my old Manolos would carry me. I'd bought them in the days when I could afford taxis. Now my feet screamed for a pair of Sketchers. The heel was in need of repair and I could feel it wobble as I tried to walk faster.

Too late. A family of hefty tourists in cargo shorts seemed to have overheard the driver as they barreled out of Lincoln Center toward the Metro station.

"It is her!" said the teenaged boy. "The Manners Doctor. She used to be married to that TV guy — you know, on *The Real Story*." He aimed his camera phone at me.

I put on my New York street face and stared straight ahead — pretending I saw nothing and heard nothing — as all mannerly New Yorkers do when sharing a crowded sidewalk. But the family kept coming at me, like a bunch of corn-fed storm troopers. I didn't know whether to brazen it out or turn and run.

"I heard she does weird sex stuff," the teen girl said.

"Shut up with that filth," said the mom.

"I'm sure it's her. I saw her on *Entertainment Tonight*," said the boy.

"Not every fancy lady is an effing celebrity," said the dad, staring at me as if I were something in a store window. "She doesn't even look like Kahn's wife. The Manners Doctor has shorter hair. And bigger hooters."

Right. I didn't even look like me because I hadn't been able to afford to go to the hairdresser for months. I'd probably lost weight too. The stress of the divorce had not been kind to my digestive tract.

At least I didn't run into any more perverts as I walked up Lincoln Square and made my sweaty way to my co-op building on 69th Street. But it wasn't a fun walk. The humidity had to be at least 90%.

Habib, the doorman, gave me a dark look when I arrived. I hadn't tipped him for over a month. As he held the door for me, he gave a smirk. A smirk—from the ever-glowering Habib. Maybe the heat really had made everybody in the City turn into lunatic creeps.

Then I saw the copy of today's *Post* on the table in the lobby.

Damn. There was a picture of me above the fold. An awful thing showing me on Jonathan's arm, looking slightly tipsy. Probably at the Emmys last year. The paper looked rumpled and discarded, so I didn't feel bad about picking it up and giving it a read. I'd made Page Six way too many times since Jonathan's scandal stirred up the media jackals, but I'd never been on page one. I couldn't imagine what they'd dreamed up to say about Jonathan and me now.

I shook the paper open I saw the headline: KAHN REVEALS TRUTH ABOUT KINKY DR. MANNERS.

What fresh hell had Jonathan invented for me now?

Clutching the paper, I ran to the elevator and slammed the button for the sixth floor, hoping nobody would rush in and try to share the car. I wanted to be alone when I read the toxic thing.

I worked on calming my breathing to prepare myself.

But there was no possible preparation for the horrible

words swimming in front of me. Jonathan had apparently told the *Post* reporter that he wasn't the only one with an edgy sex life.

He accused me of being into sadomasochism. Me. And oh my god — necrophilia and bestiality. Dead people? Animals? Where was this coming from? If anything, our sex life had been too vanilla. That's certainly what he whined about all the time. I'd always presumed that was why he'd been getting more interesting flavors from Los Angeles street hookers.

How could I have loved this man? Maybe I really was a masochist.

No. I never loved the man who gave that interview. I'd loved a Jonathan who was a kind, loving friend, and an honorable journalist. A Jonathan who hadn't existed for a long time. I guess I was the only one who hadn't realized the old Jonathan was gone.

Somehow I managed to keep the tears from flowing until I got safely into my apartment. Then I let out a wail so loud it felt as if it came from somebody other than me — some wild animal that was trapped inside and screaming for its life.

I was probably terrifying the doddery Grimsby sisters upstairs. But I couldn't stop. I yelled and crumpled the copy of the Post in to a ball, threw it toward the trash, then yelled some more. I took off my Manolos and threw them hard against my closet door.

Unfortunately, one hit my dresser and knocked half my collection of photographs on to the floor. I could hear the shatter of glass. I ran to assess the damage and saw what I'd done. I'd broken the protective glass and bent the frame on my favorite photograph. The one of me and Plantagenet Smith.

It had been taken at some debutante party over twenty years ago. When Plant and I were impossibly young and beautiful. When I loved Plant with all my heart and soul, and he loved me, I think, in his way. Before I met Jonathan. Before

I betrayed Plant by getting him to go on Jonathan's damn TV show to be ambushed.

I slid the photo from the frame. It didn't seem damaged, thank goodness. It was irreplaceable. If Plant had ever kept a copy, he'd never share it with me. He'd refused to answer my letters and calls for the past five years. He hated me for what I'd done. And I couldn't really blame him.

Stifling new tears, I stomped into the kitchen and reached into the freezer for the Ben and Jerry's. But there was no Chocolate Fudge Brownie left. Just an old half-eaten tub of Cinnamon Bun covered with icky crystals. I really didn't like Cinnamon Bun.

But it only took me about three seconds to inhale it.

Then I called my lawyer. The voice mail at Barrowman, Hodges and Fine said Mr. Hodges was not available. The creep hadn't been available for weeks now because I hadn't paid his bill, but how could I when the checks never appeared? The divorce was final three months ago. I was supposed to be getting regular payments from Jonathan. But so far I had not seen a penny. I tried to leave a coherent message, but my tongue was twisted with rage and ice-cream freeze.

I checked my own voice mail, expecting some frantic calls from friends who'd seen the article. I didn't use a cell phone anymore so they wouldn't have been able to reach me if they'd read the paper this morning.

I'd decided to stop carrying a phone when I left Jonathan. The media harassed me constantly, no matter how many times I changed numbers.

So I had the Manners Doctor write a column about the evils of portable phones and swore off them forever. I really did hate the way they turned people into blabbering idiots incapable of carrying on an uninterrupted conversation. Well-bred people should not live in servitude to electronic devices.

I liked my land line. Only a few people had the unlisted

number. It might make me a dinosaur, but I got to choose when and if I wanted to have a phone conversation.

But no. Nobody had called. Not even my mother.

That was a blessing. Maybe I could keep it from her. Thank goodness she was off sailing the Mediterranean with her new boyfriend Count Whatsis. Pure Eurotrash, but he'd keep her occupied — at least until he figured out most of the family money was gone.

I picked up the phone and dialed my realtor. She'd been a pretty good friend since I'd split from Jonathan. I met her when she helped me find this apartment.

But she didn't pick up. I couldn't bring myself to say anything on her voice mail. My assistant didn't pick up either. Just as well. She wasn't happy that I'd shut the office. I guess I wouldn't be either, if I had to give up a glamorous Manhattan job and telecommute from my parents' house in Queens. I didn't feel up to talking to any of my old friends in Long Island. I'd been kind of shunned by the social register crowd since the scandal of the divorce.

Maybe it was for the best. I had no idea what to say to anybody. And I didn't want to see people. Or for people to see me.

I was going to have to stay in this apartment forever.

If I could afford it. I looked at the stack of unpaid bills by the phone. The co-op board had sent a second notice on last month's maintenance fees. The co-op board. What were they going to do when they read the *Post*? People had been asked to vacate for much less.

I paced my two tiny rooms, banging open cupboard doors looking for something. I didn't even know what. Probably chocolate. But I didn't find anything chocolaty but two stale PowerBars.

However, I did discover the bottle of Glenfiddich Mother's drunken stockbroker friend brought when I agreed to have dinner with him last month. He'd left almost half the bottle. If there was ever a time for scotch, this was it. I poured myself two fingers and added a little water and some ice. It stung on the way down, but I felt better once I finished it. I refilled the glass and skipped the water this time.

When I was on my third refill, the phone rang.

I checked caller ID. Not a number I recognized. It had a California area code.

Jonathan. Jonathan the Monster must be calling me from his fancy new digs in Malibu. Which he much preferred to that palace we used to rent in Southampton, he'd said in his last semi-toxic missive. His lawyer must have given him the number.

The phone kept ringing.

I certainly wasn't going to pick up. I wondered if he'd leave a message. I took deep breaths, telling myself to be calm and ignore whatever sadistic nonsense he tried to pull.

Finally I heard a voice come out of the answering machine—deep and raspy—not at all like Jonathan's mellifluous broadcaster's tones. In fact, even though the voice was in a low register, it didn't sound male. And something about it was familiar.

"I hope you're not out of town, Camilla dear." An old lady's voice. "Have I reached the right Camilla Randall? The Manners Doctor? Your mother gave me your number last month when we were fundraising for the Equine Rescue Ranch. I'm Gabriella Moore."

Gabriella Moore, the actress. No wonder I recognized the voice. I'd loved her TV show when I was a child. *Big Mountain*—all about lovely horses and wayward cowboy sons. I had no idea she was still alive. I hadn't heard anything about her in twenty-five years. Why would she be calling me?

I picked up.

"Miss Moore! What a delightful surprise. I grew up with *Big Mountain*. It was my absolutely favorite TV show when I was little."

Gabriella gave her signature throaty laugh.

"Don't admit that to anybody, honey. It's like sticking a sign on your forehead that says, 'pushing forty.' But I sure am glad you're a fan. Maybe you'll be willing to help me out? I have an emergency here."

"Where? In California?" No way was I going anywhere in the vicinity of Mr. Jonathan Kahn.

"Yes. The Golden West Writers Conference. I run it here on my ranch in Santa Ynez. Festivities start on Thursday and I've just lost my only nonfiction workshop leader. Would you be interested in giving a little presentation about how to write a syndicated column? The pay's not great, but I'm sure that wouldn't matter to a Randall. It's a chance to promote your column. And don't you have a couple of books out?"

My books were out all right. Out of print. But I wasn't going to tell her that.

"Santa Ynez? Isn't that where the Reagans used to live? The Western White House and all that?" Maybe I should consider it. I'd stayed out of the spotlight as much as possible since the divorce, but my readership had been falling off. It was probably time for me to let people know I was still alive and kicking.

"Yup. Prettiest country on earth. Golden hills, fat cattle, and vineyards as far as the eye can see. Just north of Santa Barbara. This place was a dude ranch back in the 1920s. And hundreds of old westerns were filmed here, back in the day. Come on. How about a nice change of pace? And a paid vacation. All you have to do is talk about your column to a few wannabe writers. Marie Osmond had an emergency and cancelled on me so I'm really up the creek without a paddle, honey."

I was being asked to stand in for a has-been TV celebrity who wrote little sewing books. Mother would have a fit.

But Santa Barbara was far enough from Los Angeles that I probably wouldn't run into Jonathan. And going anywhere outside the circulation area of the *New York Post* would be awfully nice.

"Is it hot there?" I looked out my bay window at the sweaty, shirt-sleeved crowd on the sidewalk. Odd to see so many people gathered in this residential neighborhood.

"These hills can be toasty in the daytime, but it's a dry heat, Gabriella said. "And the nights are cool."

At first I thought the crowd down there must be tourists, since they all had cameras, but I realized what was happening when one of them aimed his camera at my window.

Not tourists. Paparazzi. Damn.

"It's a four-day conference, but you can stay longer if you like," Gabriella said. "Free room and board."

"I'd love to." I pulled the drapes shut.

Now I just had to figure out how to survive until Thursday with no Ben and Jerry's. With any luck, by the time I got back, the *Post* article would be history, and some other celebrity would be in the media crosshairs.

Chapter 2—Ghost Mountain Rider

THE FLIGHT TO CALIFORNIA wasn't too bad, considering how miserable traveling in coach was these days. But our take-off was delayed, and some mechanical drama during a layover at Dallas/Fort Worth kept us grounded for a couple of extra hours.

At least nobody in the airport seemed to recognize me. A few dogged paparazzi had followed my cab to Kennedy, and I was very ready for my fifteen Warhol minutes to be over. When we finally landed in Santa Barbara, I felt free for the first time since the story broke on Monday.

A little too free. I seemed to have been unencumbered of my luggage. At the baggage claim, I was told my suitcases had probably taken an alternate flight.

I tried to get the baggage clerk to show some interest in finding them — they were Louis Vuitton — but he looked at me with such blank boredom, I wondered if I'd ever see my things again. Thank goodness I had a few necessities in my carry-on.

I looked around the little Santa Barbara airport for anybody who looked like greeters for the conference, but saw no likely candidates. I didn't really expect Gabriella's people to wait so long. It was nearly seven. The opening reception would be going strong by now.

I flagged a taxi and told the driver the address in Santa Ynez. The unsmiling little man seemed to speak no English, but he nodded seemed to understand when I said "Santa Ynez." He repeated the name of the town with lilting Spanish inflection.

He didn't seem to be speeding, but we arrived at our destination in amazingly good time. I thanked him and gave him a couple of twenties, hoping that would be enough. He gave a sudden wide grin, jumped back in the taxi, and took off so fast I wondered if he might be dealing with some sort of bathroom emergency.

I peered through the evening gloom, but saw no sign of Gabriella's ranch—or the writers who should have been gathered for the opening reception dinner.

I didn't see any golden hills, fat cattle or vineyards, either. Nothing but the strained quiet of over-manicured suburbia.

An icky sensation ran down my neck.

I could feel someone watching me—lurking in a shadowy open garage across the street. I heard the snarl of a motorcycle engine and reached in my bag for the hairspray—a useful weapon in a pinch.

I headed for the corner with purposeful stride—or as close an approximation of stride as I could achieve in my wobbly Manolos. Under the street lamp, I saw a sign that said, "Santa Ynez Ct."

Oops. The driver must have thought I meant the Court, not the town. That's why the trip from the airport had been so improbably short. I must still be in Santa Barbara.

And I'd really over-tipped that driver.

I told myself to think positive: be grateful to the airline for losing my luggage. This would be a whole lot worse if I were carrying all those suitcases. I've never learned to pack light.

A motorcycle roared down the driveway from the ominous garage. I clutched the hair spray and re-arranged my face into a stiff smile.

The rider pulled up beside me and lifted his face guard.

"Doctor Manners? I thought I recognized you, darlin'."

He grinned, displaying a serious need for dental work.

Apparently members of the Santa Barbara outlaw biker community read the New York *Post*.

"It's me." The man took off the helmet. His look was something between cave person and aging rock star entering rehab. His eyebrows might have done damage in their own right. "From the Saloon. You're a long way from Santa Ynez, sweet thing."

He knew where I was going. This was getting creepier by the minute. I didn't see a camera, but he had to be a paparazzo. Gabriella probably put out some publicity about me for the conference and this guy had followed me from the airport.

"I don't frequent saloons." I gave him a look that, while not exactly rude, was of a chilliness that could usually shrivel a Manhattan *maître d'*.

He responded with a suggestive chortle. "Oooh, I love that talk. Come on darlin'."

I realized I was going to have to let him take his pictures. This wasn't a case of being able to close the drapes. After fifteen years of marriage to a TV celebrity, I'd learned the best way to get rid of some paparazzi is to give them what they want.

"Okay, you win." I smoothed my hair and gave him a celebrity smile. "Get out your equipment."

"In the goddam street? Doc, you are into the kink!" With an

animal grunt, he lunged in my direction. I jumped back, but he caught my wrist and jerked me toward his leather-clad chest. "I am up for some fun, darlin', but I like a little privacy. I just got paid for an '88 Norton I rebuilt for that old fart across the street."

The man's breath needed to be reported to the EPA.

"What say we hit the Saloon, then my place? I've been a bad, bad boy..."

Another pervert. I should have realized this would happen. The *Post* was online these days, like everything else. People all over the country could have seen that article.

"You're not a paparazzo, are you?" I scouted for the best way to run.

The biker looked offended. "Paparazzos? Never heard of that bike club. I'm a Ghost Mountain Rider." He pointed to the bike-riding skeleton logo on his jacket.

I edged away, scanning the garden for a nice rock or weapon-sized garden gnome.

A barking dog startled us both. A spandex-clad woman appeared in the doorway of the next house, talking on her cell phone while jogging in place. I ran to her, waving with relief. But her dog barked louder and the woman screamed at us.

"Get out, you trash!"

The dog was large, with dangerous-looking teeth—and no leash. It let out a menacing growl. The spandex woman shouted again.

"I've called 911. I can't believe it. Prostitution. Only two blocks from Montecito. Oprah lives here! Have some respect."

The dog growled again.

"Here you go, Doc!" The biker offered me a silvery helmet and pointed at his studded-leather saddlebags. "Got an extra jacket. Put it on, and you can stow your bag back there."

I looked from the dog to the biker. The dog had significantly more teeth.

A police siren wailed. I tossed my tote in the saddlebag,

shoved my arms into the huge jacket, slammed on the helmet, and launched myself onto the back of the Harley, trying not to think about the damage I was doing to my Dolce and Gabbana suit — or how much leg I was showing.

"I can't believe that woman took me for a streetwalker!" I tried for a casual laugh.

"Yeah. What a bitch! Everybody knows you are one high class call girl." The biker gave my thigh a startling slap. "Put your arms around me, darlin' and hang on!"

He wove through the congested traffic, as drivers raised middle fingers and one — I'll swear — waved a gun. By the time we escaped the city and hit the dark mountain roads, I stopped worrying about what the man intended do to me and concentrated on worrying whether I was going to live long enough to find out.

I couldn't have said if we spent hours or days roaring up the twisting highway, zooming around hairpin curves, leaning into the wind and passing cars as if they were standing still. My legs went numb first, then my hands, and soon after, my lips. The endless roar drilled through my ears to my brain until all thinking was impossible. With my arms circling the biker's thick body, the worn leather of his jacket was the only reality I could cling to.

When we finally came to a stop, we seemed to have passed through a portal of time and space and landed in the Wild West, *circa* 1895. We'd parked in front of a building called the "Maverick Saloon." Two horses were tied to the railing of a wooden sidewalk and several cowboys smoked hand-rolled cigarettes nearby. None of them took any notice of us. Perhaps dentally-challenged bikers accompanied by designer-clad etiquette columnists frequented the place on a regular basis.

"Time for a brewski, darlin'." My companion lifted me off the bike.

I followed on rubbery legs, reasoning that wherever/whenever I'd landed, I'd be safer in public than alone with the man.

As we entered, my dried-out eyeballs managed to focus on a newspaper stand next to the door. It displayed *The Santa Ynez Valley Journal*. The headline read, "Golden West Writers Conference celebrates its Thirteenth Year." Underneath was a photograph Gabriella Moore in full cowperson regalia—a bit shrunken with age, but still very much the rancher-matriarch of her *Big Mountain* days.

Santa Ynez. Here I was, after all. Miraculous. All I needed was a ride to Gabriella's resort. Did the town have taxis? Or was one expected to rent a horse?

"I'm going to have to take a rain check," I said, choosing words I hoped wouldn't offend my unorthodox chauffeur. "I'm supposed to be at the Rancho Montana Grande. You gave me such a fun ride, I nearly forgot!"

I faked a grateful smile as I checked my watch: nearly nine PM. I'd missed my evening presentation. I hoped Gabriella would be sympathetic to airline delays. I didn't want to antagonize one of the few people willing to employ me after the scandals of my divorce.

The biker looked like a little boy who'd lost the ice cream from his cone.

"Day-um. Can't you cancel, darlin'? I'll make it worth your while..."

I managed to keep my smile in place.

"Is there a public telephone nearby?"

He laughed. "You still on that 'the Manners Doctor doesn't approve of cell phones' thing?" He started to pull a phone from a zippered pocket, then dropped it back. "Aw, hell. Hop on the hog. It'll only take a minute to run you up there."

His expression darkened.

"But I ain't stickin' around. That place scares the bejeezus out of me. It's lousy with ghosts. Some ain't even got no head."

Chapter 3—The Cowboy Way

THE RANCHO MONTANA GRANDE looked as Wild West as the old Saloon. A few rustic cabins were clustered by the main entrance, and a winding dirt road led up to the "Hacienda" — a maze of interconnected buildings that gave equal representation to every stage of California architecture from homestead adobe to mid-century Palm Springs *moderne*.

The place looked odd. But then, I probably did too, as I slid off the bike in my sweaty Dolce and Gabbana, with helmet-hair, and sand-blasted make-up, and even more precarious heels. After thanking my unlikely chauffeur, I tied my hair back with a scarf, shouldered my tote bag, and headed for the lobby — as if I normally traveled via outlaw-biker Harley.

I did hope I wouldn't encounter any ghosts.

Not that I believed in them.

Much.

Actually, I've always thought it was silly to be afraid of ectoplasmic apparitions. It wouldn't make sense for a ghost to kill a live person. That would create another ghost to share the same space. Think of the housemate problems.

When I entered the lobby, nobody stared, but a few whispered together while looking in my direction. A woman with a notebook approached.

"Can I have your autograph?" She held out a pen. I reached for it, praying she wouldn't make any S/M jokes. I wanted this nonsense to be over.

But the woman walked past me without a glance, handing the pen to a tall, elderly man in a cowboy hat—an old movie star I recognized but couldn't name. I watched the old cowboy star try to escape as the notebook woman gushed admiration while asserting her entitlement to his attention. His famous face showed a combination of impatience and trapped-animal terror.

I gave my name to the little man who presided at the front desk. He handed me a gold-colored pocket folder, a room key and a faculty nametag that said "Camilla Randall, Nonfiction."

His smile was efficient and professional. I told him about my lost luggage and he assured me that everything would be taken care of. He wore a nametag that said "Alberto Gonzales, Concierge."

"You have missed the reception and evening classes," Alberto said with hint of reproach. "But the critique workshop in the Ponderosa Lounge is still in session. You may join if you hurry. Your bags will be brought to your room when they arrive."

I hurried down the corridor, barely avoiding a collision with a waiter exiting the Ponderosa Lounge with a load of water pitchers. With a quick elbow, he caught the door and held it for me. His expression was stern, but he made a charming, childlike bow.

Inside, fifty or so writers turned in their folding chairs to stare.

"If it isn't Miss Manners!" A big man boomed the greeting from a small stage. "She's moseyed down to our Cowboy Critique workshop—a little late for the party." He gave an unfunny laugh. "But it looks like she's been having one of her own."

I looked down and felt my face flush when I saw my skirt had ripped halfway up the side. The grizzle-bearded speaker—costumed as something between Texas oil man and singing cowboy—touched the brim of his Stetson.

"I'm Toby Roarke."

He motioned me to the stage.

"Better introduce yourself, Mrs. Kahn—or whatever you call yourself now."

I ignored the dig, as well as the way Roarke grinned into my cleavage. Positioning myself behind the lectern, I hid what I could of my shredded skirt.

"I'm using my maiden name again—Camilla Randall." I beamed an exaggerated smile at Mr. Roarke. "I'll be giving a workshop on writing the advice column. My *nom de plume* is the Manners Doctor. People do confuse me with Miss Manners, and I adore her, but she is about three decades older, so..."

I hoped I was making sense. My body still vibrated from the Harley's engine.

Toby Roarke harrumphed and rocked back on his Tony Lama heels.

"Any questions for Ms....um, whatever, before we get back to our critiques?"

Unfortunately, several hands waved. A pretty, over-made-up young woman in Donna Karan stood. "Can you get Jonathan Kahn to read my book?" Her speech had a Hispanic inflection. She waved a bulging gold folder. "It's all, like, kinky sex in the news business. Since you're into that scene..."

I feared my smile muscles might cramp, but I managed to say, "I'm not in contact with Mr. Kahn." So much for escaping the *Post.*

A red-faced man rose to his feet and spoke with a plummy Oxbridge British accent.

"Forget your ex, Miss Manners. I have a book that's right up your street: *"The Story of O and Zombies…"*

So the *Post* article had gone international.

A grandmotherly woman interrupted.

"Didn't you hear her? She's not Miss Manners. Miss Manners would never dress like that. Miss Manners is a lady."

Toby Roarke laid a heavy hand on my arm.

"Honey, whatever you call yourself, I don't think it's 'Cowboy.' And this is called the Cowboy Critique Workshop. That Cowboy would be, um, me. You wanna take a seat and let me get on with business?"

That would be the moment, of course, when my heel broke off—just as I stepped down from the podium. I removed the shoe and limped to a seat, clutching the shoe and severed heel. As a first post-divorce public appearance, this wasn't going well.

Roarke read from a list in a passive-aggressive whisper.

"Ernesto Cervantes. You're up to read." The room hushed, but no one stood. "Where is the lovely Ernesto?" Roarke hooked his thumbs into his tooled leather belt. "Does our peroxide bombshell have another date with Miss Clairol? I'll have to let somebody have his reading slot…"

As writers thrust up hands like eager schoolchildren, a bleached-blonde, dark-skinned young man rushed in.

"If you're fixin' to read us your deathless prose, you better get to it, boy."

The teenager's muscled chest heaved under his "Sin City" T-shirt as he made an effortless leap up to the stage. He gave the crowd an endearing grin.

I wanted to run up and save him from whatever the Cowboy had in store. In spite of a crude, tough-guy tattoo on his forearm, he looked like a vulnerable child.

"This story is called *El Despertador Looks at the Stars.*" He looked a little nervous as he started to read. "First there is a quote—'we may all be in the gutter, but some of us are looking at the stars'—Oscar Wilde said that."

"No, he didn't!" Toby jumped down from the stage, spurs jingling. Swaggering down the aisle, he let his hand brush the exposed shoulder of the pretty Donna Karan girl. "Wilde said, 'We are all in the gutter, not 'may all be.' *Lady Windemere's Fan*, Act III."

Ernesto flipped through his conference folder, looking confused, then angry.

Toby grinned. "If you're not ready, Ernie..."

The young man shot him an ocular dagger before continuing with a wild, surreal story about the cock-fighting subculture among local farm workers. His grammar wasn't perfect, but I found the story gripping.

I wanted to applaud. But the room went silent as critiquers scribbled notes.

Roarke strolled back to the lectern.

"Any comments for Mr. Cervantes?"

A fiftiesh woman in Ralph Lauren denim began.

"First, it was totally unbelievable. Nobody would bet money on chickens fighting each other. Make them polo ponies or racehorses or something. Plus the violence was offensive."

Another woman, whose beige hair exactly matched her raw silk overalls, agreed.

"I was offended by that talk about black cocks. You can't say that in this day and age."

After a wave of titters, one of a group of smug twenty-somethings spoke.

"I agree it's unbelievable. A macho guy kills himself over a sick rooster?"

Ernesto clenched his jaw. "El Despertador is a fighting cock..."

"No talk-back!" commanded Roarke. "Not till everybody says their piece." He gave his audience a conspiratorial grin. "I have to agree that nobody's going to buy all this tragedy about—well, let's face it—poultry. You can't start with a highfalutin' literary quote and end with the dying thoughts of a friggin' chicken!"

Titters exploded into guffaws.

The Miss Manners fan interrupted.

"I felt sorry for Desperado. And the boy who killed himself after he gambled away his mother's savings."

"No!" Ernesto yelled. "Not Desperado. Despertador. It means—"

Despertador. My Berlitz Spanish sent me a brain-flash.

"Alarm clock!" I blurted out. "The rooster's name is 'Alarm Clock.' It's all a joke. It's very funny..."

"So, Mr. Cervantes, doesn't that make you feel better?" Roarke gave a savage smile. "The former Mrs. Jonathan Kahn is amused by your—um—little cock."

The room went silent as Ernesto, his face taut with rage, bounded from the stage. The door closed behind him with an eloquent thud.

Toby Roarke glared at me.

"You tell the boy his story is a joke? You really are into that sadism stuff like they say, aren't you?"

I stuffed both shoes into my bag and ran after the boy. I must have been wrong about the alarm clock.

"Ernesto!" I called down the corridor. "I'm so sorry!"

A small, elderly woman grabbed my arm as I ran by.

"You look like that Dr. Manners. Are you all right?" She eyed my stocking feet with confusion and then searched my face. "The ghosts are after you, aren't they? Don't think they don't know about you. We don't cotton to perverts around here."

So—even little old ladies had read that stupid article.

This could be a very long four days.

Chapter 4—Cowboy Heaven

"ARE YOU SURE YOU'RE alright?" The old woman's hand was still firmly clamped to my arm. She continued to stare at my naked feet.

I gave her a clueless smile. Pretending I knew nothing about the *Post* article was probably the best way to handle the whole mess. I regained custody of my arm and fished my traveling flats from my bag.

"I'm fine—except for being insensitive, apparently. But the poor boy was dying in there. I only wanted to help." I stepped into the flats. They felt comforting. I looked around for Ernesto, but he seemed to have escaped to the lobby.

"The boy was dying in there?" The woman gave an anxious look at the door to the Ponderosa Lounge. "I'm Mitzi Boggs Bailey, the poet. If he's not all right, I could call 911." She pulled a phone from the pocket of her voluminous cardigan.

I tried to make an escape. "I don't think his situation is that dire. I just wanted to apologize. He may still be in the lobby. If I could catch him…"

"Gabriella isn't all right," said the woman. "Jackie Collins canceled. Gaby hates it when celebrities cancel on her. Nobody did that when she was a famous TV star."

I gave her what I hoped was an understanding nod. The conference seemed to have an awfully tough time holding on to its celebrities.

The old woman finally released my arm to reach into her large plastic tote bag.

"I'm famous, too. For my poetry." She pulled a conference folder from the bag. "But I don't go to workshops any more. Not with that Toby around."

She did have the dreamy look of a poet. Had Roarke humiliated her too?

A tall man with mocking dark eyes approached from the lobby.

"Suffering from Cowboy fatigue, you two?"

His nametag said, "Rick Zukowski, Mystery-Thriller."

"Mr. Roarke seems a little hard on the beginning writers." I tried to hide my shredded skirt with my bag, wondering if I should try to explain my state of *dishabille*. "But of course he's the expert. I'm just a non-fiction person."

Rick Zukowski, Mystery-Thriller had a delicious smile.

"Don't let that sleazebag intimidate you. God knows what Gabriella sees in him. I've heard he hasn't published a thing in decades, except as a ghostwriter." He laughed. "You ladies headed for the bar?"

"Toby's not the ghost that writes," said Mrs. Boggs Bailey. "That's Old Obadiah. You don't want to tangle with the Rancho ghosts." With a shudder, she turned and shuffled toward the lobby, clutching her gold folder to her chest like a shield.

Rick Zukowski shrugged his impressive shoulders.

"There's lots of legends about this old ranch. The foundation dates back to the *Californios*. But the craziest parts are from Prohibition, when this was a dude ranch—party central for illegal boozing. They got secret rooms and passages all over the place." He pointed to a door covered with furry brown and white cowhide. "That's the infamous Longhorn Room. Can I buy you a drink?"

"I probably shouldn't..." I wished I had clothes to change into. I felt so vulnerable without my wardrobe. "I look like a ragamuffin. I ran into some trouble getting here..."

"Car trouble?" Rick gave a sympathetic laugh. "Then you really need that drink."

I couldn't help returning his scrumptious smile. Why did I have to look like a tornado survivor when I was finally meeting a man who wasn't hand-picked by my mother?

"Dr. Manners!" Mrs. Boggs Bailey called over her shoulder. "You pay attention if the ghosts write to you. They won't put up with your shenanigans."

I wished I could explain to her—to everybody who had seen that awful article—that my entire thirty-eight years had been remarkably shenanigan-free.

Rick opened the furry door. I followed. He had a brotherly/boy next door manner that made me feel safe. But the noisy, crowded room didn't feel safe at all. With a scarred mahogany bar, spotted cowhide everywhere, and dead horned-animal heads on the walls, the place looked as if Jesse James might walk in and start shooting things at any moment.

"Quite a spot, isn't it?" Rick gave me that smile again.

"Halfway between gruesome and cowboy heaven." I tried to shake off the ghost-story creepiness. "What are those dead things on the wall—giant cows?"

"Gabriella tells me they're Texas Longhorns." He waved at a little woman with a big, platinum hairdo. Same hairstyle she'd been wearing for forty years.

Gabriella Moore was unmistakable. She sat at a table by the fireplace in conversation with a large, bearded man. "Have you met Gaby yet?"

She beamed her movie-star smile.

"Camilla!" she called. "Sorry about your airline hassles.

We've rescheduled you for tomorrow. Captain, come on over!"

Nobody turned to stare at me. I relaxed a little. Maybe not everybody had read the *Post*. I would so much like to be able to spend this four days with normal people who didn't have preconceived notions about me. Like nice Captain Rick. What was he—a sea captain? Army, maybe. His bearing seemed slightly military as he introduced me to Gabriella and the man with her, whose name was Silas Ryder.

Mr. Ryder was the owner of a local independent bookstore chain called "Ryderbooks." Bespectacled and attractive in a large, tweedy way, Mr. Ryder looked like a courtly bear as he stood and offered wine from the bottle he and Gabriella were sharing.

"Some of Gabriella's Pinot Noir? The grapes were grown right here on the Rancho." As he filled two glasses for us, a phone in his pocket rang. He glanced at the number. I braced for a conversation-halting phone call, but he excused himself. "I'd better go take this," he said, heading for the door. Good manners. I liked him.

Rick gulped his wine, looking as if he'd probably rather have a beer.

I took a sip. "Lovely," I said. "Light, with a nice blackberry-coffee finish."

Gabriella dismissed my winespeak with a wave.

"Oh, it's Toby's Pinot. I'm just an old cowgirl, but Toby says beef isn't cost-effective anymore. He's planting grapes all over the damned place. Excuse my French, Dr. Manners."

So Toby Roarke was Gabriella's significant other. Maybe that explained the alpha male behavior. But I wondered what Gaby thought about his flirtations with students like the exotically lovely Donna Karan girl.

"Dr. Manners?" Rick cocked an eyebrow at me. "Are you the famous Manners Doctor who...?"

I braced myself. But instead of telling me what a bad boy

he'd been, Rick put on an old-lady falsetto. "The Manners Doctor urges you to arrive at a dinner party ten minutes late. The hostess needs time for a glass of wine before the guests descend'." He laughed. "My mother-in-law is crazy about your column."

Okay. I had to shut down the fantasies. The man had a mother-in-law. After what I'd been through with Jonathan, I wasn't even going to smile at another woman's significant other.

Time for a change of subject. "I've heard people talking about these Rancho ghosts," I said. "Do people really believe this place is haunted?"

Gabriella gave an enigmatic smile.

"Yeah. We got us some ghosts. Obadiah and Joaquin. Obadiah Wilke was a 'forty-niner killed on the Rancho by bandits looking for his gold. Used to be a schoolteacher before he came prospecting."

"Oh, so that's why they say he's a writer?" Rick's voice had a tinge of sarcasm.

Gaby laughed. "I guess. My husband Hank, rest his soul, said Obadiah left messages scrawled in his accounts book. He thought Obadiah was trying to tell him where he'd hid his poke."

I could feel the warmth of Rick's body as we sat squished together at the tiny bar table. I hoped I didn't smell of *essence de biker*: cigarettes, leather and toxic emissions. I needed to get myself into a shower.

But Gaby kept on with her ghost story.

"Anybody loses pens or paper around here, they figure old Obadiah took it. Alberto, my concierge, says a whole lot of pens have been disappearing lately—especially his calligraphic ones. And about fifty years' worth of vintage stationery he's been saving in the back room went missing a few weeks ago."

"I'll keep my eye out for him—or them."

"Oh, you don't want to see Joaquin." Gabriella grabbed my hand. "Mean old customer. He's the one killed Obadiah. Later they chopped his head off and showed it around every bar from here to San Francisco, pickled in a whisky jar. He wanders all over these hills looking for that head."

I couldn't tell if Gabriella believed the nonsense she was spouting, or was just displaying her talent for dramatic presentation.

Rick gave a skeptical grunt.

"Joaquin Murrieta? Got a lot of haunting to do, that dude. Legends put him everywhere from Orange County to Yosemite."

Gabriella let go of my hand, but she still wasn't smiling.

"Take it from me: that is one ghost you do not want to mess with. He'll give you nightmares."

I stood. "I'm afraid I'll have to brave the supernatural dangers and find my room. It's two in the morning, my time."

Gabriella stopped me again.

"Does Alberto have you in one of those awful little rooms under my apartment? We wanted to put you in a suite, but there was a mix-up. Stay put for a minute. I'll check and see if we've had any cancellations."

"I'm sure it will be just fine..."

Gabriella pointed at my vacated chair with an authoritative finger as she took a phone from her vest pocket.

"I've given Silas the John Wayne room, so he doesn't have to drive all the way home tonight. He's been trying to locate some more Jackie Collins titles, but we don't need them now."

I sat, wishing I weren't so aware of Rick's eyes on my naked thigh.

"I'm sorry to hear about Miss Collins' cancellation. Is she ill?"

"Beats me." Gabriella pushed a button on the phone and put it to her ear. "Toby got a call from Jackie's people just before his workshop started, so he didn't have time to tell me.

You'd be amazed how often these folks cancel at the last minute."

She clicked off the phone and gave a weary sigh.

"Alberto must be away from the desk. But we've got a fantastic replacement for Jackie: Plantagenet Smith, the screenwriter, fresh from his Oscar win. Silas came to my rescue. He met Plant at a San Francisco book fair last year. We've never had an Oscar winner at the conference before."

My head roared. Plantagenet. Here.

"Mr. Smith is... here?" I tried not to let my emotions show. It had been five years, but he wasn't likely to have forgiven me.

Chapter 5—Reunion

RICK LOOKED UNIMPRESSED at the mention of Plantagenet Smith.

"Is he the dude who wrote that crazy thing about Oscar Wilde and Calamity Jane?"

Gabriella grinned. "I knew Westerns would make a comeback someday...oh, Plant wanted me to give you this." She pulled a note from the pocket of her suede vest.

My hand shook as I opened it.

"My darling Camilla—Longing to see you. Tragic about you and Jonathan. See you ASAP. We can compare sagas of tabloid hell."

My eyes stung. Could he possibly have forgiven me?

"Is he going to join us?" I hoped my voice didn't sound shaky.

"I invited him," Gabriella said. "But he said somebody tailgated him over the pass, and all he wanted was a shower."

Gabriella rolled her eyes as if this indicated serious wimpiness on Plant's part. "We put him down in the Zorro cabin—the one with the fountain out front."

I jumped up.

"But it's about a ten minute walk, hon," Gabriella called as I made for the door. "Ask at the desk for someone to take you down in a golf cart."

I'd wanted to patch things up with Plantagenet for so long, but when I was still with Jonathan, I was afraid Plant would tell me to leave him—and when I finally did it, I felt too needy to be good company.

As I approached the front desk, Alberto—engrossed in a pile of legal-looking documents—waved me away.

"I have spoken with the airport. Your luggage will be here by morning. I can do nothing more tonight." He dismissed me before I could thank him.

A walk down the hill might get the knots out of my body from the crazy motorcycle ride. The haunted-ranch stories made walking alone a little creepy, but anyone who could be frightened by a headless ghost had never been stalked by a paparazzo.

◊ ◊ ◊

The wind had a chilly bite, but the exercise was warming. I began to relax, breathing the tang of fruit in the clean night air as I walked the dirt road between the regimented stakes of grapevines. Zorro was easy to spot—the flashiest of six Spanish-style cabins nestled in an oak grove at the entrance to the Rancho. A three-tiered fountain dominated the courtyard in front. Lights glowed from inside.

A brand new Ferrari nestled in the space beside it. Plant did love his cars: this must have been his Oscar-win celebration buy.

I knocked on the door, but heard only the splash of the fountain. The other cabins were quiet and dark. I was about to knock again when I checked my watch. Nearly midnight. Any sensible person would be asleep. I turned to make a polite escape.

But with a creak, the door opened and I saw a death-pale Plantagenet, wearing nothing but silk boxers.

"Camilla? Oh, dear God!"

His look made me want to run all the way back to Manhattan. I wished he would be angry—scream at me—do something besides give me that horrible blank stare.

"I'm so sorry," I said. "Please believe me: I had no idea of what Jonathan would do to you on his show. He told me he wanted to talk about your Tony award, not your sex life."

"Ancient history, darling." Plant made a gesture as if he were waving away a bug. "It was my own fault for putting off coming out for so long." He peered out, as if he thought we might be watched, then grabbed my arm, pulling me forcefully into the cabin.

"I really am sorry." I said again. I didn't know why he was being so rough.

"Darling, it's nothing compared with what Jonathan has done to you. You must be going through a hideous time since that awful story came out."

We were in a small sitting room, where an erotic gay film showed on the muted television. The couch and chair were strewn with clothes. The Ermengildo Zegna jacket looked as if it might belong to Plant, but the Nikes and "Sin City" T-shirt did not.

Ernesto.

I'd interrupted Plant in bed with Ernesto Cervantes. This was more than awkward. I glanced at the closed door that must lead to the bedroom.

"Plant—I don't know what I was thinking. It's the middle of the night…"

He still had a grip on my arm.

"Please stay. I found him like this. There's blood…"

Now I saw the Zegna suit was smeared with red.

Plant opened the door to the bedroom.

I froze.

Ernesto Cervantes lay face down on the red-spattered sheets of Plantagenet's bed. A small gun glinted in his hand next to what was left of his blonde, damp head. Under the sheets, he appeared to be naked.

And quite dead.

Chapter 6—Wilde in the West

PLANTAGENET'S HANDS SHOOK as he grabbed a pair of khakis from the suitcase that lay open on the floor, his face as pale as his cropped, silvering blonde hair.

"What...happened?" I tried not to look at all the blood.

"Roarke." Plantagenet croaked the name like a curse. "The Cowboy. He did this. Evil old toad."

"What do you mean? Toby Roarke is rude and unpleasant, but he couldn't have done this. His workshop is still going strong—at least it was an hour ago." The scene felt surreal. The film on the television didn't help. "Do you mind if I turn that off?"

Plant flushed as he pulled on his trousers and struggled with the zipper.

"Do. Yes. It was on when I got down here—with the volume way up. I could hear the grunts and groans from halfway up the hill. I guess I hit the mute instead of the off button trying to shut it up." He picked up the remote and the

TV clicked off. "You were there? At the Cowboy Critique workshop?"

"It was awful. Ernesto read an intense story, and Roarke laughed at him. Everybody did. I guess I did too, but I thought the rooster's name was supposed to be funny, and Ernesto ran out..."

"Creep!" Plant's face went from gray to purple as he yanked on the stubborn zipper. "Smug, narcissistic old bastard!" He screamed this last word loud enough to be heard at the top of the hill.

"Don't you think we should call the police or something?" It was horrible to think Ernesto might have committed suicide because of his humiliation in the workshop—and that my alarm clock comment might have added to his pain.

Plant finally looked at me. He seemed to see me for the first time.

"Darling, I know Jonathan's ridiculous stories must have devastated you, but have you taken to rending your raiment?"

He always could make me laugh. Even in the worst of circumstances. And this pretty much qualified as the worst. I gave him a half smile.

"Long story. My luggage is taking in the sights of Dallas. Or Denver. Nobody's quite sure, so I missed the limo and had to travel via motorcycle."

He grabbed me in a bear hug.

"Darling, it's so good to see you!"

His arms felt safe and warm, in spite of the gruesome scene around us.

"You forgive me, then? For luring you into Jonathan's clutches? I had no idea he'd invite your ex-boyfriend to tell the world you're gay."

"Of course I forgive you." Plant gave me a sweet, familiar smile. "Jonathan Kahn is a muckraking sleazebag, and I was furious at the time, but the truth is that coming out was the best thing I ever did. I thought I could straddle some sort of

Kinsey fence, but right after the fiasco on Jonathan's show, I took a job with a theater in San Francisco, and met somebody..."

"That's fantastic! So you're in a committed relationship now?" My eyes rested on Ernesto's clothes. "Um, sort-of committed?"

"It didn't last forever, but he was the one who got me interested in the stories about Oscar Wilde's San Francisco visit, and when I found out that Calamity Jane had been in town at the same time, I had to write about it and...well, you probably saw that Ferrari I've got parked out front."

"It's a lovely car."

Okay, I'd pretend this was a normal conversation. Plant was probably in shock.

"*Wilde in the West* is brilliant: the script, the cast...Gwyneth has never done better work."

Plant picked up a key ring from the coffee table.

"Oh, God, the Ferrari. I gave Ernesto these keys—so he could drive my Ferrari down from the Hacienda while I checked in with Gabriella."

He fell on the couch as if the wind had been knocked out of him.

"Do you suppose he killed himself out of some kind of envy? Could this be about a goddam car? A talented kid with his life ahead of him?"

I hugged him again and tried not to notice that his zipper was still entangled in a bit of shirttail.

"Shouldn't we pull ourselves together and call the police? Even when it's a suicide, they have to—you know—do their police things."

"As soon as we do, it will be all over the media. Poor kid. It's going to look so sordid. I don't know if he had a family here, but that will be so awful for them..."

Plant ran his fingers though his cropped hair, as if he still had the long-forelock preppy cut he wore in his younger days.

His breath went ragged.

"He didn't want to sleep with me—not really. He wanted to actually be me: that bleached hair; his obsession with Oscar Wilde. I kept saying, 'I'm too old for you sweetie.' But then he told me about Roarke. Goddam closet queen. Old enough to be his grandfather—feeding off the boy's youth and talent—like a damned vampire."

"Ernesto—and Toby Roarke? That John Wayne-wannabe is gay?" The sexual ambiguities of Plantagenet's romantic life had always confused me. "Ernesto was involved with both of you?"

Someone banged on the door.

"Are you all right?" said a voice.

Plant froze.

Chapter 7—The Mask of Zorro

AFTER MORE LOUD KNOCKING, Plant seemed to remember himself and rushed to open the door in that automatic way of people who didn't grow up with servants.

"Hello," A familiar voice said. "I'm Mitzi Boggs Bailey, the poet. Are you all right? I heard somebody shouting over here. Did you see the ghosts?"

"We're fine, Mrs. Boggs Bailey."

I stuck my head out the cracked-open door. I thought she probably wouldn't deal well with the recently deceased.

"Everything's fine. No ghosts. Sorry about the noise."

I tried to ease the door shut.

"There are too! The ghosts—I saw them. Plain as day. Both of them."

Mrs. Boggs Bailey pushed the door wider and tried to come inside. She wore a remarkable pink nylon peignoir that looked as if it might have belonged to Doris Day *circa* 1963. She still clutched her gold folder.

"Joaquin was here," she said. "Mean old customer. And he had Old Obadiah with him. Joaquin says we have to be quiet or they'll take Gabriella to the hoosegow."

Plant stepped up to try to close the door again.

"Sorry we disturbed you." he said. "And your nice ghosts. Sleep well."

"You're not Jackie Collins." Mrs. Boggs Bailey held her ground. "Jackie Collins was supposed to have this cabin. That's why I'm in Roy Rogers. I wrote a cowboy play. A play that's a poem. Its name is *Under Deadwood*." She presented her folder to Plantagenet. "I wanted to show it to Jackie because it would make a great picture. She knows everybody who's anybody."

"I'll, um, be happy to read it later, but—"

Mrs. Boggs Bailey continued to wave her manuscript as Plant hid his lower torso behind the door, hiding the still-resistant zipper. Finally he accepted the folder as the old woman went on.

"I don't want Roy Rogers now. I don't like your kind. You make too much noise. You and the girl who looks like Dr. Manners and the boy who was dying in there. There's a name for that—having sex with dead people. It isn't nice."

Plant handed me the folder with a raised-eyebrow look of wonderment.

"Uh, why don't you take that up with Gabriella in the morning?"

"I can't. Gabriella's in trouble. The Sheriff is going to take that old girl to the hoosegow. That's what Joaquin told me. I heard you having sex. People with cars like that always make noise when they have sex." She turned and pointed at the Ferrari. "My husband and I used to run a motel. I should know."

I heard a whirring sound from the road, and a light seemed to float toward us as a golf cart emerged from the dark.

"Are you all right?" Mrs. Boggs Bailey called out.

"What's the problem, Mitzi?" I recognized Gabriella's throaty voice. "Alberto said you phoned him with an emergency."

I stepped outside and shut the door behind me so Plant could deal with his zipper. Gabriella climbed out of the cart and strode toward us, the big silhouette of Silas Ryder looming behind her.

"An emergency. Yes," said Mrs. Boggs Bailey. "I heard him shouting: that man who isn't Jackie Collins. I wanted Jackie to read *Under Deadwood.*"

"Mitzi, dear, you shouldn't bother Mr. Smith at this hour." Gabriella grasped Mrs. Boggs Bailey by the shoulders and turned her around, like some child's mechanical toy. "I'm sure he'll be happy to look at your lovely play after he's had some rest. Tomorrow you can move back up to the Hacienda." She winked at me over her shoulder. "Good night, dear. Our Mitzi can get a little confused."

"He had his fly open. They were having sex," said Mrs. Boggs Bailey, as Gabriella steered her toward the cabin next door. "A *ménage a trois*: The girl who looks like Dr. Manners and the man who isn't Jackie Collins and the boy who was dying in there. They made the most disgusting sounds, and shot off their guns. The ghosts carried him away. Obadiah and Joaquin. They were fighting mad — not that I blame them..."

"Silas!" Plant called from behind the door as the big man began to follow Gabriella. "Silas, I've got to talk to you. Now!"

Silas stifled laughter as he and I went back inside the cabin.

"Poor old Mitzi is on a roll tonight with the ghost stories, isn't she?"

His expression changed when he saw Plant's face.

Plant pointed at the bedroom.

Silas took a step, then froze.

"Roarke," he said in a choked voice. "God damn Toby Roarke." He looked as if he might cry. "Ernie acted tough, but he was so damned fragile..."

"We really have to call the police," I said softly.

Silas didn't seem to hear.

"I tried so many times to make him get rid of that damned gun. I told him he'd never put the gang life behind him until he let go completely."

"Why didn't you make him get rid of it?" Plantagenet's voice sounded harsh. "He worked for you—didn't you have any leverage?"

Poor Ernesto. A gay gangbanger. His life couldn't have been easy. And he was somehow involved with Silas. Was Silas his lover too? With so many admirers, why hadn't Ernesto turned to one of them before taking such a tragic step?

"How does Roarke seduce these kids? Damn! I could kill that slimeball. Kill him!" Silas pounded the wall in fury.

A crash came from the bedroom on the other side.

Plant rushed into the room and emerged with a framed black and white photograph—its protective glass cracked. It showed Gabriella Moore with a man in a Zorro costume. Scrawled across it said, "To Gabriella from Guy Williams."

"Guy Williams!" Plant sounded dazed. "An autographed picture of Guy Williams! I was so in love with him when I was a kid. Did you know his real name was Armando Catalano? What a sad time—a Latino had to put on an Anglo mask to play a Latino hero." He choked on tears that were not for Mr. Williams/Catalano.

Silas took the picture and handed it to me, as if I had some secret feminine knowledge of how to deal with such things. I placed the picture atop some papers on the desk and eyed the phone. It was an ancient hotel phone with no dial. I supposed you had to pick it up and ask for an outside line, even to call 911. A cowboy telephone. A heavy thumping on the outside door made me jump. Were the police here already?

But it was Mitzi Boggs Bailey again.

"You look like that perverted Dr. Manners," she said. "Are you all right?"

I sighed. "Yes. I'm fine. It's very late…"

"I don't want that man to have my play," she said. "He's not Jackie Collins."

Plant pointed to the papers on the desk.

I lifted the broken photograph frame and unearthed the gold folder, handing it through the crack in the door.

"Good night, Mrs. Boggs Bailey. Sleep well." I closed the door and leaned against it with relief. Silas and Plant stood hugging each other like frightened children. "Is one of you going to call the police," I said. "Or should I?"

"Not the police, the Sheriff," Silas said. "Santa Ynez is under the jurisdiction of the Santa Barbara Sheriff-Coroner. Solvang has the nearest substation, but they may have to send somebody down from Santa Maria. He picked up the desk phone and asked for an outside line.

"I bumped into Ernesto in the lobby — literally." Plant collapsed on the couch again. "He was tearing down the stairs like a lunatic, waving one of those gold folders everybody's got, babbling about how he was going to get back at Toby for something. I told him to go to my cabin and cool down. I let him drive the Ferrari while I registered at the desk, then I walked…"

He picked up the keys again.

"As if two minutes driving somebody else's car was going to make anything okay."

Silas put down the phone. "Somebody will be here soon."

Plant turned to me.

"You should get back up to the Hacienda before the Sheriff's people arrive. After all your nasty publicity, I'm sure you don't want to be involved in something like this…"

He tossed me the keys.

"Here. Drive the Ferrari. It's too late to be out there walking by yourself. At least the damned car can do somebody some good."

I accepted the keys. He was right about the bad publicity, of course. And I knew better than to argue with Plant when he was in big-brother mode.

Chapter 8—The Captain

OUTSIDE, THE NIGHT WAS deathly still. Everything looked eerie in the amber glow of the security lights.

Across the courtyard, a sliver of light appeared between dark curtains. I could see Mitzi Boggs Bailey peeking through. Probably looking for more supernatural apparitions.

I grabbed the car door handle and was surprised it opened without the key. Ernesto must have been in such a hurry to self-destruct that he hadn't bothered to lock it. I slid into the leather seat and grabbed the wheel, with its signature prancing horse in the center. The 360 Spider convertible smelled like luxury—like success. Maybe it had driven Ernesto to suicidal envy. I felt pretty envious myself. Even when Jonathan came through with my money, there would be no Italian sports cars in my immediate future.

I was at the hotel parking lot within a minute or two, grateful I hadn't needed to make that spooky walk again. I made sure the car was securely locked. No matter how Plantagenet felt now, I knew how precious this car must be to a self-invented man who grew up in a New Jersey slum as a nobody named "John Smith."

Inside, the lobby was empty now, except for a young Hispanic man behind the desk, fiercely scribbling in a notebook. He said he knew nothing about my luggage.

I wasn't looking forward to a night without my things, but I set off through the maze of corridors and covered walkways toward my room. I found myself walking down a long, narrow corridor decorated with framed black and white photos of actors in cowboy hats. After I'd passed dozens of autographed pictures of long-ago stars with names like Ty Hardin and Will "Sugarfoot" Hutchins, I realized I was lost.

A sudden shout made me jump.

"Hey Doc!" said Rick Zukowski. "How was the reunion with the Oscar-winner?"

"Fine," I lied. I didn't want to talk about Ernesto's suicide with some military man who would see the situation in terms of black and white.

"Did the Oscar-winner blow you off? Success can change people."

"No. Plant was lovely. I just can't seem to find room fourteen."

Rick pointed at a door that led to a covered walkway which joined the central building to a newer wing. He put a warm hand on my back to guide me. I tried to ignore the tingles I felt from his touch. I did not want to feel like that about any other woman's husband. Not after what I'd been through.

"So, Captain, is your wife a fan of my column, as well as your mother-in-law?"

"My wife is — not alive."

"I'm — so sorry!" There was no right thing to say.

"Car accident. A moron driving an SUV and texting flattened her Hyundai like it was a Coke can. But, hey, that was over a year ago. I've healed up some. I still hate texting, though. In fact, I never carry a phone unless I'm on duty."

"I'm with you there. I don't even own a cell phone. The Manners Doctor says they encourage narcissism, intrude on polite conversation, and destroy the privacy necessary to a civilized society."

We'd nearly reached my room.

"Do come to my talk tomorrow." I dismissed him with a cool smile. Even if he was available, all I wanted now was sleep.

I fell onto the bed, still in my suit, and drifted into a bizarre dream that involved Zorro — riding with me on the back of a Harley. I accidentally pulled off his mask. His face and head were a mess of blood. Something pounded in my head and wouldn't stop. I forced my eyes open, but the noise grew louder — sounding like fierce knocking on my door.

Someone was indeed knocking on my door.

"Camilla Randall?" A commanding voice forced me back to consciousness. "Santa Barbara County Sheriff's Department."

I stumbled to the door. Outside stood two uniformed officers. So much for Plant's hopes of keeping me out of the investigation.

"Are you Camilla Randall Kahn, also known as Dr. Manners?"

I nodded.

"Would you like to come with us, Miss Randall?"

"Not really. I'm awfully jet lagged. And my luggage still hasn't arrived." I looked down at my disastrous suit. "Could we put this off until tomorrow?"

"No, we couldn't, Miss Randall." He peered into the tiny room as if he expected to see a pile of corpses inside. "Are you going to come peacefully?"

Chapter 9—In the Jailhouse Now

A PAINTING OF A RED windmill hung on the wall of the tiny room where I sat in the Sheriff's substation. I had no idea what a windmill was doing out here in cowboy territory. All I knew was that if I stared at it long enough, the blades started to spin. I'd been staring quite a while now, since I had nothing else to do but drink nasty coffee and wonder if what was left of my skirt would hold together.

When I was first brought into this place—some sort of deputy Sheriff's office—I'd been questioned by the portly officer in charge, whose nametag identified him as D. Sorengaard. His questions were remarkably clueless. He didn't seem at all interested in the suicide and kept asking me how long I'd been drinking in the Longhorn Room and whether I'd taken any "clients" to my room. I tried to be polite, since he seemed good natured enough, and explained the "Doctor" name I used was purely metaphorical. I told him

I was just a newspaper columnist and had no clients of any kind.

When he finished, I thought I'd be allowed to go back to the hotel, but I'd been kept in this tiny room for hours. Maybe I shouldn't have left the suicide scene before the police arrived, but this seemed harsh treatment for such a minor offence.

Finally, the door opened again and a man in plain clothes appeared. He had large, rodent-like teeth and a bad comb-over. He introduced himself as Detective Fiscalini. He plunked a cardboard file box on the table and sat next to me as if he planned to stay a while. I couldn't stifle a yawn.

"Would you prefer I call you Camilla Randall, Mrs. Kahn, or Dr. Manners?" he said, bringing his chair closer to me than I thought polite.

"Ms. Randall will do nicely." I didn't like his condescending tone.

He pulled a plastic bag from the box and placed it on the table. It contained what looked like the scarf I'd been wearing earlier. I touched my hair. When had I taken it off?

"Have you seen this before, Ms. Randall?"

"Of course. It's Hermes. One of the few I have left." I'd been selling off some of my designer scarves at a resale shop in Queens. Along with most of my shoes and bags. Seeing my favorite scarf encased in an evidence bag made me feel a bit tragified.

"And these?" Detective Fiscalini produced two more plastic baggies. A smaller one contained the remains of a cell phone that looked as if it had been smashed with a large, blunt object. A larger plastic baggie contained a gun. A very big gun. He placed it next to the one containing my scarf.

"What an awful-looking thing. Did somebody hit that poor telephone with it?"

"Please answer my question. Have you seen either of these items before?"

I assured him I hadn't.

"If you've touched them, Forensics will find your fingerprints. Would you like to rethink your answer?"

"I don't recall that I've ever touched a handgun. Certainly not that one. And the Manners Doctor does not approve of mobile telephones."

The phone looked like a cheap pre-pay throw-away and the gun bore no resemblance to the one Ernesto had used to kill himself.

"These items were inside Plantagenet Smith's vehicle. Locked inside. Can you explain how they got there?"

He leaned over me, looking like an inquisitive gopher.

"I have no idea." It's not easy to be polite to a man who is so blatantly invading your space. "I do know the Ferrari was locked, because I locked it. It was unlocked when I got in, but I was careful to lock it when I got up to the Hacienda. I figured Ernesto had forgotten, because he was so stressed."

"He was stressed? How do you know that? Did you know the deceased well?"

"I didn't know him at all. I heard him read a story in the Cowboy Critique Workshop. A pretty good story, I thought. Of course, I could be wrong. I'm often wrong. Especially about men. And I certainly was wrong about the alarm clock…"

Sleep-deprivation was making my conversation less than coherent.

"But you do know Plantagenet Smith?"

"Of course. He and I are old friends. But we haven't seen each other for about five years. Ever since he appeared on *The Real Story* and my husband confronted him with his ex-boyfriend. It was horrible. I'm sure you heard about it on the news."

"Did you come to Santa Ynez to re-unite with Mr. Smith now your divorce is final?"

I shook my head.

"I had no idea Plant was going to be at the conference. As I said, we've had no contact for five years."

"No contact. And he suddenly appears at the same conference as you?" He peered into my eyes. "Isn't it true you two were once engaged to be married?"

"Oh, my. That was nearly twenty years ago." The man sounded as if he were interviewing me for *Entertainment Tonight*, not investigating a suicide. "That was before I married Jonathan—which is probably why Jonathan has never liked him. And, obviously, it was long before Plantagenet came out as gay. Even to himself. I think he was sort of experimenting with heterosexuality."

The detective's dark little eyes revealed nothing.

"Experimenting. Is that what you and Mr. Smith were doing in bed with Ernesto Cervantes' body last night? A little experiment in necrophilia?"

I sighed. Okay, this guy had read the *Post* article. I shouldn't be surprised. But I refused to play his game.

"Detective Fiscalini, I'm afraid my jet lag is playing mind tricks on me." I gave him a Manners Doctor smile. "I thought I heard you accuse me of having sex with Plantagenet Smith? And a dead person?"

"You deny it?"

"Yes. I also deny being from the planet Zog."

The Manners Doctor would not have approved of that last sentence. After all, Detective Fiscalini might actually be from the planet Zog.

"But you do admit that you drove Plantagenet Smith's Ferrari from the scene of Mr. Cervantes' murder to the Hacienda at 2 A.M. this morning?"

"I drove the Ferrari up the hill, locked it, and left it in the Hacienda parking lot. Which I told the officers who brought me here. But I don't know about any murder. Ernesto Cervantes committed suicide. Anybody who saw his body would know that. And the boy had just been humiliated in front of half the people at the conference by Toby Roarke. Silas

Ryder said he was fragile. Teenagers can't always put experiences like that in perspective. They think the humiliation will go on forever. The Manners Doctor has often written about the importance of good manners when dealing with teenagers…"

"Silas Ryder? The owner of the Ryderbook stores? What is your relationship with Silas Ryder?"

Before I could answer, D. Sorengaard reappeared to summon Detective Fiscalini somewhere. Maybe back to the planet Zog.

Left alone with the windmill again, I began to empathize with Don Quixote's vendetta against the things. I had no idea how the detective imagined I was involved in Ernesto Cervantes' suicide—or why he used the word murder. I could only hope the nonsense wouldn't make it into the press. I could picture the news leads—

"KINKY DR. MANNERS DETAINED IN GAY SUICIDE SHOCKER"

Or "KAHN'S KINKY EX INVESTIGATED IN NECROPHILIAC RING"

Maybe the windmill picture hypnotized me into some sort of sleep, because the next thing I knew, D. Sorengaard was shaking my shoulder.

"Okay, Dr. Manners. Time to go. You got some big shot waiting for you."

I rubbed my ear where it had been resting on the table. D. Sorengaard gave me a rather sweet smile. Something about it was familiar, although I couldn't think why.

"Move your tail, honey. They sent brass up here to take you back to L.A."

"Brass?" I shocked myself back to reality with a sip of coffee—even more toxic at room temperature. "Did you say 'back to Los Angeles'? I haven't been there in years."

"Whatever. A honcho from the L.A.P.D. says he wants you for questioning. He's waiting in a car outside."

"Someone from the Los Angeles Police Department wants to ask me questions?" I followed him into the outer office. This sounded ominous.

"L.A. wants you—and L.A. can have you. Me, I've got a suspicious death on my watch and a bunch of anti-grape-crazies about to invade."

"Anti grape-crazies?" I envisioned a crusade against purple lunatics. What did he mean by "suspicious death"? He was as bad as Detective Fiscalini.

He sighed. "Yeah. Big anti-vineyard protest. Remember when the tree-huggers used to hate ranchers because cow-farts killed off the rain forest? Now they hate 'em for getting rid of the cows and planting grapes. No pleasing these people."

"So where do I go?"

He pointed to the double doors that led outside.

I had no idea what to expect. Was I going to be accused of some even more heinous crime?

Chapter 10—Police Questioning

A DEPUTY ESCORTED ME OUTSIDE. Whoever I was going to meet up with in Los Angeles, I hoped they had better coffee.

He walked me along a concrete walk past a green lawn and out to the street.

But I saw no sign of the L.A.P.D.

In fact, I seemed to have been transported out of California completely—to a misty, fairytale world of thatched gingerbread-y cottages with windows full of teddy bears, gnomes, and wooden shoes. The breezes wafted with the aromas of baking pastry. Down the street was another windmill—a three-dimensional one—about two stories high. I watched the windmill's paddles turn slowly in the gentle breeze.

A lone green Saturn was parked at the curb, the back door open. I got in, while the deputy went around to the driver's window and exchanged a few monotone grunts of cop-speak with the man at the wheel.

As the deputy returned to the building, I had the creepy realization that the man in the driver's seat wasn't wearing a uniform. I kept my hand on the door handle.

He pushed a paper bag through the headrests.

"Cheese or ollalieberry?" he said. The bag smelled of fresh coffee and pastry. I let go and took the bag. Inside was a take-out coffee cup and two of the biggest Danish pastries I'd ever seen.

"I hope you like your cappuccino with chocolate sprinkles." He turned to look at me. "It's the only way they serve it in this town."

It wasn't a policeman. It was Rick Zukowski, Mystery-Thriller.

"Rick!" I said. "The deputy thought you were somebody else. We have to find the L.A.P.D. They're going to question me —"

"They already have," Rick said, still grinning. "The question was: cheese or ollalieberry?" He peeked into the bag. "You gotta decide, because I'm starving."

"You're from the L.A.P.D?"

"It's a fact, ma'am." He pulled an impressive badge from the pocket of his faded denim jacket. Captain. Not of the deep blue sea, but the thin blue line. That was where that air of authority came from. Was he going to arrest me? It was too humiliating.

"You think I'm a murderer? And a necrophiliac dominatrix?"

Rick's warm brown eyes stared at me through the headrests. I couldn't tell if he was trying not to laugh or seriously trying to picture me in the role.

"Necrophilia? What — they get their complaints from late night comics?"

Late night comics. That's probably why everybody knew

about the *Post* article. Some comedian had got hold of it. Damn. That could only make things worse.

"Apparently. Is that what you're going to arrest me for?"

"I'm not going to arrest you."

"Then what are we doing here?"

I decided to take the Danish with the purple jam center. It was buttery and warm and the jam tart-sweet and wonderfully gooey.

"We're eating Danish pastry. Just out of the oven." He took the bag and pulled out the remaining Danish. He took a large bite before starting the engine.

"You got D. Sorengaard to release me by pretending the L.A.P.D. wanted me?"

I leaned forward so I could see him better between the head rests. I was trying to process this new information about Rick. A policeman-writer. A sensitive warrior. Intriguing.

"I flashed my badge to speed things up, but they had nothing to hold you on. They hauled you in on an iffy complaint from a semi-intelligible cell phone call. Awful reception in these hills." Rick munched cheese Danish while he drove us through the cutesy streets.

"They got a complaint about me? Who made the call? It wasn't my ex-husband, was it?" Was Jonathan subjecting me to some new humiliation? After the *Post* article, I knew he was capable of anything.

Rick laughed. "Jeez, you two are having some battle, aren't you? Not that I blame you for dumping him. Not many wives would stick around after a video of her husband getting a b. j. from a Sunset hooker made it onto You Tube. But I gotta have some sympathy for the guy. Those amateur paparazzi are a menace with their phones."

"If Jonathan didn't make the call to the Sheriff's people, who did?"

"Mitzi Boggs Bailey. She called in a complaint against you and Smith and a dead guy who drove an orange Mustang. She said you three were having such noisy sex that she couldn't sleep." He chortled. "And I thought your reunion hadn't gone that well..."

If I hadn't had my hands full of coffee and pastry, I would have hit him.

"That was pay-per-view! Plantagenet and I did not have sex, noisy or otherwise! Besides, it's a Ferrari and it's not orange; it's burgundy. Anyway, I didn't know sex was against the law in—" I looked around at the cutesy shops. "Garden Gnome Heaven or wherever we are."

Rick laughed again. "Solvang. We're in Solvang. A little bit o' Denmark on the Central Coast of California." He turned right and pointed at a sign that said 'San Marcos Pass.' "We're on our way back to Gabriella's Rancho. Sex is legal in both places, as long as you're not scaring the horses or disturbing the peace. Especially the peace of someone related to Gabriella Moore—Mitzi's her sister-in-law, you know."

That explained a few things.

"But blowing people's heads off isn't legal anywhere that I know of."

His voice came at me like buckshot.

"I hear the kid you and the famous screenwriter were having that threesome with got his head blown off last night. You want to tell me about that?"

My mouth went so dry I couldn't swallow. Finally I managed to wash things down with a cappuccino that was more chocolate sprinkles and foam than coffee.

"There was no threesome! And no sex. Except on some TV movie Ernesto was watching. Mrs. Boggs Bailey must have heard the soundtrack—and I don't know—maybe she went over to complain about it and saw the body. But she says she saw ghosts too, so who knows?"

I gulped more coffee.

"But no—I don't particularly want to talk about it. A boy committed suicide. It's tragic. But please don't pretend to be my friend when you only want to interrogate me." Why had I flirted with this man? "Are you working for that Fiscalini person—is that why you're here? Some good cop/bad cop thing?"

"I'm here buying you breakfast and taking you back to the Rancho." Rick turned and gave me a silly grin. "Do you know you have chocolate sprinkles on your nose?"

Chapter 11—Meanwhile Back at the Ranch

WHEN RICK AND I GOT back to the Rancho Grande, the parking lot was jammed with cars and vans with media logos. A knot tightened in my stomach. And I'd thought I could avoid all this horror by escaping New York.

Reporters accosted me as soon as I opened the car door, pressing around me as I tried to make my way to the Hacienda. They kept asking me questions like, "Are you romantically involved with Plantagenet Smith?" and "Are you and Plantagenet into necrophilia as well as S and M, Dr. Manners?"

Poor Plant was getting slimed by Jonathan's *Post* interview along with me.

Rick escorted me through the crowd and into the lobby with practiced efficiency. I was glad to be in the company of a policeman, even such an infuriating one.

"Thanks," I said as I stopped at the desk for my room key. "This is all such nonsense. They must be starved for news around here."

"I'm sorry Ms. Randall," said Alberto, the little concierge. "You are no longer in room fourteen A. That room is not available." He was engrossed in lettering a sign that said, in elegant calligraphy, "GUESTS ONLY & NO REPORTERS."

"My room is not available? Where is Gabriella?" Was I being given the boot because of Mitzi Boggs Bailey's delusions?

"Miss Moore is out. She says you can have Roy Rogers. No extra charge." Alberto put the final touches on his ampersand.

"I should hope not. I'm supposed to get free lodging," I gave a grumpy sniff. "First my luggage disappears and now this."

Alberto silently pointed with his Rapidograph pen. My set of ancient Vuitton suitcases and laptop case were carefully stacked behind the desk. I ran to them. It felt like being reunited with family.

Rick picked up my two largest bags.

"Roy Rogers is very nice. Sleeps six." Alberto gave a phony smile.

I gave him a cold look.

"I don't plan on doing any entertaining."

"Don't be upset about the room change," Rick said. "The place is full. Gaby probably wants to get Mitzi away from the crime scene. The old girl has already screwed things up for the i-team with that call to the Sheriff about your..." He raised his eyebrows in feigned shock, "Zombie sex *ménage a trois*."

"Screwed it up for the investigators? What about me? Look what that old woman's delusions have..." I stopped. Rick's mention of "zombie sex" had quieted the lobby to an eavesdropping hush.

Now I knew the punchline of the most recent late-night jokes.

Rick hurried me out to his car.

I apologized for my crankiness when we were safely in his Saturn.

"You seem to have a lot of practice with crowds."

"I was a rookie beat cop during the O.J. trial." Rick started down the winding drive to the cabins. "I learned a lot about dealing with scandal-obsessed reporters. Since then, I've been assigned to dozens of celebrity cases. It's absurd how the smallest thing can explode into a scandal once the media get hold of it."

The cabin area wasn't as crowded as the Hacienda, and I couldn't spot any lurking reporters, but all the cabin parking spaces were taken by what looked like the investigation team. Several determined-looking workers in Sheriff's Department uniforms stood inside the yellow police tape barrier surrounding Zorro and its environs.

Rick had to park a few hundred yards up the hill, but didn't complain as he grabbed my suitcases and started down the road. I had the laptop bag and make-up case as well as my tote, which made for an awkward load as I trudged after him. The warming sun beat down bright and hot.

"Too bad we had to shoot the horses, Dusty." Rick put on a stagy cowboy drawl. "But at least we got all your bricks in these here saddlebags."

"Sorry. I tend to overpack. I had no idea how people would dress out here in the Wild West—especially right down the road from the old Reagan Ranch. I didn't want to look shabby if I was going to run into a bunch of Republican *grande dames*. They are the Manners Doctor's fan base after all."

Rick laughed. "My mother-in-law's a Democrat, and she's your biggest fan—swear to God. But everything I've heard about you is so different."

Uh-oh. This was it. He was going to ask if anything in that

article was true.

But he just grinned. "You seem real. You know, down-to-earth."

"I am real. So is the Manners Doctor, in a way. Most people have an inner child. I have an inner great aunt."

He had a delicious grin. He even carried my bags into the bedroom and lifted the biggest one onto the folding luggage rack.

"You've been so kind," I said. "I don't know how you managed to be there exactly when I needed you, but thanks. If I can do anything for you…"

He laughed. "I wish I could claim to be psychic, but actually Gaby sent me this morning. She felt awful about Mitzi's call to the Sheriff, and if she could have picked you up herself, she would have."

He leaned closer, smelling of Old Spice.

Mr. Stowe, my favorite stableman when I was growing up at Randall Hall, used to wear Old Spice.

Rick looked into my eyes a moment longer than necessary. I wondered if he was thinking about kissing me.

"Actually, there is something." He gave a nervous laugh.

"Sure." I wouldn't mind a goodbye kiss. Those big brown eyes were melty.

"If you could—look at my novel? I'm supposed to show it to somebody tomorrow, and if you had any suggestions, or catch any typos…"

Chapter 12—Foul Play

MY HEART DID A LITTLE embarrassed sinking. Here I was thinking a hot policeman was interested in me.

But all he wanted was for me to read his silly novel. It was bound to be awful. First novels always were.

"I'm sure it's great. Great!" I said with feigned enthusiasm. "But I'm no kind of expert. Unless you've got a character who's worried about where to seat an ex-mother-in-law at a third wedding, or how much to tip the galley crew after a sailing party..." I started bustling around the room, unzipping cases and opening drawers. "You'd be better off asking Toby, or one of the other fiction people."

"Toby charges an exorbitant fee, and everybody else is furious that I'm getting a big advance on an unfinished manuscript. They say that never happens to a new writer."

"Advance?" I stopped mid-bustle to look at Rick in this new light. "You have a contract? Congratulations. You must find all these amateur workshops boring."

"Believe me, I need workshops. I've got a great agent, is all. Lucille Silverberg. She's going to be here this weekend. In fact, she was due last night, but she got hung up in L.A., thank goodness. I don't get a penny until I've finished the book, and I'm going crazy trying to end it. It's up in the car."

I watched him sprint up the hill to the Saturn. That whole exchange was odd. Usually writers with agents were too far up the food chain to bother with conferences—especially a Z-list one like this.

Over at the Zorro cabin, the Ferrari sat in its former spot next to the fountain. Two of the Sheriff-Coroner's investigators were pulling out the seats, looking for God-knew-what. Plant must have been moved out of the cabin. As soon as I got some sleep I had to find him and ask about the mysterious gun and that smashed phone Detective Fiscalini claimed he found in the Ferrari. Right now I was too sleepy to make sense of any of it.

Rick rushed back in.

"Here it is." He presented me with another of the ubiquitous gold folders. "Except the last four chapters. They're still in progress. I'd appreciate any comments you've got."

I set the folder on the coffee table with ceremony. "I'll bet everybody here is sick with envy. These people would kill to get an agent. How did you do it?"

"Dumb luck. My agent found me. Or Toby did. He sent Luci a short story I wrote about busting a Hollywood sex party—you get a critique from him as part of the conference—and I guess he went nuts over it, because the next thing, Lucille Silverberg was on the phone, offering me a contract to expand the story into a book."

"Congratulations. I didn't know agents did that."

"She and Toby are tight, is all. She's going to be the main speaker on Sunday. I think most of the people here came to meet her. She's a big shot in New York publishing, I guess."

I only semi-stifled my yawns, but Rick didn't seem to be getting the signal it was time to go. His face looked tense.

"You're not going to help Plantagenet Smith if you withhold evidence, you know."

I didn't like this on/off policeman thing.

"Don't be silly. I'm not withholding anything. I'll be happy to tell Detective Fiscalini and his investigators anything they want to know. Nobody asked, but I did witness Ernesto being humiliated in front of everybody, and he took it very hard. Then he went down to Plant's cabin and — who knows why — but he shot himself. Plant was his idol. I suppose he was afraid he'd never have that kind of success, so he..."

Rick's words finally sank in.

"What do you mean — help Plantagenet? What's happened to him?"

"He was taken to the county jail for questioning early this morning. Fiscalini is pretty tight-lipped, but I got some information out of Sorengaard. It wasn't a suicide. Definitely foul play."

"It wasn't suicide? But, who could have killed him?" This wasn't making any sense.

Rick gave me a strange look. "From what he told me, it's looking a whole lot like your friend the screenwriter killed the Cervantes kid. Did they have some kind of tiff? Just tell me what you know, and maybe I can help."

I flopped down on the couch — my head full of the horrible image of Plant in his Zegna and Ralph Lauren, sitting in a smelly, seedy cell: the ghost of Cary Grant trapped in some Spaghetti Western nightmare. So unfair.

"I know Ernesto shot himself. I saw it." I looked up at Rick — all stony-faced policeman now. Did he really believe Plant could be a murderer?

"You saw it? If you witnessed the death, you should tell the investigation team. They're still collecting evidence in the cabin over there. I can go with you."

Why was he so dense?

"I don't mean I actually watched. But I did see the boy humiliated. And I saw the body. And the gun that killed him. He had it in his hand when I got there."

"Smith held the weapon when you arrived at the cabin?"

"No." I was getting annoyed now. "Ernesto—his body— did. A silver-colored gun was in his hand next to..." I didn't want to revisit the memory. "It was on the pillow. Silas said it was left over from Ernesto's gang days."

"A .22 caliber pistol?"

"It was a gun. The kind that makes people dead. They're sort of one-size fits-all, aren't they?"

"Not exactly. A .22 at point-blank range can certainly kill, but from what I could get out of Sorengaard, it seems like half this kid's head was blown off. He said they found another gun that could have made the wound—a King Cobra .357 magnum. They found it in Smith's Ferrari, along with a scarf that belongs to you. The car you drove up to the Hacienda— after the murder. You want to tell me about that?"

"I can't tell you what I don't know." I couldn't hide my anger. "When the detective showed that big gun to me—it was the first time I saw it."

Rick stared at me as if he were accessing an inner lie detector.

I didn't like his attitude.

"Even if it is murder—which I can't believe—why suspect Plant? There's no motive. The boy was hot and had a crush on him. They were about to have great sex. How can the Sheriff's people be so stupid?"

Rick sat in the chair opposite me.

"Actually, these local guys seem like a pretty bright bunch. They don't have a big pool of possible suspects. Gaby says no one would have been around the cabins at that time of night, except Mitzi Boggs Bailey. Conference guests usually stay at the Hacienda and these cabins are for workshops and VIPs"

"Plantagenet wasn't down here either. Gabriella can vouch for that. She'd just talked to him before you and I met her in the bar. He'd have walked down the hill, since he'd given Ernesto his car. That takes at least ten minutes."

"Yes, Gaby met him in the lobby a little after ten. I was there, too, checking for messages. I didn't know who Smith was at that point, but I figured he had to be one of Gaby's VIP celebrities, with all that Italian tailoring on him. She invited him to join us in the bar, but he said he wanted to shower and 'decompress' because a couple of geezers had tailgated him all the way from the San Marcos Pass."

I remembered Gabriella had mentioned the tailgating. Plant hated that.

"Your friend Smith was already upset, and then Ernesto rushed in, furious about Toby. He said some choice things in Spanish that I wouldn't want to repeat."

"To you? You knew him?"

"No, but you couldn't help noticing—a Latino kid with that bleached hair and the gang tattoo. He was shouting that stuff to everybody, mostly to Smith. He probably thought nobody understood."

"He yelled at Plant? They were fighting?" Plantagenet was the most non-violent man I knew, but everybody has a breaking point. I suppose something awful could have made him snap.

"No. They were arguing about Toby. Smith calmed Ernesto down and the kid took off in that Ferrari. I went up to my room and edited for about a half hour, and when I came back down to join Gaby for a drink, Smith was gone. Nobody knows what he and the boy did after that."

"I do. Plant walked down to his cabin, trying to decide if he was being ethical sleeping with a fan who obviously hero-worshiped him. Ernesto had time to get undressed and tune in an erotic movie on the television. He left the Ferrari unlocked, so he may have been in a hurry about it. But if you're planning to be dead in a few minutes, I guess you don't worry about car thieves."

"The car was unlocked when you went to drive it up the hill?"

"Yes. That's why I was especially careful to lock it when I got up to the parking lot. But I guess I left my scarf in there. It must have fallen off."

I touched my hair where the scarf had been. It felt sticky with road dust. "I'll die if I don't get a shower. Now. I'll talk to you later, okay?" I was desperate for some time to collect my thoughts.

Just as I managed to get Rick out the door, the phone on the desk rang. It was Gabriella.

"Sorry to bother you hon, but I'm wondering if you'd mind giving your presentation tonight for the paying customers instead of this afternoon. I need somebody to fill Plantagenet's slot."

I tried to focus.

"Plant's slot? He's still in jail? They really think he had something to do with Ernesto's death? That's so stupid. Don't they know it was suicide?"

"Nope. At least the Sheriff doesn't think so. The studio's sending up their lawyers, but it looks like they're charging your old friend Plantagenet with first degree murder."

All I could do was grunt my agreement.

First degree murder. Were these people all insane?

Chapter 13—The Desperate Alarm Clock

AFTER A LONG SHOWER, I managed to sleep a bit. Probably because I tried to read Rick's snoozerific novel. He might have a big name New York agent, but *Blue Rage* by M. J. Zukowski was not going to make any best seller lists that I knew of. I wondered what this Luci Silverberg person saw in it that I didn't.

The bedside clock said five fifteen when I woke up, feeling a little sick as the memory of the horrors of last night came back: the terrible image of Ernesto's body. How could it have not been a suicide? There had to be another explanation for the gun stuff people kept talking about.

I turned on the television. Flipping through channels, I caught a clip of Plantagenet accepting his Academy Award last February. Then an awful one of him getting out of a black and white Sheriff's car. I felt a familiar constriction in my neck. It felt like watching the weepy court-house step footage of my own divorce hearing they played over and over last fall.

The reporter's voice confirmed Gaby's dire pronouncement.

"Oscar-winning writer Plantagenet Smith is being held for questioning in the death of his protégé, nineteen-year old Ernesto Cervantes, who was found shot to death in Mr. Smith's bedroom at Gabriella Moore's resort in Santa Ynez last night."

The screen showed a still shot of a tough-looking dark-haired Hispanic boy.

"Mr. Smith, an openly homosexual writer, denies that the death was the result of a lovers' quarrel."

The picture changed to a sunny sidewalk outside a Spanish-style public building, where Silas Ryder, looking large and rumpled, blinked nervously at the camera.

"Silas Ryder, the Central Coast businessman who employed the deceased at one of his bookstores, stated that Ernesto Cervantes had no relatives except an uncle in the state of Sinaloa in Mexico. Mr. Ryder said Cervantes was a promising writer and a popular student at Cuesta College in San Luis Obispo.

"He was a good kid. A sweet kid." Silas looked uncomfortable as he squinted at the camera. "He'd lost both his parents, and got involved with gangs before he was in his teens. But he'd put that all behind him. He was a good worker and had a talent for storytelling, but like so many writers, he could be self-destructive."

The newsperson cut him off. Too much information for TV, of course.

All anybody would hear was that Ernesto was "sweet." They'd hear that as "gay" and dismiss the whole story as sordid—just as Plant predicted. The reporter didn't even let Silas finish what he probably intended to say about Ernesto's suicidal tendencies. They wanted a drama, and they'd cast Plantagenet as the bad guy: a gay celebrity for the media sharks to feed on.

Of course, if it really was murder, Plant was an obvious suspect. And that was an awfully big gun they found in the Ferrari. Plantagenet had been alone in the cabin with the body when I came in. Plus his suit had that blood on it.

No. I wasn't going to let my mind go there.

I picked up the remote and was about to click off when I saw the face of D. Sorengaard, giving a harried look at the camera. The newscaster was saying, "…In other news: more protests today in Santa Ynez, as environmental activists chained themselves to the ancient oaks that are slated to be cut down for more vineyards…"

I turned it off. I'd think of some way to help Plant, but first I had to get myself together for my talk. I wasn't going to be speaking to a small group of non-fiction writers as planned. Plant's presentation had been advertised to the public, and tickets had been sold. People would be coming from as far away as Los Angeles to see an Oscar winner, and all they'd get was the Manners Doctor.

My stage fright built as I reviewed the notes for my speech. I paced the room, lecturing the faux mission furniture on the rigors of daily column writing and warning the autographed photos of Roy Rogers and Dale Evans about a life that's always on deadline.

I dressed in my brown Chanel suit and strappy cobra skin sandals — the things I'd planned to wear for my talk when it was scheduled for the evening after the opening reception. Now I wasn't sure about the sandals. There was a lot of walking to do around that crazy hotel. I had a pair of pumps that would be more comfortable. Fendi pumps. Conservative, but chic.

If Plantagenet were here, he would have helped me choose.

Plantagenet. Always kind. Always helpful. Not a killer. It couldn't be true.

Something Mrs. Boggs Bailey said flashed in my memory:

"They shot off their guns," she'd said. Guns, plural. Could there have been a gunfight?

Maybe Ernesto had tried to shoot Plant—to rob him, maybe—and Plant was forced to shoot back. Anybody might do that if he/she happened to have a weapon handy. Which apparently Plantagenet did.

Which wasn't at all like him, but maybe I didn't know him anymore. It had been a long time. Rick was right that success changes people. Look at Jonathan.

Was my taste in men so abysmal that I'd chosen a killer for my gay best friend?

I had to get through dinner before my talk. I doubted I could eat much, but Gabriella made it clear she expected me to join the faculty in the dining room. I changed into the Fendi pumps and touched up my make-up again.

I recognized the golf cart driver she sent to pick me up. He was the young man who had been furiously writing in his notebook at the front desk last night. He wore a nametag that said "Miguel". His face, a dark teak-brown above his white long-sleeved shirt, looked nervous.

He helped me into the cart with careful ceremony.

"Can I ask you something, Ms. Randall? I heard you were there—in Mr. Roarke's workshop—when Ernie read that story. The guy who got shot—he read a story about a rooster. Do you remember?"

El Despertador Looks at the Stars. Yes. I thought it was very good. A little rough around the edges, but original and moving. Was he a friend of yours?" No wonder Miguel had that tense look. He was grieving.

"Kind of. He helped me sometimes with spelling and stuff. And titles. I never can come up with titles. That's why I gave him the story to look at. He put the fancy quotation on it and that 'Looks at the Stars' stuff. Me, I called it *The Desperate Alarm Clock.* He said that wasn't literary enough."

"You wrote that—the story about the rooster?"

Wow. Ernesto didn't write the story.

I suppose there was some small relief in knowing I'd been right about the alarm clock, but it kind of wiped out the possibility of suicide. Writers might be a self-destructive lot, but they didn't kill themselves over other writers' rejections.

"Yeah. Ernie didn't tell me he was going to read it in the Cowboy Workshop, but I guess he didn't have time to write something of his own. He does that sometimes. I heard a bunch of obnoxious TV writers talking about it at lunch. They said you liked it."

"Yes. I did. You're quite a writer."

And Ernesto had been quite a liar.

Chapter 14—The Hole in the Wall

THE HACIENDA PARKING LOT was packed with even more media vehicles. Now I understood why they'd been asking me all those questions about Plant—news of his arrest would have been out by the time I arrived this morning.

I didn't know how I was going to get through the melée into the hotel, especially since the media crowd was augmented by a large, unkempt crowd carrying picket signs.

But an unfazed Miguel drove up onto the lawn and followed a footpath around to the back of the main building, where he parked behind a laundry van. He led me through a utility yard to a door marked "Employees Only."

"What's going on out there?" I whispered as we entered a dark corridor.

"A protest. To save the trees. Mr. Roarke cuts down oak trees to plant his grapes—then the owls, foxes, squirrels—they got no place to live. So the college kids and the old hippies—

they carry signs. Plus there's a bunch of TV guys who want to put everybody on the news. Oh, did you want to be on the TV news—for publicity?" He stopped and gave me a polite, questioning look.

"Oh, no. Absolutely not."

Amazing to think some people might see this as a marketing opportunity.

"Me neither. I'm legal, but I don't need no questions."

He led me past several offices, including one with a plaque on the door with a star that said "Miss Moore"—obviously a souvenir from her actress days. We then walked past the busy kitchen, where we were greeted by the bowing waiter who had held the door for me when I first arrived. He waved a soapy hand as he washed a stack of pots and pans. He said something in Spanish to Miguel, but Miguel rushed past.

"Don't mind Santiago," he said. "The guy is a dork. From Guatemala. Don't speak no English. His Spanish sucks, too."

Behind a heavy wooden door and there was another hallway, where linoleum gave way to guest-territory carpeting. Miguel stopped at what looked like a solid panel in the wall and took out a set of keys.

He inserted a key into a bit of carved scrollwork, and the whole panel started to move—a cleverly disguised door. I followed him inside to a small banquet room furnished with fabulous Art Deco antiques. Miguel laughed, giving me a smile over his shoulder.

"Crazy, huh? They call this room the Hole in the Wall—after the hideout of Butch Cassidy and the Sundance Kid—every name in this place is from old western movies.

The room didn't look so much like a gunslinger hideout as a 1920s speakeasy. It had polished mahogany wainscoting, red-flocked wallpaper and a spectacular art deco chandelier.

"Miss Moore asked me to bring you this way because of the reporters." Miguel said. He obviously saw me staring at the molded glass-and-bronze chandelier. "This part of the hotel was built during the Prohibition, when this was a dude ranch. I guess Hollywood bigshots came up to party all the time. This room is so secret it's not even in the building plans. Miss Moore doesn't even show it to most of the guests. You must be special."

Noise of a key in a lock in a panel opposite suggested that somebody else was special, too. The panel slowly opened and Rick Zukowski stepped inside.

I made a startled noise.

"I hoped you might be in here." Rick laughed "Gaby sent me out to do a search and rescue. She was afraid you might have been ambushed by the hostiles out there." He nodded at Miguel and said something in fluent Spanish.

Miguel gave a quick nod and let himself out the panel we came in.

"Impressive, Mr. Zukowski," I said. "You talk Spanish like a native."

He gave me that cute grin.

"I am a native. L.A. born and bred. My mom was born in Mexico. Zukowski was a salesman from Ohio, traveling through." He studied my outfit. "You look fantastic. Wow. Really great."

He kept staring and grinning. Nice to know I still had it.

"Thank you." I bestowed a quick kiss on his cheek. "I'll be a little less nervous knowing I look okay."

He looked into my eyes for a moment, then gave me a kiss back—long and sweet. Amazing how much I'd wanted him to do that. His body felt strong and safe. I clung to him for just a moment too long, then felt embarrassed.

I covered by telling him about Miguel's revelation about the rooster story.

"I know it looks bad, but it doesn't mean Plant is guilty." I went for a businesslike tone. "The killer didn't have to be staying at the resort. The cabins are close to the road. Maybe it was a passing driver."

Rick obviously didn't buy it.

"Somebody driving a country road in the middle of the night says, 'I think I'll stop in here for a minute and use a guest for target practice, then toss away my thousand-dollar gun'?" He scrunched his face as if he were thinking hard.

He ushered me out the wall panel he'd come in. It led to the corridor with the pictures of Will "Sugarfoot" Hutchins and the other old cowboy stars.

Rick seemed to have a thing about the cowboy myth being ripped off from Mexicans. He told me how ranch is short for *rancho*; and chaps are *chaparejos*; and "hoosegow" is bad spelling of *juzgado*.

"And what makes a cowboy a cowboy? His cow? No frickin' way. It's his horse. 'Cowboy' is just Anglo for *caballero*. A horseman. The great American cowboy is a Mexican horseman."

He was probably right. He seemed to be right about most things. Which I found annoying. I didn't want to let him be right about Plant.

"Silas said Ernesto was self-destructive. Maybe he did commit suicide after all." I knew how lame that sounded as soon as it came out.

"Silas Ryder said that? How well do you know him?"

There he was, back to being the interrogating policeman again.

"I met him last night in the Longhorn Room, same as you. Later, he came down to the cabins with Gabriella. Plant showed him the body, and Silas called the Sheriff's Department. He thought it was Toby's fault, just like Plant did. He was so mad he knocked Zorro off the wall."

"Silas Ryder is the one who vandalized the Guy Williams photo?" Rick pondered this as if it held some significance. "Did he say anything anti-Latino?"

I didn't like where this was going.

"Why are you asking me all these questions about Silas? He

seems to be the only real friend Ernesto had."

"People are usually killed by the ones closest to them."

Was that true? All I could do was shudder. It was obvious Silas knew Plant pretty well. Silas might have known Ernesto was going down to Plant's cabin. He could have killed Ernesto and then tossed the gun into Plant's car.

Rick looked at his watch. "We'll be late. Gaby will kill me."

He closed the door to the secret room and locked it, hiding the key in a piece of scrollwork near the top that seemed to have been built for the purpose. No one would have known the door was there.

"So you suspect Silas of killing Ernesto—just because they were close?" I followed Rick down the corridor. "Do you have any other reason?"

Rick shrugged. "Silas Ryder was also the last person to see Mitzi Boggs Bailey."

I wondered if I'd heard right. "What do you mean, the last one—what's happened to her?" The poor old woman. She'd been so terrified of those ghosts.

Rick stopped and looked at me.

"Hasn't anybody told you? Mitzi Boggs Bailey disappeared from her cabin last night. The old girl's gone missing."

Chapter 15—Maverick Jesus

WHILE WE HURRIED TO the dining room, Rick told me what he knew about Mrs. Boggs Bailey's disappearance. Apparently after Plant was taken to Santa Maria, Silas found Mitzi in the parking lot, harassing the investigators about the noise. Silas offered to walk her back to the cabin to wait until they could get a room ready for her at the Hacienda.

That didn't sound very suspicious to me. I know Rick was trained to think in terms of statistics, but I didn't want see Silas as a murderer. Plant obviously liked and trusted him.

"That must have been why they moved me out of room fourteen," I said. "They were getting it ready for Mitzi."

"Could be. Anyway, when Miguel sent a cart down to get her, Mitzi was gone. So was Silas. But the old girl has gone missing before. There's a search and rescue team looking for her now."

I offered a few encouraging words, but all I could think was that if Ernesto had been murdered, a killer was out there wandering those hills. And because it was pretty unlikely that Silas or Plant had killed Ernesto, Mrs. Boggs Bailey was in awful danger. She might very well have seen the killer when she was wandering around talking to her "ghosts." I wished Rick seemed more worried.

"Jeez," he said when we finally got to the Fiesta Hall dining room. "I can't believe they didn't save you a seat." He nodded at the big, round head table.

It certainly looked crowded. In fact, the short wiry man who called himself, "Herb Frye the Sci-Fi guy" had squeezed in an extra chair, wedging himself between voluptuous Vondra DeHaviland, the romance novelist, and a greeting card verse expert from Fresno who looked as if she'd rather be enduring a tax audit. Beside Toby sat the pretty Latina girl from the workshop—overdressed in a Donna Karan cocktail dress from a few seasons ago, with her eyes ringed in enough black eyeliner to make a raccoon jealous.

On Toby's other side, the amazingly stoic Gaby soldiered on, wearing the mask of gracious hostess.

Vondra waved Rick over to where his entrée sat waiting.

"Go," I said. "I'll be fine at another table. I'll see you at my talk. I hope you can be there?"

He gave me a quick kiss. Not much more than brotherly, but there, in front of everybody, it felt like a declaration of affection. He countered the intensity of the moment with a laugh.

"Of course. How could I face my mother-in-law if I missed it?"

The Miss Manners fan waved at me and pointed to an empty chair next at a table of memoir-writing senior citizens. But several of her companions gave me icy looks that indicated they'd probably heard the late night "zombie sex" jokes.

As I looked around for another spot, the red-faced

Englishman from the workshop rose from a table nearby and accosted me.

"These waiters don't seem to speak a word of English. Could you tell that young man that I require tea, not coffee, and that I'd like my beef cooked—not practically alive and mooing?" He pointed at one of the waiters bringing out trays of tri-tip barbeque and beans. "I thought I was coming to America, not Mexico. Will you tell me why the towns, the food, the language, everything here is all bloody Mexican?"

"I suppose it's because the Mexicans were here first." I tried to ignore his implied racism. "But I'm afraid I don't speak much Spanish either. I had the same trouble with my taxi driver on the way here."

The man had that angry-tourist look that hovered between anguish and rage. I looked around for a way to escape him.

I spotted a free chair at a table with the smug twenty-somethings from *Cowboy Critique*. They must be the "obnoxious TV writers" Miguel mentioned. One was wearing a much laundered T-shirt with a *Vampire Diaries* logo and another had a baseball cap from *Criminal Minds*.

As I sat down, they stopped their animated conversation about how New York agents scorned Hollywood screenwriting credentials. The *Vampire Diaries* woman nudged *Criminal Minds* as he used his sourdough toast to scoop beans and salsa from his plate.

She handed him a fork.

"She's the Manners Doctor, dickhead; don't act like some brain-eating zombie"

There was a snort from the leather-jacketed alpha male of the group, and his cohorts joined in. More fans of late-night TV.

I armored myself with a Manners Doctor smile.

"Please go on with your conversation, and enjoy your meal. The Manners Doctor is just a character I use when I write—a voice. Besides, the Doctor says good manners are about respecting other people, not judging them."

But the smugsters ate in silence. I wondered if they were intimidated by my Manners Doctor persona or busy picturing me in some kinky sex act. I kept looking over at Rick, adorably goofy as he laughed at the Sci-Fi guy's jokes.

Finally one of the smugsters spoke. He had a remarkable number of piercings in his nose and eyebrows.

"I'd watch myself around Captain Road Rage, Doctor. He may have got himself a fancy agent, but he's still a menace to society."

"I'll keep that in mind." I helped myself to more salsa. "And who is Captain Road Rage?"

"Captain Maverick Jesus Zukowski." *Vampire Diaries* gave a sarcastic laugh. "Of the L.A.P.D."

Maverick Jesus — M. J. Zukowski. What a name to live with. I steeled myself for whatever snark the smugsters were planning to hurl at him.

"How come that creep hasn't been fired?" said Pierced Nose.

"I read they keep him twiddling his thumbs behind a desk or something. Maybe that's why he's written a novel," said *Criminal Minds*.

I had to ask. "Why do you call him Captain Road Rage?"

The alpha smugster gave a knowing laugh.

"I know it's hard to keep the L.A.P.D. horror stories straight, Doctor — but this guy was a division captain — a big honcho in the department, and one day last summer he went postal: started chasing a black guy down the 405, siren blaring — and when he caught up with him, he hauled the man out of the car, roughed him up and cuffed him — screaming at the poor guy for texting in his car. Stomped the phone to bits — a brand new iPhone."

"But another driver got it all recorded on video and sent it to KTLA — busted!" said *Criminal Minds*.

The smugsters laughed happily as I tried to swallow. I

remembered seeing that blurry bit of video myself, on some evening news program. Horrifying. I looked over at Rick, now smiling kindly at Vondra. Could he really be the same man?

Toby Roarke stood and clinked his glass.

"We've had a terrible tragedy in our literary family," he said in ponderous tones. "We shall all miss Ernesto Cervantes, who came to us last year as a scholarship student and was showing so much improvement in his writing—"

I wondered if Ernesto's "improvement" was the result of stealing Miguel's work.

"I would like to ask for a moment of silence, while we all remember Ernesto's beautiful spirit."

As everyone's head bowed, I did think about Ernesto—as well as Plantagenet in his jail cell. I also thought of Mitzi Boggs Bailey, lost in the hills, with darkness coming on. And Rick. Could he really be that terrible person? How could I be such an awful judge of character? The moment of silence went on and on. I sneaked a glance at the room and was startled to see Toby Roarke's gnarled hand creep around the tiny waist of the Donna Karan girl and slide down to her knit-encased bottom.

I couldn't stand it. I had to get away from Toby and his morbid farce, as well as Rick Zukowski a.k.a. Captain Road Rage. I'd go find a rest room and run through my speech one more time.

I dashed out the door and ran down the corridor to the lobby.

But I'd forgotten what would be out there, lying in wait.

Chapter 16—Squirrel Murderer

Apparently the only reason we'd been allowed to eat in relative peace was that Gabriella had posted guards at the end of the corridor to keep the reporters at bay — well, not actual guards, but a couple of kitchen staff, including Santiago, the "dorky" bowing Guatemalan.

He looked fierce and professional as he gave a sharp warning glance at a young man with blond dreadlocks.

The young man wore a T-shirt that read "STOMP OUT GRAPES."

He must be one of D. Sorengaard's anti-grape crazies.

Gabriella's plan seemed to be that the reporters were to stay herded into the lobby and the vineyard protesters were to be kept outside in the parking lot, but of course the protesters were infiltrating, hoping for publicity.

And now I was walking straight into three videocams and God knew how many still cameras. Not to mention the grape-stompers.

"There she is!" somebody said. "Dr. Manners!"

Microphones poked at my face. People crowded into a blur. I tried to push the microphones out of my way, but more kept coming.

One hit me on the nose.

"Did you witness the murder of Ernesto Cervantes? Why did Plantagenet Smith murder his lover?"

I touched my wounded nose, hoping it wouldn't bleed on my Chanel suit. I turned back, trying to make my way back to the dining room. Even watching Toby Roarke play cowboy with his new pet student would be better than this.

But now the way was blocked. Reporters pushed around me. Panic tightened my chest.

"Have you told the police everything you know about the murder, Dr. Manners?" said somebody with a bigger microphone than the rest.

"I'll be happy to talk to the Sheriff's people again, if they ask me, but I didn't see any murder!"

The room went quiet and reporters crowded in. Now I was going to have to elaborate.

"It didn't look like a murder. It looked like suicide. And after the way he was treated…"

I caught sight of Gabriella, pushing through the crowd toward me. She'd been through so much, with her sister-in-law missing, her conference in shambles, and who-knows-what happening in her vineyards. I certainly didn't need to add to it by saying angry things about Toby.

"I have to go," I said, trying to protect my nose from further microphone assault. "I have nothing more to say at this time. Come hear my presentation tonight. In the Ponderosa Lounge at seven-thirty. I don't know what time the doors will open." I looked questioningly at Gabriella.

"All public talks have been canceled!" Gabriella's voice sounded as big and loud as it had herding cattle on *Big Mountain*. Some of the microphones rushed toward her. "Ms.

Randall's talk tonight has been rescheduled for a later date. For enrolled attendees only. Full refunds will be mailed to all single-event ticket holders. I repeat: all public events have been canceled until further notice."

Finally, enough reporters migrated toward Gabriella that I was able to push my way back toward the dining room.

"Hey Doc, what were you going to say?" It was the dreadlocked man with the "Stomp out Grapes" T-shirt. "You said the dead kid was mistreated. Care to elaborate on that?"

I tried to escape. "No I don't. I...misspoke."

He gripped my elbow.

"Cut the crap, Doctor. I think you know what a fascist that guy really is. You know how old those oak trees were that he cut down? Four, maybe five hundred years old. And you know what happens when they plow deep enough to plant vineyards? Everything dies—owls, foxes, squirrels. He's murdering them. Like he murdered this gay dude."

"Your police escort is here, Ms. Randall," said a Joe-Friday voice. A strong hand grabbed my other elbow.

I turned and saw that cute grin. Captain Road Rage's grin. I stiffened.

"Oh, man, the pigs are here?" Grapes said.

"Oink," said Rick, pulling out his badge.

The blond dreadlocks disappeared into the crowd.

"Alberto has a golf cart for you out back, but not enough staff to drive it," Rick said. "Most of his employees are illegals, so they evaporate when law enforcement shows up. Okay if I play chauffeur?"

I nodded, although I avoided meeting his eyes, not sure if I wanted him to know I'd found out he was the road rage cop. Maybe he'd flipped out because of his wife's death. He did say she was killed by a cell phone-using driver. I so hoped he wasn't the racist the alpha smugster implied. People who hate are so dangerous to everybody.

Rick led me to the Hole in the Wall shortcut. I had a

moment of panic as he led me into the room — realizing I really didn't know a thing about this man. I was alone with Captain Road Rage in a secret, hidden room.

But he led me quickly through the staff quarters and out to the golf cart.

He seemed to sense my fear, but not the reason. He gave my shoulder a pat.

"Gaby said you were stressing."

He let down the vinyl windscreen to keep the photographers from getting a clear shot, although a few trailed behind once they spotted us.

"Are you upset that Gaby and Toby rescheduled your talk again? The decision wasn't just theirs. The Sheriff's department wants to keep the public away as much as possible, with the investigation going on. Not to mention the complications provided by the protesters. Those folks might have heckled you off the stage. You don't need 'squirrel murderer' and 'tree assassin' added to the bogus accusations against you."

I hoped the accusations against him were bogus, too.

"Did Toby really cut down five-hundred-year-old oak trees? Those trees would have been here when this was Indian land: no cowboys — not even *rancheros*. When you think that only a hundred and fifty years ago banditos were roaming these hills..."

"And some of them still do," Rick said with a chuckle. "And one's got no head." He started whistling the theme from *The X-Files*.

"They were very real to Mrs. Boggs Bailey." I was not in the mood for jokes.

"Sorry," he said in a more serious tone. "But I doubt her disappearance has anything to do with ghosts — not that she isn't in danger. If she witnessed the murder, she could be a target."

A thought came to me. "She did keep calling Ernesto the

dead boy. I thought she'd misinterpreted what I said about him 'dying' in the critique workshop, but maybe not. Maybe she did see him. She could have walked into the cabin and seen his body, or maybe she even witnessed his death."

He shrugged and shook his head.

"Mitzi isn't coherent a lot of the time. Her dementia seems fairly advanced."

By the time he pulled the cart in front of Roy Rogers, the photographers seemed to have given up. Zorro was still surrounded by the Sheriff's yellow barriers and the investigators' van sat in the lot next to the Ferrari. On the front gate was one of Alberto's elegant signs that said—

"PUBLIC EVENTS CANCELED. TICKET HOLDERS TO PLEASE CALL FOR REFUND."

At the door to my cabin, I reached for the key in my bag, but pulled out the wrong key—the one to Plant's car. He'd given it to me less than twenty-four hours ago. How could things have gone so wrong since then?

"Damn!" I tossed the key back, rummaging furiously for the door key, which seemed to have evaporated.

"Hey, it's going to be okay," Rick said, his hand light and warm on my shoulder.

His comforting touch made me feel like a kid in need of a good cry. But I was not going to let it happen. Certainly not in front of Captain Road Rage.

Rick reached in his pocket and pulled a pack of tissues that had a picture of Kermit the frog on it. He handed me one.

"Kermit?" I said.

"Yeah, I've got a Little Brother, Jamal—you know, with the Big Brother program? Jamal's got allergies like you wouldn't believe. And he's crazy for frogs."

Finally I found the cabin key. I opened the door and accepted the tissue.

"Things will look better tomorrow." Rick looked down at me the way he must look at the snotty-nosed frog-lover.

"Now, don't stay up all night reading that brilliant blockbuster novel." He laughed as he pointed to his manuscript, which I'd left scattered over the couch.

I nodded and blew my nose on a little green Kermit.

He brushed my lips with a kiss—just a quick one, but it was enough to leave a tingle.

"I've got a lot of writing to do tonight. Still got five chapters to go, and Luci is going to expect the full manuscript when she gets here tomorrow." He gave a nervous laugh. "I'd sure rather spend some time with you."

But I was glad he left so quickly. I needed to figure out how I felt about Captain Road Rage—without his body so near. I didn't do well when I let my hormones do the thinking. I picked up his manuscript and sat at the desk, wondering if it held any clues to who the real Rick was: "Captain Road Rage" or the guy with a "Little Brother" named Jamal?

I looked at the dial-less phone, wondering if there was a way for me to contact Plantagenet. Maybe I could call Silas. I picked up the phone. Alberto probably had a number for him.

There was a busy signal. The switchboard must be jammed. I'd try again later.

But what if Rick was right in suspecting Silas? He had disappeared from the bar just about the time of the murder. He left because he had to answer a phone call—I'd thought he was so polite, but maybe he was just being a very clever killer.

Setting down the receiver of the useless phone, I wondered if it was time for the Manners Doctor to relent about cell phones. Most people wouldn't be inconvenienced by the quaint lack of technology in the Rancho's phone system because they carried their own. Too bad they only made me furious.

With an awful chill, I flashed on the smashed phone Detective Fiscalini showed me. Obviously somebody besides me was furious at telephones. It looked as if it had been attacked with a hammer. Or stomped on.

The smugsters said that Captain Road Rage had stomped on his victim's iPhone.

Could Rick have attacked Ernesto—for texting and driving? Maybe something about Ernesto's driving triggered some uncontrolled rage response in Rick. His wife had only died a year ago. He must have a lot of unhealed grief.

And Rick hadn't accounted for the half hour between when he saw Plant and Ernesto in the lobby and when he met me outside the Ponderosa Lounge.

I wiped the memory of tingle from my lips. Rick Zukowski could be a psycho killer.

And I might get the prize for the world's worst taste in men.

Chapter 17—Cranially-Challenged Ectoplasm

I READ THE REST OF Rick's novel, trying to find clues to his Captain Road Rage alter ego. I don't know what I expected—somebody killed for distracted driving, maybe. Righteous rage.

But his Captain Iggy Sanchez was such an upright, uptight, perfect-citizen type—except for his weakness for Scandinavian pastry—that even his mother-in-law would probably be bored. I managed to slog through police report prose describing celebrity bust after celebrity bust—mostly because I recognized the thinly disguised A-listers and their whispered-about proclivities. But when the manuscript ended in the middle of chapter twenty-four, I didn't have any further insight into Rick's capacity for murderous rage.

I also couldn't figure out how he'd managed to interest the great Lucille Silverberg with such a snooze of a book.

I felt trapped in the little cabin, and could have used a walk. I stepped outside for a moment, but every shadow in the deserted place made me jump. Even the investigators' van was gone, although they'd left up their yellow tape barrier. I wondered if they planned to do any more investigating. If Plant wasn't a murderer, then someone dangerous was out there in the dark.

Captain Road Rage?

Silas Ryder?

A headless ghost?

Nothing made sense. I went back inside, did some yoga, took a long bath, then popped one of the Ativans I'd brought for the plane. I finally fell into drifty sleep.

But I woke to odd sounds: footsteps, then a rustle. From out in the sitting room.

My body went cold. Somebody was out there.

In the dark, I could make out something in the outer room. Someone outlined by the yellow parking lot light that bled around the curtains at the front window — a figure in the doorway, very tall, wearing a long coat or cape.

But it had no head.

The ghost. Joaquin. Real cranially-challenged ectoplasm. Here. In my bedroom.

I lay still, my heart pounding, and listened for the sounds again. Nothing. Maybe the headless figure was just a trick of shadow.

No. I was aware of something else — not exactly through sound or sight — but I could feel it: breathing.

Ghosts didn't breathe, did they? Certainly not headless ones. How could it be a ghost? I didn't believe in ghosts, headless or otherwise — did I?

No. What I did believe in was the insanity of the celebrity-crazed media. Clarity came to my drugged brain. Had I locked the door? If someone was in my cabin, it had to be some sneaky creep with a camera.

Now I was just plain mad. I wasn't going to let some paparazzo terrorize me. I made a quick roll to the edge of the bed and slid from under the bunched-up covers onto the floor. I fell on something hard: the Cuban heel of one of the Fendi pumps I'd been wearing earlier. I pulled it from under my butt and hung onto it. It might make a threatening-looking weapon.

"Go ahead, roll your damned camera, you media slime!" I shouted. Let the Bozo get a nice shot of an unmade bed.

But there was no camera—just a gasp and another floorboard creaking.

I hurled the shoe in the direction of the creak.

I heard a shattering crash, then a squawk and a yelp. Something crouching in the shadows suddenly stood tall and menacing by the door. With a quick flash of yellow light, the door opened and slammed shut.

After a few moments, I could hear nothing but the pounding in my own chest. Quieting my heartbeat with steady breaths, I grabbed the other pump and felt the satisfying weight of the stacked leather heel. I crept around the bed and peered out.

I peeked through the curtains, half expecting to see some Sleepy Hollow horseman taking off down the road. Instead I saw a vintage sports car speeding toward the gate. It was too dark to read the license plate. But the color could have been orange.

Mrs. Boggs Bailey's orange Mustang.

I stood by the window, shivering in my Oscar de la Renta charmeuse chemise, still holding my shoe. I ran back to the bedroom and flicked on the light. I could see my shoe had knocked over a ceramic lamp shaped like a cowboy boot. It lay in shards all over the braided rug.

But the intruder was gone. Whoever—whatever—had been here was definitely gone. And so was something else: Rick's novel.

Rick's manuscript had disappeared. I'd left the gold folder with his pages inside on the coffee table. It wasn't there. Rick's Sominex novel—who on earth would steal that?

This was more than creepy.

I started to pick up my hurled pump, but stopped myself. The investigators would want everything left the way it was, pieces of cowboy-boot lamp and all.

The investigators. If I hadn't just seen a supernatural apparition, I had seen a criminal—probably Ernesto's killer—drive off in an orange Mustang. I needed to call the Sheriff's people right away. I reached for the phone on the desk.

But the signal was still busy—probably still jammed with calls from the media. Poor Alberto.

But no way was I going to stay alone in the cabin. The headless thing—whatever, whoever it was—could come back at any time. I needed a working phone. Now. As soon as I got back to work next week, The Manners Doctor would reverse her position on mobile phones.

I peeked out the window again.

No headless persons of any kind.

But behind the barrier ribbon I saw Plant's Ferrari—blood red in the amber light.

The key to the Ferrari was still in my bag. The "barrier" was just a flimsy plastic ribbon. After I explained to the investigators that my life was in danger, they'd have to understand why I needed to cross it, wouldn't they?

Whatever had been in my cabin: ghost, paparazzo, murderer, book thief, or anti-grape crazy, I would be insane to stay here and battle it alone.

Chapter 18—A Cowboy Cut Down in his Prime

I GRABBED A SWEATER AND jeans, jammed my feet into my flats, and put on my watch. It was nearly one AM. I hoped something would still be happening up at the Hacienda. Maybe reporters were still hanging around. This was one time I'd be glad to see them.

Clutching my other Fendi pump for protection, I cracked open the door and listened to the night. Not a sound but the chirping of crickets, and the ribbitting of a lonely frog. I ran through the courtyard and ducked under the police barrier tape. When I unlocked the Ferrari, I was relieved to see the investigators had replaced the seats. I backed out of the courtyard and drove up the curvy road way faster than I should have.

When I got to the Hacienda, I was actually disappointed to see the parking lot half empty. I had hoped for the safety of a crowd. But the protesters seemed to have left. So had the reporters. Gabriella must have cleared them out.

With the pump for protection, I crossed the lot and entered the lobby. It was eerily unpopulated as well. Even Alberto had disappeared. The phone receiver lay on the desk, off its cradle. I put it to my ear, but couldn't get a dial tone—just silence. For a moment, I thought I heard somebody breathing on the line.

I dropped the thing and stifled a scream.

I'd have to go to the Ponderosa Lounge. The late-night Cowboy Critique workshop might still be going.

At this point, I'd welcome the sight of any other human, even Toby Roarke. I couldn't imagine a dead lover would stop him from doing his duty as resident tyrant. One of the workshoppers might call the Sheriff for me.

I wondered how I would explain the shoe I was carrying and steeled myself for jokes as I pulled open the doors.

But the Ponderosa Lounge was deserted and dark. Only a few half-empty water glasses on the table showed that a workshop had taken place. They glowed faintly red in the light of the "Exit" sign above the service door.

Maybe people were in the Longhorn Room—a few late-night drinkers. At least it wouldn't be empty like this. I walked quickly down the hall.

But one of Alberto's hand-lettered signs had been taped to the bar's cowhide door, "BAR CLOSE 11 PM DUE TO STAFF SHORTAGE."

Staff shortage. The waiter Miguel said he was legal, but obviously most of the workers here were not. They must be Mexicans working here without proper papers, and of course they'd evaporated at the sight of law enforcement.

Pulling on the horseshoe-handle, I peeked inside. Maybe somebody was nursing a last drink. But the bar was as dim as the lounge, illuminated by another red Exit sign.

I didn't notice the wall until I turned to go. Scrawled across the furry cowhide wainscoting I made out what looked like city-street graffiti—crude blood-red letters, and a familiar image: a snake with horns—and the face of a devil—just like Ernesto Cervantes' tattoo.

Then I saw Toby Roarke.

He lay in front of the fireplace—face down, surrounded by a pool of dark ooze. Pinning him down was a huge object, flat on one side. At first I thought some strangely-shaped table had been placed over his lower back. But when I got closer, I saw that somehow, horribly, one of the animal heads had fallen from the wall above.

And under it lay the Cowboy himself, dead, impaled by the terrible horn of a Texas Longhorn steer.

I stared at the bloody body. For a moment, my brain didn't comprehend that the screeching in my ears was the sound of my own screams.

Someone came through the door behind me. I clutched the shoe and prepared to defend myself.

With a click, the room flooded with light. Raising the pump, I turned to see one of the maids with her hand on the light switch. The girl's screams rose above mine as the bright light made the scene all the more horrific.

"*Viboras!*" the girl screamed. "*Viboras! Madre de Dio!*" She crossed herself as we stared at each other in horror.

I heard footsteps, as someone came running down the corridor outside.

It was Miguel—the waiter who'd written Ernesto's rooster story. He had a concierge jacket thrown over his waiter uniform.

"Don't hit her!" Miguel said, grabbing my arm. "What has she done?"

The maid shook her head and said something in Spanish. She pointed at the wall. After a quick intake of breath, Miguel crossed himself too.

"You have hit Mr. Roarke with this?" he said, roughly seizing my shoe. He closed the door behind him and put a comforting arm around the sobbing maid.

"Of course not," I said, trying to take the shoe back.

"When did this happen?" Miguel wasn't letting go of my shoe.

The door under the exit sign banged open. A voice shouted in the darkness.

"Bar is closed! Please read the sign!"

Alberto the concierge, wearing neatly pressed pajamas and robe, marched toward us and gave Miguel a short, angry bark in Spanish. He turned to me.

"I am surrounded by imbeciles. My staff is gone, running from *la Migra*. The police tear everything apart. Those dirty people with their signs—and the crazy reporters, always ringing the phone! It is no wonder my head is full of hammers..."

Miguel did nothing but point at the horror by the fireplace.

Alberto's words stopped. We hardly breathed as he walked toward Toby's body.

Avoiding the spreading patch of blood, Alberto leaned over to study the steer head that impaled Toby so obscenely. Then he stood back to look at the crude blood-red painting on the wall. Finally he spoke—hissing something in a choked voice.

"Viboras."

Alberto whispered something to Miguel. He took my shoe and handed it back to me, then gave a comforting pat to the maid's shoulder. He sent Miguel and the maid out the staff door he had come in. Then he turned to me.

"You found...this?" His voice cracked.

I nodded.

"Did you see the Viboras? A gang?" He looked into my eyes, sharing my fear. "Any suspicious boys—Latinos?"

"No, but..." I wanted to tell him about my ghostly intruder and the orange Mustang, but Alberto's eyes were opaque—full of as much horror as they could take. He guided me out of the room with automatic courtesy, his face a mask.

"Come," he said, opening the door. "We must call the Sheriff. I hope the telephone lines are free. Before I went to bed, I left the phone off the hook. All night, reporters kept ringing the phone as soon as I put it down. When I left, some television man was on the line, refusing to hang up, so I left him there."

His voice rose to a cry as he opened the door to the hallway, and nearly collided with a pack of awakened writers. I squeezed out behind him, but was pinned against the furry door by the crowd.

"Stop!" I grabbed the elbow of the *Vampire Diaries* smugster, whose curious hand reached for the door handle. "You do not want to go in there."

"Oh, right. God forbid you'd have to share story rights, Doctor."

"Back to your rooms, please," Alberto said to the gathering conferencers, his voice firm again. "It is not a problem for you. Go back to your rooms."

"I heard people screaming," said Vondra DeHaviland, pulling a diaphanous pink negligée over an equally flimsy night dress. "What's going on here? Where's Gabriella? Where's Toby?"

"Not together, I'll bet," said Herb Frye the Sci-Fi guy, with a wink at Vondra.

Alberto gave a pleading look at the two workshop leaders.

"Miss Moore is with the Sheriff's search and rescue team, looking for her missing sister-in-law. Please take the guests back to their rooms." He gestured at me to go down the hall to the lobby.

But I could hardly move through the increasingly unruly crowd.

"It's those tree people, isn't it?" said the Miss Manners fan. "I saw them on the eleven o'clock news. They had an old woman tied to a tree. Dancing around like a bunch of devil worshipers, chanting about rapes. Or grapes. Or something."

"I knew we shouldn't have come. It's conference number thirteen," said one memoirist to another. "Didn't I tell you it would be bad luck?"

"Where are the police?" said the woman with beige hair.

Alberto looked as if he might pass out. "You must make them go to their rooms." He left in the direction of the service wing.

I turned and faced the crowd, blocking the door.

"Everyone needs to go back to their rooms. Now."

The alpha smugster came at me with defiant eyes.

"What's in there, Doctor? What are you hiding? Got some S/M party going on? A little stomping? Some foot fetish action?" He came at me, reaching for my pump.

I shoved him back. "What part of 'NOW' don't you understand?"

He lost his balance and fell backwards.

"Herbert, help me. These people have no sense," Vondra said as she stepped out of the way of the falling smugster.

There was no more smugness in the young man's eyes as he picked himself up from the carpet and fled. He actually looked frightened of me. The rest of the writers followed. I heard whispers and the word "dominatrix" as they scurried away like so many shooed-away chickens. I have to admit to a small feeling of satisfaction.

But behind me the door pushed open, nearly knocking me over. Mitzi Boggs Bailey barreled through, followed by Miguel, his jacket still unbuttoned.

"Dr. Manners isn't all right," the old woman said, pointing at me. "I've told her before that her kind is not welcome here."

Mrs. Boggs Bailey was still clad in her Doris Day quilted peignoir, now much the worse for wear. Her wispy gray hair was tangled with oak leaves, and her face smudged with mud and soot.

"I was on TV," she told me. "To save the trees and the squirrels. We got tied up and they had cameras. Now I'm more famous than you, Miss phony Dr. Manners!"

"I'm supposed to take Mrs. Boggs Bailey to her room," said Miguel. "Reporters are keeping Miss Moore outside. But Mrs. Boggs Bailey doesn't like the room..." He lowered his voice. "I have not told Miss Moore about...Mr. Roarke. Alberto said he will speak with her." He gave a weary sigh. "Can you take Mrs. Boggs Bailey to the lobby? I will see if I can get another room."

The lobby was deserted, and the phone was still off the hook, but I could see major activity in the parking lot outside. Gabriella, flanked by Silas and Rick and a number of young people in orange Search and Rescue shirts, spoke to a crowd of reporters.

Rick and Silas. Together. Helping Gaby. They looked chummy. I hoped that meant Rick had stopped suspecting Silas.

A few moments later, the front doors burst open and Gabriella stomped in, looking as if she'd been herding cattle over the mountain. Rick followed after doing some crowd control with a knot of reporters outside.

"I don't like her," Mrs. Boggs Bailey said, pointing at me. "She's bad news."

"You leave her alone, Mitzi," said Gabriella. "Where the hell is that Miguel? Isn't he supposed to be on the desk? And Toby? If he didn't cut the workshop short tonight like I told him..."

"Oh, Gabriella!" What could I say?

"What is it?" Rick ran to me. His eyes showed nothing but concern. If he knew about Toby, he was a remarkable actor. I wanted to cross him off my list of suspects. Somehow the froggy tissues seemed to trump the road rage.

"There's been a terrible, um, accident," I said, relieved to be able to let him comfort me.

It wasn't an accident, but I didn't know what to call it—a gang killing? The word murder wouldn't come out.

"Did somebody hurt you?" Rick eyed the Fendi pump.

"Not me. Toby, he's..." I pointed toward the Longhorn Room with my shoe.

Gabriella made a noise as if someone had hit her and started down the hall.

"Stop her!" I pushed Rick in her direction.

But he wouldn't budge. "What's wrong? Why shouldn't Gabriella go to the bar?"

I didn't know how to begin.

"Don't let her see what they did in there. It's too horrible."

"They? Who are they, and what did they do?"

"Alberto the concierge thinks it's a gang. Vigoras. Viagras, something like that. They left a snake on the wall. In blood."

"A snake on the wall?" Rick eyed my shoe. "You were going to kill it with that?"

"No. The snake is a graffiti — graffito."

"It's Toby," said Mrs. Boggs Bailey. "He's not all right. He's got a cow head on top of him. Dead as a doornail. Serves him right, scribbling on the walls like that."

Chapter 19—Disturbing the Peace

I THINK IT WAS RICK who finally called the Sheriff. He cleared the crime scene and Detective Fiscalini and two uniformed officers showed up about twenty minutes later. Rick met them in the lobby, looking professional as he muttered with them in staccato cop-talk.

Gabriella sat behind the desk, the color of chalk, not saying a word, and Alberto hovered while Mrs. Boggs Bailey chatted into the phone about the pleasures of being tied to a tree while chanting environmentalist slogans.

I sat in one of the lobby's big leather chairs, cradling my shoe. It was somehow comforting. Much resoled, but designer Italian leather just the same.

The coroner's team arrived a few minutes later. Alberto led them all off in the direction of the Longhorn Room, except for one of the uniformed officers who stood guard at the door as Rick helped clear the non-guests from the parking lot.

I let out an unladylike yawn. "Sorry," I said.

"You should be sorry," said Mrs. Boggs Bailey. "You and your kind." She put down the phone and walked over to the officer. "You should arrest her." She pointed at me. "She's not all right, that phony Dr. Manners. You should arrest her for disturbing the peace."

"Mitzi, What the hell are you talking about?" Gabriella had suddenly come to.

"Her!" said Mrs. Boggs Bailey, pointing at me. "She pretends to be Dr. Manners, but she's not all right." She looked me up and down. "At least you changed out of that other dress. Your boobs were hanging out. Disgusting."

The officer looked uncomfortable. He gave a glance at Gabriella.

Gabriella stood. "That is Camilla Randall. She's the Manners Doctor. She doesn't disturb the peace. She helps make the world a nicer place. Mitzi, go to bed."

"I can't. I haven't had my whisky sour. You know I like a whisky sour before bed." She came out from behind the desk and walked slowly toward my chair. "You're a degenerate. You were disturbing the peace at the Saloon. People there don't like your kind."

Gabriella strode toward us, holding up a hand to the wary officer.

"Ms. Randall hasn't disturbed anybody's peace. My sister-in-law Mitzi has disturbed people's peace. And I—God knows—have disturbed people's peace. I disturbed Toby Roarke's peace. You want to see somebody whose peace got disturbed; you go right down that hallway. You'll see disturbed peace, all right."

During this speech, Gabriella's voice steadily increased in decibels. But she choked on her own words and her voice went to a whisper. "He never wanted to be a cowboy. Me—I wanted him to be a cowboy. But he was an artist. A poet. A sweet, kinda limp-wristed poet—and, oh Lord, did I disturb that man's peace!"

I stood to put an arm around Gabriella's shoulders, trying to give comfort as she went on, through her tears.

"You want to know who killed him, really? It was me. I killed his soul."

I held the weeping Gabriella in my arms as the deputies stared.

The lobby filled with a terrible silence.

Outside we could hear Rick talking with a couple of reporters. They raised their voices, but Rick's stayed calm.

Rage-free.

That was reassuring.

Mrs. Boggs Bailey picked up the phone again.

"Gaby's crying," she said. "Gabriella Moore, the TV star. She's not all right. Her boyfriend's dead. You wouldn't believe the blood. All over the walls. I thought it was that Dr. Manners who did it, but Gaby says she killed him herself. I'm not surprised, the way that Toby runs around."

Gabriella pulled away, back to her imperious self.

"Mitzi, get off the phone right now. You're going to bed."

"You don't have to shout." She spoke into the phone. "Sorry, I have to go now. But it was nice talking to you, Mr. Kahn."

"Kahn?" I nearly jumped over the desk. Had Jonathan been the media jackal who refused to get off the line? Had he been listening the whole time? I should have realized he'd be all over this story, once he got wind I was involved.

I grabbed the phone and shouted into the phone.

"Jonathan, if you broadcast one word of that — one solitary word — I am going to kill you, do you hear me?"

Detective Fiscalini's voice came from the hallway.

"Let's not have any more killing, Ms. Randall. It's been a long day." His gopher face looked weary as he bustled into the lobby with one of the investigators.

Gabriella gave me a pat. "Don't worry. I doubt there's

anybody on the line. Mitzi has a rich imagination when it comes to her phone conversations. Yesterday, she was on the phone with Joaquin Murrieta for hours. Alberto, do you want to take her to her room?"

"I want the Ronald Reagan suite. Or Frank and Jesse. You said I could have the James Boys. Miguel wants me to stay in room thirteen. But I won't. I don't need any more bad luck. I already lost my play. I think the ghosts took it."

Alberto gave Gabriella an apologetic look. "I'm sorry. The James rooms have been given to Detective Fiscalini for his investigation."

"But Gaby promised!" said Mrs. Boggs Bailey.

"That was before you went AWOL, Mitzi." Gabriella's tone was not open to argument.

As Mrs. Boggs Bailey and Alberto disappeared down the corridor, Detective Fiscalini pointed at my Fendi pump.

"Can I see that?" I held it out for his inspection as he pulled a plastic bag from his jacket pocket. "Is this the shoe you've been threatening people with?" He spoke with the nonchalance of someone asking the time of day.

"What are you talking about? I didn't threaten anybody! I just told them to go to their rooms."

Detective Fiscalini took a pen from his pocket and poked it into the shoe's toe box, dangling the pump from his pen before dropping it into the bag like so much dog poo. He examined it through the plastic.

"It's got quite a distinctive heel. Are we likely to find any wounds on Mr. Roarke's body that correspond to this heel, Ms. Randall?"

I couldn't believe it.

"You think I committed that horror? With a Fendi pump?"

He continued in the same infuriatingly conversational tone.

"You discovered Mr. Roarke's body, right?" He perched himself on the arm of the chair. "Did you have an assignation with Mr. Roarke in the Longhorn Room tonight?"

"Assignation?" I looked over at poor Gabriella. "What a ridiculous idea! Mr. Roarke was Gabriella's... significant other."

Detective Fiscalini gave me his blank gopher-eyed look

"You're barking up the wrong tree, Fiscalini," Gabriella said. "She's not Toby's type."

Rick came inside as the reporters' car finally took off from the lot outside.

Gaby put a hand on Detective Fiscalini's shoulder as if he were an old friend.

"Frankie, I could use a drink. I don't suppose you're going to let me in the bar?"

"Not a chance. It's a crime scene."

"What if I take Ms. Moore up to her apartment?" Rick said. "I don't think anybody should be walking around here unescorted when we could have a serial killer at large in the building. If you need to talk to her again tonight, maybe you can interview her upstairs? She's had a terrible loss..."

As Rick escorted Gaby away, Detective Fiscalini resumed his armchair perch.

"So what were you doing up here at the Hacienda at midnight, Ms Randall?" He looked down at me, leaning in a little too close. "The staff say that you're staying down in the cabins. What was so urgent that you would violate a crime scene and steal a car to drive up here? That must have been some hot date."

I leaned away. He had awful coffee breath.

"I did not have a date. And I wasn't stealing. Plant gave me the keys."

"Then why did you go into the Zorro cabin looking for them?" Detective Fiscalini was beginning to look more like a rat than a gopher. "Do you know the penalties for interfering with a crime scene, Ms. Randall?"

"I didn't go into the Zorro cabin! I'm very sorry about taking the Ferrari, but I didn't have a choice — I was dealing with a headless ghost!"

Detective Fiscalini's inquisitive little eyes looked scornful.

"Or something," I added.

"You had a date with a headless ghost?"

After taking a careful breath, I repeated my story. Fiscalini looked at me as if I were making no sense at all. The only thing that interested him was the Mustang.

"Are you sure it was orange?"

I nodded.

When he finally dismissed me, he asked me not to leave the area.

"What about my shoe? And the Hermes scarf? It's quite valuable, you know."

"The evidence will be returned when you've been eliminated as a suspect."

He gave me such a fierce look that I rushed out of the lobby to escape him.

Did he possibly imagine I'd done that to Toby Roarke?

Chapter 20—The Burberry Ghost

I WAS HALFWAY DOWN THE hallway before I realized I
had no place to go. My first room was presumably still "not
available." But I wasn't going back to the Roy Rogers cabin
with whatever horrors were lurking out there. And the floor
would be littered with broken bits of cowboy boot lamp.

I had a thought: the Hole in the Wall. I'd probably be safe
in the hidden banquet room. I hoped the key would be in its
hiding place. Maybe I could stretch out on the carpet. Miguel
said even most of the staff didn't know that room was there.

I walked quickly through the maze of corridors, trying to
find the wood paneling that hid the door to the secret room. If
only I'd been paying more attention to the route and less to
Rick and his seductive kisses. I turned down a hallway I
thought looked right, but soon realized I was in unfamiliar
territory. Every creak and thump in the old place brought me
closer to panic.

I tried taking calming breaths.

But I heard a coyote cry from the hills outside, then a bang from somewhere ahead. Hard to get calm when you're lost in a maze with a murderer on the loose—or maybe a whole gang of them.

No. This would not do. I'd never find the Hole in the Wall without a map.

I didn't have much choice than to go back to the lobby. Detective Fiscalini might treat me like a criminal, but at least I'd be safe. I hoped I could find my way back.

At the end of the hall ahead I glimpsed a woman. She looked familiar. I wanted to call to her, but realized I'd probably cause more panic if I woke the guests. I walked faster, trying to catch up, but the woman turned a corner and disappeared from view.

Now I heard footsteps coming from behind me. Somebody who was breathing heavily.

Somebody closing in behind me.

I ran toward the woman as fast as I could.

"Miss?" I hissed, in as loud a whisper as I dared. "Miss? Could you help?" I turned another corner and saw the woman at the other end of the hall. She looked tall and elegant, and wore her hair in a long blond bob like mine. "Please?" I hissed louder.

But a heavy hand on my shoulder stopped me.

"Camilla?"

I turned and saw Rick Zukowski.

"What's got into you? I've been chasing you all over."

I told him about the woman.

"Did she look like that?" He pointed ahead.

Now I could see an ornately framed mirror hanging at the end of the hallway.

"A tall, elegant woman who wears her hair just like yours?" He gave a gentle laugh. "Camilla, you've been running after your own reflection. There's a mirror at the end of most of these hallways." There was no trace of his usual mocking tone. "You've had a shock. It's understandable. I'd say it's time to get some sleep."

Maybe he was right. Maybe I was stressed. Or going crazy. But it was awfully strange that the woman in the mirror wore a Burberry coat. I did own a Burberry coat in that exact style, but it was back in my closet in New York.

Right now, I was wearing a baggy black sweater and jeans.

Rick walked me down the hall, away from the mirror, with its apparently supernatural powers. He seemed to think I needed wine. He carried a big bottle of Fess Parker Frontier Red, topped with the signature coonskin hat. He put an arm around me, but I pulled away.

I still didn't know if I could trust somebody called Captain Road Rage.

"Come on. It should help you relax and get to sleep. Alberto let me choose a bottle from the dining room in exchange for giving up my suite to Mitzi. I don't know beans about wine, but Jamal is gonna love the frog-sized headgear."

He seemed to be taking me to his room. Okay, I could either spend what was left of the night with ghosts, demon-possessed mirrors, or a presumably armed man with anger management issues. Who also liked little kids and cartoon frogs.

I sighed and went along.

He led me down the hall toward the 1950s wing where I had stayed the first night.

"Mitzi was raising heck about staying in room thirteen, so I said I'd take it and let her have Ronald Reagan. I hope you're not superstitious."

"In the last twenty-four hours, I've seen a headless ghost, two dead bodies, and my oldest friend has been hauled off to jail. I've been suspected of prostitution, necrophilia—and from what I could gather from that detective's questions—committing homicide by shoe. How much worse could my luck get? You want me to be afraid of a room number?"

"Right. Thirteen is just a number." Rick squeezed my shoulder as he slid his arm around me.

His arm felt good.

But the room wasn't thirteen at all. It was fourteen A, my old digs—right under the stairs that led to Gabriella's apartment—next to the ice machine. Probably the worst room in the hotel.

" 'Fourteen A' must be a hotel euphemism for thirteen."

Rick ushered me inside. I sat on the quilt-covered double bed while he opened the wine and poured a healthy amount into two bathroom tumblers.

Wine and Ativan. Not a good combination. I'd forgotten about taking the pill earlier. I soon found myself babbling to Rick about my encounter with the headless ghost.

"Are you sure you weren't dreaming?" He sat beside me on the bed—the room was too small for a chair. "Sometimes stress can trigger what they call 'waking dreams'."

He spoke in his infuriating, calm-down-now-ma'am policeman voice.

"In my experience, supernatural beings without heads don't usually get scared off by ladies' footwear." He gave me a quick kiss on the forehead like I was a five-year-old. "And it's never a good idea to interfere with a crime scene, even after the investigators have left. After they get the lab results back, they may have to go back for more samples. That's why it takes a couple days to release a scene."

I didn't want to be patronized.

"So arrest me. But the phone didn't work. And this place was deserted. Did the whole conference move down to the vineyard protest?"

"I think most of the conference folks crashed early. Murder tends to make people unsociable. Besides, Alberto closed the bar right after dinner because he had no staff, and nobody wanted to hang out in the lobby—with all those reporters and protesters around. Only a few diehards stayed around for the Cowboy Workshop. About ten o'clock, Search and Rescue called Gaby to say they'd found Mitzi at the vineyard protest, but they were having trouble convincing her to come back. So the rest of us who were hanging around went to help Gaby bring her back—well, except Toby."

Rick gave a grim laugh.

"He said he was tired, but apparently he had a heavy date with a longhorn steer."

I looked away. The image was too raw.

"Sorry," he said, getting up to refill his glass. "That was insensitive. But Toby was acting sneaky. I'd been wondering if he had something going with that girl he sat with at dinner."

"The Latina girl in Donna Karan? I thought so too." I watched Rick pour wine. "Mrs. Boggs Bailey didn't want to be rescued?"

Rick laughed. "Not hardly. It was all a party to her. That protest has become quite the media event. Even your ex was there."

My body went rigid.

"Jonathan Kahn—my ex-husband—he's here? In Santa Ynez?"

I'd thought things couldn't get much worse. I'd been wrong.

Chapter 21—Vipers

I TRIED TO FORM COHERENT words as Rick smiled down at me, oblivious to the fact my head felt about to explode.

"Mitzi Boggs Bailey trying to save the squirrels is a national news story?" I said. Well, sort of sputtered. "Jonathan Kahn is covering rural agriculture stories?"

Why hadn't I seen this coming? We were only a couple of hours north of Los Angeles — now the home base of his show.

I had to pray Jonathan didn't know I was here.

Or anything about my night at the Solvang Sheriff's substation.

Or that I was a murder suspect.

I tried to will him from my brain. With any luck, he was on his way home by now.

I jumped when I heard a thump outside.

"Do you think they're out there — those Vigoras, or what ever they're called?"

"Viboras." Rick spoke with perfect Spanish inflection. He jumped up and started to pace, nervously pulling at his sleeve. "It means snakes — vipers. But that part isn't making sense to me. Of course Fiscalini doesn't want to part with a lot of information to an L.A. cop, but it looks as if his guys have found the murder weapon: a cast iron frying pan."

"A frying pan — he was killed with a kitchen utensil?" This was hard to believe, with all that gore.

"Yes. From what I could see, Toby was probably bludgeoned to death somewhere in the service wing, then dragged to the Longhorn Room. Any self-respecting gangbanger would use a knife or a gun. And Miguel says the paint used for tagging the scene was stolen from the utility closet. Rust-oleum Equipment Red. Taggers would have brought their own paint."

"Equipment red? So on the wall — that was..."

Rick gave a half smile. "Not blood. Just the work of a tagger who didn't know how to use spray paint without leaving a bunch of drips. Another reason I don't think it's gangbangers."

"Toby was bludgeoned to death? But the cow head...?"

"Looked to me as if it was done post mortem. That could be a gang thing, but I've never known them to stray this far from their turf, especially to kill a stranger. They usually kill over specific things — territory, drugs, girlfriends." He gave a dry laugh. "I don't suppose you've been romantically involved with any Latino dudes lately?"

I felt myself blush and looked away from his dark, Latino eyes.

"No. Tattooed gangsters aren't exactly my type."

I turned away. It was too late in a very difficult night to even think about romance.

I looked around the room and saw Rick's things — his suitcase open on the dresser. Inside was what looked like a gun holster sticking from between athletic tee shirts and a pair of Nikes. This was his room and there was no place for me to stay except in his bed. Did he really expect me to sleep with him—tonight?

He was pacing again, rolling down his shirtsleeves, although the room was too warm, if anything.

He grabbed the wine and refilled his glass.

"Right. Your type is city boys in Italian suits. Like Kahn and the Oscar-winning screenwriter. Hey, is it true you two used to be an item? Smith goes both ways?"

I wasn't sure I wanted to have this conversation.

"Plantagenet is bisexual, yes, but that doesn't mean we still have any kind of spark going. We've been friends for too long. He's like a brother—which is why it's absurd for that detective to think that I'd kill Ernesto out of jealousy—or whatever nonsense he thinks."

Rick took a sip of wine. "I doubt he thinks that. In fact I'm pretty sure Fiscalini likes the Viboras for both murders. He thinks they made Ernesto an example of what happens when you try to leave the gang life, then killed Toby because he seduced Ernesto into a gay lifestyle."

"Plant's not a suspect anymore?"

"My money says he'll be released in the morning. It's a lot easier to convict a bunch of street kids than a Hollywood celebrity."

Rick's voice had a negative edge.

"You think Detective Fiscalini is wrong? " I said. "It wasn't a gang?"

Rick shook his head.

"I'm not saying the Viboras aren't capable of vicious violence and homophobia, but I can't fit them into any scenario that would reasonably result in that crime scene."

"Killing people and 'reasonable' don't go together in any scenario I can think of." It all seemed more senseless by the minute. "If it's not a gang, who is it? You don't think I did it? With my little Fendi pump?" I couldn't stifle a large yawn.

Rick put down his glass.

"Hey, we've got to get some sleep. The Hacienda's still full, so I told Fiscalini you'd be staying in my room." He gave me another one of those nervous little smiles. "The Ronald Reagan suite, where I was staying, has a sitting room with a fold-out. When I let Mitzi take it, I didn't realize there would be only one bed here. I'll go see if I can find the maid who moved my stuff down here. Hotels usually have an extra room or two—someplace funky next to the kitchen, or under the stairs—someplace they only use for emergencies. But I don't know…"

He looked around the cramped room.

"This might be it. But I'll…um, see you in the morning."

On another night I might have been disappointed. But I was so exhausted, I think I may have fallen asleep before he shut the door.

Chapter 22—A Woman Scorned

I WOKE TO THE METALLIC sound of a key in a lock.

And the creak of old floorboards.

Pushing sleep-fog from my brain, I lay very still, trying to maintain the rhythm of my breath as I listened to the doorknob being jiggled.

I heard the key-in-the-lock sound again and jumped out of bed and flicked on the light. Somebody was trying to break into the room. And me without even a shoe for a weapon.

But maybe Rick had a gun in his suitcase. I was pretty sure I'd seen a holster in there...

Another noise. From somewhere down the walkway outside. Then a metallic bang and a crunch.

I felt around in the suitcase, and found a dark molded plastic case underneath his neatly folded jeans. It was the sort of case Jonathan's overpriced tools came in. I opened the lid, and there it was. Not a shiny, cowboy gun. Thi s was Darth

Vader black and felt heavy and cold in my hand.

The floorboards creaked again right outside. I heard the thump of footsteps. Someone was out there. Maybe the someone who had committed two horrific murders.

I had to get out of this trap before they broke in. The ancient lock did not look as if it would hold against much. I clutched the gun and opened the door.

At the end of the porch, something moved in the shadows behind the ice machine.

"Hold it right there." I raised the heavy gun with both hands.

"Where did you get that?" said a growly voice. I held the gun steady.

A figure emerged from the darkness.

Rick. Looking furious and scary.

"That's my weapon, isn't it?" His voice sounded thick from sleep. "You stole it?" He took a step toward me. "Talk about a woman scorned! Jeez...I know it sounds lame, but I really do have one hell of a headache. That's why I'm getting ice. An ice pack on the back of the neck sometimes helps...Camilla, you gotta give me my gun."

"Woman scorned?" Now I was furious, too. "Don't flatter yourself."

"I'm sorry, but I'm not used to women creeping into my room at two A.M.." He gestured at the door behind him. It was numbered fourteen B. "Now give me the gun."

"You're staying in fourteen B?" He must have had some kind of waking dream.

"Okay, if you want to pretend you wandered into the wrong room, fine..." He massaged the back of his neck.

"I don't know what you're talking about. I've been asleep since you left. Somebody woke me up trying to get into my room. I haven't left it until just now."

"Fine. Whatever." He leaned an arm on the icemaker. His body looked relaxed, but his eyes were fierce. But before I could as much as blink, he leaped toward me and with dance-like grace, twirled me around. In one quick move, he grabbed me from behind, yanking back both my arms in a painful grip.

"I'll take that," he said, as he pulled the gun from my fingers.

His grip was painful. Now his anger management issues had to surface?

"You could have asked. There is no need to be rude."

He didn't move. I knew there was no point in fighting him, so I stood quietly and waited for him to get over it.

That was when I smelled patchouli—layered with tuberose and apricot. Very girly. And very weird if this woman in his bed had been a dream.

"Is that her perfume? The woman who climbed in bed with you? Couldn't you tell it wasn't me from that scent?"

Rick released me and stood back, his gun pointed at me as if I were a criminal. He sniffed his shoulder.

"I don't know. It's a lady's perfume. You wear perfume."

"I wear Chanel. Chanel is light and classic. This is heavy. Retro-trendy. Not me at all." A thought came to me— "This woman who came in your room—was she wearing a Burberry coat—you know the fawn and cream plaid with the red stripe?"

Rick lowered the gun a little.

"How should I know? It's pitch dark in there. Maybe it was one of the damned ghosts."

"It wasn't a ghost. Ghosts don't leave scents as far as I know. There has to be another explanation. In spite of that thing I saw without its head, I don't believe in ghosts."

An eerie creak came from the wall across from the ice machine.

We both froze as some ghostly force slid open a piece of the solid wall. If I'd had the breath to speak, I would have taken back those last words.

Chapter 23—Requiem for a Cowboy

RICK TRAINED HIS GUN ON the ghostly wall, his body taut and threatening.

"There you are, you two." Gabriella's voice.

She stepped out of the shadows. "So you got together after all! I thought it was a shame when Miguel said you wanted separate rooms. You can put the gun away, Captain. I'm not a gangster."

"I didn't know you had an elevator there," Rick said.

I studied his shadowed face as he put his gun in his jacket pocket. The set of his jaw showed anger: Captain Road Rage.

"They used this for loading booze back during Prohibition," Gabriella said. "This wing was the barn then. We rebuilt the lift for Hank's wheelchair, in his last days. Toby insisted we keep it working. Most of the time, I prefer the stairs. But tonight, I guess I'm just weary. Fiscalini's making such a mess of my office. I don't know why. Toby hardly ever set foot in the service wing."

She headed for the ice machine and slid open the metal door.

"Speaking of Toby, I have a favor to ask of you two."

She seemed to be fishing around in the ice for something.

"You want to reach in there, Rick? Your arms are longer than mine. I think I felt it—a bottle of champagne. Well, sparking wine anyway. *Blanc de Noir*. From our first Pinot harvest. I've got some more in the cellar, but it's not chilled."

As if this were a routine request at three-thirty in the morning, Rick knelt in front of the ice machine and reached inside.

I glanced into the shadows. Was the phantom woman still here, hiding?

Rick's arm went deeper into the ice machine.

"The old goat used to stash a bottle or two in here when he had a rendezvous with one of his students," Gabriella said. "I think he used it as a signal—'bottle in the ice machine, coast is clear' —something like that. I have a feeling he was planning a little tryst tonight, poor bastard."

"Is this it?" Rick pulled out a foil-topped bottle and handed it to Gabriella.

She cradled it like a child. I wondered if she was going to cry.

"Well, come on." She started toward the elevator. "It's not the greatest champagne in the world, but it won't kill you." She held the doors open and gave us a stoic smile. "Please come up. It's a promise I made to Toby. "

"I don't think so..." Rick rubbed his chilled hands together.

But Gabriella went on. "He was sure I'd outlive him, even though I'm twelve years older. He made me promise that the night he died I'd drink a toast to him with a bottle of our *Blanc de Noir*."

Rick started to speak again as he looked helplessly at his watch.

But I knew better than to argue with Gabriella Moore.

◊ ◊ ◊

Her private apartment upstairs merged the Western theme with mid-century Rat-Pack luxe. Directly across from the elevator was a bar padded in red leatherette, with six matching stools. The bar was backed by sleek mirrored shelves and lit with a wrought iron chandelier.

I could almost smell the Lucky Strikes and gin.

A wall of books and a mahogany desk made a cozy nook in the opposite corner. While the large part of the room was clean and orderly, the writing nook was a mess of piled papers, books and dozens of those gold-colored folders. On the corner of the desk, a big old wood-grained answering machine flashed an urgent red light.

"Sit! Sit!" Gabriella waved us toward the bar stools.

She handed the champagne bottle to Rick.

"Why don't you do the honors, Captain? Glasses are behind you. Look at that phone machine, flashing away. That's an unlisted, private line—but every session, some kid trying to get on the reading list always manages to get hold of it. No matter how many times Toby says, 'You gotta be there to sign up at the end of the workshop or no reading'..."

She stopped herself.

"Said. He said. Used to say...." Her eyes moistened as she turned away and took a quick breath. "Open the damned champagne, Rick."

"Yes, ma'am." Rick sounded less than enthusiastic. He rubbed his neck before picking up the bottle.

"What's the matter? Head hurt?" said Gabriella.

"Yeah," Rick said. "You mind if I make an ice pack with some of those cubes? I've got a heck of a headache, even if some people don't believe me." He directed the last remark at me.

"I never said I didn't believe you!" This was getting annoying. A murderer was out there, lurking—and he was feeling sorry for himself because some woman came on to him in the dark. I kept wondering if he'd met the Burberry woman. I knew she couldn't be a hallucination.

But he just ignored me as he opened the small fridge, emptied a tray of ice into a dishtowel, rolled up the towel and draped it around his neck.

"Your mama never tell you about aspirin, Rick?" Gabriella gave a dry laugh.

"I don't have any of my medications." He perched on his stool. "All my stuff is in somebody else's room. Somebody I was trying not to disturb."

I could only roll my eyes.

Gabriella gave Rick a motherly pat.

"Toby usually has a few aspirins stashed in his desk for hangovers." She started searching in the writing nook. "You want to get some champagne glasses, Camilla?"

I found no proper champagne flutes, but there were some saucer-shaped glasses that I supposed were what Gabriella and Toby used. I put two on the bar and grabbed the third as the cork exploded toward the ceiling with a loud "pop". I rushed to catch the fountain that spurted from the bottle.

"Damn!" Rick jumped as the wine splashed on his shirt. The dishtowel fell from its perch on his shoulders.

I scrambled to pick up the ice and rolled it back in the towel.

"Rick, you've got to believe it wasn't me in your room." I handed him the towel. His pale yellow shirt was covered in damp, pink blotches. He pulled away, as if I intended to hurt him. Did he believe the stupid *Post* article after all?

"Listen, Captain, I'm not whatever the late night jokesters are saying. It's just my ex-husband's lies. The media can print any stupid thing, and there's nothing I can do about it without a whole lot of money for lawyers. Which I haven't got."

Rick gave a grim smile and settled back on his stool.

"Yeah. I've been there. You know that so-called road rage

video of me they played a million times on TV? They left out the part where I busted that dude for an illegal weapon. He'd been threatening an old farmer in a slow-poke truck for miles. He was the one with the goddam road rage. The department knows I was just doing my job, but because the tape got to the media before the truth did, I gotta live in a cage labeled "dangerous weirdo" my whole damned life."

That helped. I got back on my bar stool, too.

"Oh, hell!" Gabriella gave a low moan from the writing nook. "It's not here!" Her voice sounded close to tears.

Rick ran to her side.

"It's only aspirin, Gaby. I'll live."

"Not the aspirin." She continued her frantic search. "It's gone—the folder with the Montgomery manuscript. It was supposed to be right here on top of the desk. Toby promised he'd have it ready tonight. He's ghosting a memoir for Walker Montgomery. Walker came by last night in a tizzy, demanding to see the pages Toby had promised him. He's coming back for them tomorrow. Damn, where did that old goat put it? You do not piss off Walker Montgomery."

"Walker Montgomery, the anti-gun-control guy?" Ick. Walker Montgomery was one of those old-time TV tough guys who hadn't mellowed with age. President and spokesperson of a national gun club.

Then I remembered: "He was here last night—the night I arrived? I saw some old TV star in the lobby. I couldn't place him."

"Probably him. He and Toby some big brouhaha just after the reception. He stomped out of here like he planned to kick the place down with his own little feet." Gabriella tossed papers around, looking old and tired. "It could be still here, I guess—in any one of these folders, but they're not labeled. I over-ordered our Golden West folders last year, so Toby uses them for everything... Damn. Luci Silverberg will be here tomorrow—finally. But if the deal's off with Walker, she is going to have a conniption fit."

At the mention of Luci's name, Rick massaged his neck more intensely.

"Gaby, what do you say we have our toast and get a little shut-eye? It's been a long day."

Gabriella looked up from her rummaging. "What happened to your shirt?"

All Rick could do was point to the champagne sitting on the bar.

"Exploded on you?" Gabriella returned to the bar and studied the bottle. "I'm surprised. I never thought this vintage had that much pep."

She sat on a stool next to me and picked up a glass, handing me another.

Rick lingered by the desk. He seemed fascinated by a grimy-looking Rolodex full of dog-eared address cards.

"Come on, Captain. It's almost sunrise, for goodness sake. Camilla looks exhausted." Gabriella petted my hand. "You don't have to go back to those god-awful rooms. We only keep the fourteens for emergencies. You can both sleep up here. There's plenty of room, if one of you doesn't mind sleeping in Toby's room. In fact..."

Gabriella set down her glass again and disappeared down a hallway.

"I'll only be a minute."

I sipped wine, glad to be here with Rick. I had to admit I felt safer with a man who carried a gun. Especially if he didn't suffer from uncontrolled rage after all. But I wished he'd understand that his encounter earlier in the evening hadn't been with me.

And that I hadn't imagined that intruder in the Burberry coat.

Rick flipped through the Rolodex.

"I wouldn't want Walker Montgomery as an enemy either." He grinned at me over his shoulder. "Do you remember him on that old TV show? What was his name? Tom Colt—that P.I. who killed ten people every week and never got collared?"

"I remember he had a crazy car that turned into a boat." I don't know why I remember trivia like that. After all that had happened tonight, we were playing trivia games.

"The amphibious red Mustang! It was awesome. Especially on those Hawaiian beaches. Amazing—those beaches were always empty except for bad guys waiting to be shot."

"Not Hawaii. Florida—Palm Beach. It was called *Eye on the Beach*." Gabriella reemerged from the bedroom. "Before that, Walker starred in a cowboy show called *The Brazos Kid*—but you're both too young to remember that one—here."

She held up a Ralph Lauren pullover tennis sweater.

Rick's attention was still on the Rolodex.

"Wow. You still keep in touch with all these folks, Gabriella? This reads like a Hollywood 'Who's Who'."

"More like a 'Burbank: Who's Over'. Bunch of TV has-beens. All of 'em writing their memoirs. Except they can't write, so they come to Toby."

Gaby tossed the sweater at Rick.

"Why don't you put this on? Never been worn. It was too big for Toby, so it might fit over those shoulders of yours."

"Toby was ghosting for all these names?"

"Ninety percent gave up after the first interview. But Toby liked having all those celebrities in his personal file."

She came at Rick with the sweater.

"Oh, come on, Zukowski, don't be so modest."

She started unbuttoning Rick's shirt and pulled off one sleeve.

"Hey!" His voice was sharp. "Gabriella, for chrissake!"

He pulled the shirtsleeve back on, but not before I saw a long, nasty scar that snaked up his left arm.

"Are you afraid Dr. Manners wouldn't approve of a lady stripping the clothes off a wet policeman?" Gabriella gave her growly laugh. "Fine, be damp, if you like, but this is a nice sweater. Cost me a bundle. Toby never wore it." She headed back to the bar. "So are you going to help me drink this hooch or what?"

Rick headed toward us, rebuttoning his shirt. He smoothed his left arm with his right hand, as if tracing that scar.

It was a gesture I had seen before — recently,

It was exactly the way Ernesto Cervantes had traced his devil snake tattoo.

Gabriella raised her glass.

"To Toby Roarke," she said. "One sweet man, when he wanted to be. And a fine poet. Pretty good ghostwriter, too."

"To Toby's ghost," Rick said. "May he rest peacefully." He winced as he raised his glass, grabbing the back of his neck again.

"Oh, damn! I forgot your aspirin." Gabriella set down her glass and was off to the writing nook again. "Now where did I put that...? Oh, hell. I hit the damned button."

From the telephone answering machine, the ghostly voice of Toby Roarke said he wasn't in right now and asked the caller to leave a message — then, after a beep, another man's voice spoke, staccato with anger: the famous gravelly baritone of Walker Montgomery. After a jumble of shouts, one phrase came out, icy and clear —

"Toby Roarke, if you don't have that stuff for me tonight, you are a dead man!"

Chapter 24—Free but Never Cheap

"WAKE UP, SLEEPING BEAUTY," a voice whispered.

I felt warm lips brush against my cheek.

I stiffened. "Rick?" I hadn't had enough sleep. "What time is it?"

"It's past noon, and you'll hate yourself if you sleep through this beautiful day."

The voice wasn't Rick's.

I opened my eyes to see Plantagenet, back-lit with the sunshine that streamed through the open window of the bedroom of Gabriella's apartment.

"You're out of jail!" I threw my arms around him. "Was it awful?"

He hesitated. "Let's say that when they talk about overcrowding in California jails, they aren't just being whiny." He smelled freshly showered.

"Oh, Plant, things have been so strange — so awful.

I hugged him, not wanting to let go. I didn't know how I'd survived the last five years without him. "I'm so glad you're free!"

"Free but never cheap." He gave a little laugh as he looked around the room. "You seem to have landed in some pretty nice digs. Did your friend Captain Road Rage share the, ah, accommodations?"

"Of course not!" I sat up and tried to look as dignified as one can in an Oscar de la Renta charmeuse chemise. "That road rage stuff isn't true—and I hardly know him." I had to remind myself of that. I especially didn't know what to make of that snaky scar I'd seen him try to cover up last night.

"That's why his name was the first one that came to mind when a man woke you with a kiss?" Plant laughed. "I don't blame you, darling. A cross between Jimmy Smits and Jimmy Stewart—what's not to like? But I'm glad you're not intensely involved, since Lucille Silverberg seems to be busy staking a claim."

"Luci Silverberg has arrived? Good. Gaby will be so relieved. And she's Rick's agent, not his girlfriend. Not that I care." I kissed Plantagenet's cheek. "You and I have to spend some time together in New York, or San Francisco—soon. Somewhere safe. No more wild west for me."

Plantagenet put on an expression of exaggerated hurt. I forgot his recent fame came from his revival of the Western film.

"Oh, but I adored your Oscar Wilde-West movie. Such a clever plot. Do you think Oscar Wilde really could have had an affair with Calamity Jane?"

Plant laughed. "Why not? They were both in California in the spring of 1882—both in their late 20's. He was bisexual. She was a cross-dresser. Nobody can prove it didn't happen." He checked his watch. "Better get going, or I'll be in trouble."

Not good news. "The police don't still suspect you, do they?"

"I meant with Gaby. I have no idea what the Sheriff's people think. All I know is that at ten this morning, one of the deputies told me I was free to go, and there was Gabriella in her Cherokee, ready to give me a ride back here."

He made a move toward the door.

"And, um, Toby? Did she say…?"

He nodded. "She told me the terrible news, and said the Sheriff seems to think Ernesto's gang killed him — Ernesto, too. She said the gun they found in my car was stolen by a gang, who probably killed him for attempting some upward mobility. A terrible, terrible tragedy, but at least it seems to be over."

It sounded so sensible when he said it that I felt stupid telling him what Rick said about gangs and frying pans.

"I'd better leave you to dress, darling," Plant said. "Gabriella had all your things brought up from the cabin." He pointed to my Vuitton bags, neatly stacked by the door. "She wants us down in the dining room ASAP. I think she wants to show me off. I don't know if it's to let people know I'm out of jail, or because she's so desperate for some kind of celebrity to parade in front of the paying customers."

"Why isn't Gabriella parading the great Luci around?"

"Luci's off in town having a private moment with your maverick police captain."

"Maverick?" I laughed, although I felt a twinge of jealousy when he talked about Rick and his agent. "That's his real name, you know — Maverick Jesus Zukowski."

"Yes. I know. So does Luci. That's why she's taking him to the Maverick Saloon. She thinks it will make a great setting for a photo shoot." He stood by the door and pointed to my luggage. "By the way, apparently Rick found a manuscript of yours mixed in with his things. Gaby said it's on top of your laptop case."

He left before I could tell him I was the only person in the place who did not have a manuscript to hawk.

My suitcases were indeed stacked by the doorway, a gold folder laid on top. Probably the notes for my talk. Sweet of Rick to put them in a folder for me. I so much didn't want to think he was some kind of gangster. Of course in East L.A. a kid might fall in with the wrong crowd. And he had removed the tattoo, if that's what caused the scar at all.

I scrambled into my Chanel suit and cobra skin sandals and jammed the folder into my tote. So Rick was at the Maverick Saloon. I wondered if outlaw bikers would be included in the photo shoot.

And more important—I wondered how attractive Luci was.

Chapter 25—A Message from Inmate C33

DETECTIVE FISCALINI HAD SET up shop in the Frank and Jesse James suite on the ground floor and was questioning the conference-goers one by one. They were still parading in and out by the time we finished lunch.

I wondered if that was routine or if Fiscalini wasn't as sold on the gang theory as Plant seemed to think.

After lunch the red-faced Englishman accosted me.

"I can't believe this!" He clamped an angry hand on my forearm. "Those cretins are holding us hostage. We've been ordered not to leave. Any of us. As if this place weren't stressful enough—besieged by the media, devoid of the promised celebrities, infested with murderous gangs." He sighed with martyred pain. "And now the local constabulary insists on interviewing every single one of us about where we were when Toby died. Can't you do something?"

I forced a polite smile as I tried to peel his hand from my

arm. I wanted to tell him a lowly presenter had no more authority here than he did, but that might have made him angrier. I suppose he still hadn't got any proper English tea.

"I'm afraid we all have to do what the Sheriff's investigators want," I said.

"I'm going to call my solicitor," he said, taking a phone from his pocket. "And I suggest Miss Gabriella Moore should do the same. I saw those CSI people swarming around her apartment about an hour ago." He pulled me closer and hissed in my ear. "I wouldn't be surprised if the old girl did them in herself—Toby and his Mexican toy boy."

Gaby's apartment. I hadn't thought about it, but of course they'd be going through Toby's things for clues. And my things were strewn all over the bed. A Manners Doctor no-no.

By five to two, I finally escaped the Ponderosa Lounge, where the great Luci was scheduled for her two o'clock talk. But she hadn't appeared.

Neither had Rick. I wondered if they were still partying at the Maverick Saloon.

Plant held Gabriella's hand, saying reassuring things about how he could give his talk now instead of tonight if Luci was a no-show. Most of the crowd was already seated, and the buzz of conversation was uneasy.

I sat next to Plantagenet and Gabriella, keeping an eye on the back door for Rick. But it was Mitzi Boggs Bailey who burst through the door. She made a bee-line toward us.

"Are you all right?" she said to Plantagenet.

"Why, yes," Plant said, rising to give the old woman his seat. "It was an ordeal, but it's over. I'm hoping the investigation will…"

"You sit down," Mrs. Boggs Bailey said. "She's the one who has to move." She pointed at me. "I have to sit next to the play writer. I have something to show him."

"Mitzi," Gabriella said sharply. "You can talk to Plantagenet about your play later, but now is not the time."

She turned to me. "Hon, if you don't mind, sometimes it's better to humor her."

"It's not about my play." Mrs. Boggs Bailey plopped herself down in my vacated chair.

I stood by, not quite sure where I should go.

"It's a message," the old woman said. "An important message."

"From Luci?" said Gabriella. "Did you take a phone message from Luci? Saying she'd be late?"

"No, it's not from anybody named Luci." Mrs. Boggs Bailey leaned toward Plant. "It's from Obadiah. He must have put it in my chifforobe last night. I thought it was my play, but when I opened the folder, I found this." She reached into her gold folder and pulled out a thin, ancient book, wrapped in a couple of sheets of equally antique writing paper. She handed it to Plant. "You want to know how I knew it was for you? It said the-ater. Right there on the address. The Platt The-ater. San Francisco. You live in San Francisco. Don't you, Mr. Smith?"

As Plant examined the contents of the folder, an amazing change came over his face. It went very white, but his mouth spread into an ever-widening grin.

"Dear, sweet God in heaven."

His hand shook as he handled the fragile yellowed paper, covered with faded, spidery handwriting.

"Plant, what's wrong? Do you need some water?" said Gabriella. "Mitzi, where did you get this stuff?"

"I got this from Old Obadiah," said Mrs. Boggs Bailey. "I told you. He put it in my chifforobe. The ghosts must have got into my room last night, because they left stuff, both of them. You don't want to look at the junk from Joaquin. It's filthy. But see?" She pointed to the bottom of the letter. "See where Obadiah signed this one?"

"The return address is the Platt all right," Plant said, giving a nod as he continued his zombified stare at the document.

"That's where he gave his talks."

"Who? Where's the Platt Theater?" I was a little tired of Mrs. Boggs Bailey's dramas. I finally decided to sit in a chair in the row behind Plantagenet.

"It's where Oscar Wilde gave his lectures in San Francisco," Plant said in a strange, flat voice. "In 1882." Plant opened the book. His voice had gone to a whisper. "It's a Smithers First Edition of *The Ballad of Redding Gaol*, written by C33!"

"Not C33," said Mrs. Boggs Bailey. "It's signed Obadiah Wilke. "See right there on the letter—and the book." She grabbed the yellowing paper and showed it to me.

The signature did indeed look as if it said "Obadiah Wilke."

But it could also have read "Oscar Wilde."

Plant's voice was still breathy. "C33 was Oscar Wilde's inmate number when he was imprisoned in Reading Gaol. Smithers was afraid to even print Wilde's name after the scandals—and he only published eight hundred copies. They sold out in three days."

"Then for God's sake be careful!" Gabriella barked at Mitzi and handed the letter back to Plant.

"What is it?" somebody said, as a crowd began to gather around.

Plant cleared his throat and read the flyleaf of the book.

"To my dear S. S. 'We may all be in the gutter, but some of us are looking at the stars.'"

He then showed the handwriting on the letter. "Platt Theatre, April 1, 1882. My dear Sharpshooting Songbird—".

He stopped, his voice overcome with emotion again.

"Dear God, they're dated almost twenty years apart. Not only did they have some sort of friendship, but it went on for nearly twenty years!"

"Who?" A number of people chimed in as I said it.

"The Sharpshooting Songbird..." Plantagenet beamed. "Otherwise known as Miss Martha Jane Canary: Calamity

Jane. They must have met just the way I imagined. Listen!" He began to read the letter:

"Although I am most grateful, Miss Canary, for your offer to "put a slug of lead between the eyes" of the *Alta Californian's* cretinous reviewer, Mr. Ambrose Bierce..."

Plant turned to me. "Oh, darling, this is priceless. Just priceless. This proves my theory is true. They did know each other. This must have been what Ernesto texted me about when I was on my way up here. He said he had something to show me that proved I was a genius. I thought he meant my writing tips, but it was this! Oh, Gaby, listen..."

But Gabriella wasn't listening. Her attention was on a commotion at the back of the room.

"Here she is!" someone said in hushed reverence.

Plant stopped reading and the crowd hushed as Rick Zukowski paraded down the aisle with a tiny, remarkable woman on his arm. Clad entirely in skin-tight New York literary black, the woman sported a Lulu Guinness flower pot bag, an expanse of cleavage, a large, elaborately frosted hairdo, cowboy boots, and huge, dark-rimmed glasses.

The effect was a cross between Dame Edna Everedge and Rocky the Flying Squirrel. The woman whispered something to Rick, grinned, and stood on her tooled-leather tiptoes to give his cheek a kiss—just as he had kissed mine in the Fiesta Hall just last night. Staking a claim.

So. He was her property now. Fine. I didn't need to be involved with anybody who believed I climbed into men's beds uninvited. Especially if he'd been affiliated with the Viboras. They said people never could really leave one of those gangs.

"So sorry we're late, everybody." Luci waved at the crowd. Her nails were acrylic talons, lacquered a blood-red that matched the petals on her bag.

Gabriella hurried to the lectern to introduce "the president of New York's famous Silverberg Literary Agency—Lucille

Silverberg!"

The crowd applauded wildly as Rick—casually elegant in a leather blazer I hadn't seen before—escorted the diva to her place at the center of the stage. He avoided my eyes as he took a seat next to Gabriella behind Luci's podium. I could hear his too-new leather jacket squeaking as he shifted in his folding chair.

Luci opened her mouth to speak, but her Lulu Guinness bag began to play the theme from *Star Wars*. She gave everyone a beneficent smile as she reached in and clicked off her phone and turned back to her notes.

"Finally!" the Englishman whispered, settling into the seat beside me on the aisle. "Finally they're giving us something worthwhile."

Luci's talk went over its allotted time. To hear her tell it, she had been responsible for the biggest book deals of the last decade, from the memoirs of a serial killer's mistress to Johnny Rotten's upcoming children's book. She got more and more self-aggrandizing as she went on, finally introducing Rick as her latest discovery as he shifted and squeaked behind her. She announced that his thinly disguised memoir, *Blue Rage*, was going to "expose more scandals than the Washington madam's date book" and asked him to speak a few words.

He gave a nervous laugh and said he needed to save all the words he had in him for the book. Obviously he hadn't finished those last chapters.

I glanced at my watch, and saw it was nearly four—time for my own much re-scheduled talk. I couldn't imagine that any conference-goers would leave Luci's august presence to hear my little presentation, but it would be wrong not to be at my post at the announced time.

I tried to signal my departure to Plantagenet, but he still looked dazed as he fingered the Oscar Wilde treasures.

Onstage, Gabriella took control. Reaching for the

microphone, she boomed: "Thank you, Ms. Silverberg. We've taken advantage of your kindness too long..."

I made my escape up the aisle. Unfortunately Christian Louboutin had not designed his shoes for stealthy exits. I was only halfway to the door when I heard Luci's New York bark interrupt the toupee man's whine.

"Dr. Manners—don't go," Luci shouted. "We must talk, dear. Please stay!"

I felt every eye in the room on me. I turned to face the great Luci.

"Ladies and gentlemen, this lady is a national treasure," Luci announced. "Camilla Randall, otherwise known as the Manners Doctor, is soon to be one of the most successful writers in the business—if she listens to me."

Now I knew the woman was not only narcissistic, but insane. All my instincts told me to run, but I was frozen there, like the proverbial deer, about to be crushed by an oncoming truck.

Chapter 26—An Eye on the Ranch

I TEETERED ON MY STILETTOS as Lucille Silverberg's words echoed through the hushed room.

On the stage, Gabriella, ever the rescuer, fought Luci for the microphone.

"The Manners Doctor's presentation on writing the syndicated column will begin in just a few minutes in the Belle Starr banquet room," she said. "The question period is over. Thank you all so much."

I rushed down the aisle as fast as my heels would carry me. Luckily, the crush of people mobbing Luci allowed me to escape. I'd almost made it to the Belle Starr room when somebody came up behind me.

Somebody who squeaked like new leather.

"Camilla, I gotta talk to you." Rick panted for breath. "About Luci..."

I did not need this.

"Rick. I have a talk to give. I'll be happy to discuss your friend Luci later, but not now, if you don't mind."

I opened the door to the banquet room, but I was too late. Luci was marching on us, her pack of manuscript-wielding admirers trailing behind.

"Camilla, dear—just a moment of your time before you start?"

I grabbed Rick's leather-clad shoulder and pushed him toward Luci's entourage.

"Captain Zukowski—how about some crowd control?" I slipped inside and tried to pull the door shut behind me.

But Luci pushed past Rick and into the room. She came at me in an overwhelming cloud of Lancôme *Hypnôse*, her hands waving in that way of women who spend too much of their paychecks on their manicurists.

"Camilla, you are looking so...oh, so brave, dear!" She squeezed my hand and squinched up her face as if she were about to cuddle an adorable puppy. "Chanel couture? Christian Louboutin sandals? No one would ever guess you're destitute. That poor policeman out there thinks you're way out of his financial league. You should clue him in. You do know he's gaga for you?"

"Ms. Silverberg, perhaps we could chat another time? I have a talk in five minutes."

"How does six figures sound to you, dear?" Luci kept smiling at me, ignoring the fact her Lulu Guinness bag was again playing its tinny *Star Wars* fanfare. "With ten grand up front. Right now. You could do with a few extra dollars, couldn't you?"

She pulled out a phone and said, "Can you hold, sweetie?"

She turned back to me. "I'll bet you'd like to pay the overdue fees on that dinky west-side co-op of yours."

How did she know anything about my bills?

"Darling, I can't talk now. I'm in an important meeting," Luci said into the phone.

I was about to lose my temper.

"My husband—my ex-husband—is slow with his payments. It's just a cash-flow problem. The lawyers have to hammer things out."

"Do you honestly think Jonathan Kahn is going to pay you one cent of that settlement? You know his lawyers can keep on…"

I had heard enough.

"Madam, I have no idea what you want, but if you came in here to impress me with your bad manners, you may consider your mission accomplished. Now you may go."

"Oh, sweetie—" Luci squinched her face again. "You're so cute when you get that Dr. Manners thing going. I'm sorry. It's just that I so much want to represent your book. Ten thousand dollars. Right now. Think about it."

Luci's game was getting more ridiculous by the minute. I knew agents didn't pay writers up front. Publishers did. And it took months, even years to sell a book to a publisher.

"Ms. Silverberg, I am the one person at this conference who does not have a book to sell. If Captain Zukowski has told you otherwise, he was lying."

"But we already have the pictures, dear. All you need to do is supply the text." Luci took a small envelope from her flowerpot bag. "That is, unless you'd like someone else to write it…?" She pulled a photograph from the envelope.

My throat closed.

The picture was kinky porn—grainy and unfocused, but the subject matter was unmistakable—a naked woman spanking a man with a leather paddle. No. worse than naked. She wore nothing but a riding helmet, Chanel pearls and a pair of strappy sandals. The man showed naked buttocks above lowered khaki trousers.

The woman bore more than a passing resemblance to me, although she wore way too much make-up and her breasts were obviously surgically enhanced.

And there was no mistaking the spankee. It was Jonathan. I recognized the scar on his right buttock from when he took a bullet in Nicaragua in the 'eighties.

Phony as it was, this travesty could make all those lies about me look true—and destroy what little might be left of my professional life.

"That's not me," I said when I could make the words come out. "And why blackmail people with no money? That can't be lucrative for you."

"Who said anything about blackmail?" Luci waved her red talons. "I'm offering you money. And the chance for a little revenge. Who looks worse in that photo—you or your ex?" She gave a nasty smile. "Or, if you just wanted to supply the text, we might not need the picture..."

I had no idea what diabolical scheme the woman was proposing, but all I wanted to do was run. Jonathan's stupid lies were terrorizing me wherever I went. Would I have to move to another country? Another galaxy?

I tried to show no emotion and reached into my bag for my make-up—hoping I could paint on a mask of cool indifference.

"Ms. Silverberg, I have a talk to give." I opened my lipstick. "The Manners Doctor does not approve of women applying make-up in public, but you leave me no choice."

Loud knocking startled me. The door flew open, but instead of the conferencers, I saw an image from my childhood—a tanned, grinning face I once knew well.

But now it looked over-laundered and wrung dry.

That must have been why I couldn't quite recognize him that first night in the lobby. He extended a big, wrinkled hand.

"Walker Montgomery ma'am," he said. "Gaby said you girls were having a confab in here. Sorry to interrupt."

I sensed hostility in his bone-crushing handshake, but his trademark grin didn't waver. He turned to Luci.

"You having trouble with that phone of yours? Had it

surgically removed from your ear?" He pretended to search under Luci's hair. "I've been calling you for hours, Lucille."

Luci didn't appear pleased to see the famous star.

"What the hell are you doing here, Walker?" She clutched her flowerpot bag as if she expected him to mug her.

"I'm trying to watch my manners in front of this beautiful young lady. I suggest you do the same." He grabbed Luci's elbow in what appeared to be a friendly gesture, but Luci looked as if she'd been pinioned by a wrestling hold. "Now Luce, would you be so kind as to give me a few minutes of your time?"

Star Wars called from Luci's handbag. I could think of nothing but the horrible photograph inside.

Luci re-established her smile and pulled out the phone to look at the number.

"Let's say a few, um, uninterrupted minutes of your time?" Mr. Montgomery grabbed the phone as Luci's face turned the color of the satin roses on her bag.

He kept grinning.

"If you won't take a call as important as mine, I'm sure you don't need to take that one." With some difficulty, he found the off button and silenced the phone. "I read in the Manners Doctor column that the mobile phone is the abomination of our current era. I agree. No machine should take precedence over real human contact."

I wondered if he counted his precious guns in the category of "machines" but did not want to risk angering a man so famous for his gun collection. Besides, he had what looked like a recent scar over his left eye that suggested he might also engage in hand-to-hand combat.

"Come on, Lucille. We have some unfinished business to discuss." Walker's big arm encircled Luci's shoulders in a way that was at the same time casual and menacing. "And this young lady has a presentation to give. Pleased to make your acquaintance, Dr. Manners."

He escorted Luci out into the melee of her waiting fans.

"Luci! Ms. Silverberg, would you read my manuscript? Please, Luci…" I recognized the voices of several smugsters.

I expected them all to follow her, Pied-Piper-like, but a rush of writers pushed into the little banquet room, scrambling for seats. Rick came toward me, his face dark with emotion, but before he could speak, Gabriella, just behind, grabbed his elbow.

"No way can everybody fit in this room," Gabriella said. "Captain, run and tell Miguel to keep the Ponderosa set up. I'll round 'em up and head 'em back over there. Camilla, did you get that?"

I did, but just barely. My mind was still reeling. I couldn't figure out what Luci wanted from me. It was more than bizarre that she offered to give me money instead of extort it. Was she mixed up with the murders somehow, or was the place simply a magnet for dangerous lunatics?"

"Dr. Manners? Head 'em up; move 'em out?" said Gabriella.

All I could do was nod.

Rick took my arm. "Please tell me you didn't sign anything Luci gave you?"

I shook him off. "Of course not. As you ought to know, I don't have a book to sell. I wish you'd tell your precious agent that."

"Go!" Gabriella said to Rick. "Before we get stampeded."

Chapter 27—Newsbabes

I FINALLY MANAGED TO get myself back to the Ponderosa Lounge, as did most of the writers.

Plantagenet hadn't moved from his seat and was still studying the contents of Mrs. Boggs Bailey's Oscar Wilde find, cell phone to his ear. Mrs. Boggs Bailey sat at the end of the row watching him like a proud mother.

"Are you all right?" she said when she saw me approach. "Why did you come back? He can't let you read Obadiah's letter, because he has to take it to Silas."

Plant clicked off his phone and put it in his pocket.

"I'm not going anywhere, darling. I caught Silas at one of his stores nearby. He's on his way back here."

I guess my relief showed. He stood and kissed my forehead.

"Don't look so forlorn. I wouldn't miss your talk for the world. But I'm eager to get somebody to look at this stuff to find out if it's the real McCoy. I think this must have been what Ernesto was talking about on the night he died. He kept saying he had something spectacular to show me. Silas has a first edition *Redding Gaol* himself, locked up in his safe, so he can authenticate it pretty easily. I hope he can do the letter too. It's the real prize—it would prove my imaginary friendship between Oscar and Jane really happened."

I felt the flutter of stage fright as I looked up at the podium.

"I think I'd better get up there and say something to these people."

Plant looked behind him. "Looks like you've got a full house. Except for Ms. Silverberg."

I looked at the crowd. He was right. No Luci. She must still be in the clutches of Walker Montgomery.

Plant grabbed my arm and pointed in the direction of the stage.

"Uh-oh. It looks like Captain Road Rage may be living up to his reputation."

Gabriella and Rick stood in front of the stage engaged in what looked like a heated argument. Without giving me a glance, Rick stalked out of the room. Plant was right about his obvious anger. It was just as well Rick preferred Luci to me. The two of them could have lovely rages together.

Gabriella had mounted the stage. She took the microphone and gestured to me. "Ladies and Gentlemen, thanks for your patience. Without further ado, here is Camilla Randall to tell you about the column she writes under the famous *nom de plume*, the Manners Doctor."

I climbed to the stage, clutching my folder, and looked out at the sea of faces, most of whom were probably in the audience only because of Luci Silverberg's delusional remarks. All they were going to get was some information about how to write a syndicated advice column from a columnist whose own syndicate was likely to drop her, after all this hideous publicity.

I opened my folder, took a deep breath, and froze. As I read the words on the page, I felt my whole life passing before me—

"*Newsbabes*: a chick lit novel by Lourdes Donna Inez Carillos."

It wasn't my folder. There was no speech inside. It had been mixed up with some other writer's manuscript.

I was going to have to wing it.

I made myself smile, cleared my throat and tried to think of something.

"The Manners Doctor likes to quote Lord Chesterton, who said that the people with the best manners are the ones who can make the largest number of people feel comfortable under the most uncomfortable of circumstances. So I'm going to make this short. We've all had a trying couple of days..."

Thank goodness for Lord Chesterton. I somehow stumbled through most of what I'd planned to say—almost glad Rick had run out on me. I decided to drop the final segment I'd planned—about how to write for the growing ethnic teen market—since there were not many non-whites or teens present, unless you counted Toby's Donna Karan girl, who was now wearing lipstick precisely the color of Pepto Bismol. Her accent might come from Latin America, and she was probably still a teenager, but her blank mask of grief—or maybe fear—showed she didn't hear a word.

Nobody did. The crowd grew more restless and noisy, as—inexplicably—more and more of them appeared—none of them Rick or Luci. But I could see people lining up along the back wall.

I closed and asked for any final questions.

"Yes, I have a question," said a heart-stopping, familiar voice from the back of the room. "It's for Gabriella Moore."

My head roared. I could hardly bear to look. My ex-husband.

"Oh, look!" said Mrs. Boggs Bailey, jumping up from her

seat next to Gabriella. "It's that Jonathan Kahn from the TV. And some folks with cameras! And all my squirrel friends!"

I couldn't breathe.

There he was: Jonathan.

He was as impossibly handsome as ever, in full camera-ready make-up, with every silvering hair in place.

Obviously he was here to disrupt my presentation. Nothing seemed to be beneath him these days. Did Luci know he'd be here? Is that what the photo was about?

A furious Gabriella turned around in her front row seat as Jonathan walked up the aisle, with his crew and a rag-tag mob of protesters and newspeople trailing behind.

"Gabriella Moore?" he said into his microphone. "Why did you kill your lover, Toby Roarke?"

Chapter 28—Outlaw Cowgirl

AS THE CAMERA CREW MOVED in on her, Gabriella let out such a string of curses that I feared several elderly memoirists might faint. I hung to the lectern for support myself, suffering from equal parts fury and embarrassment. How had I ever been married to Jonathan Kahn?

"You have to let the whole world trespass on my property?" Gabriella roared, looking at the crowd of reporters, protesters and looky-loos streaming in the doors. "Who opened the gates for you, Kahn? What the hell are you doing on my ranch?"

"I had telephone authorization from a Mrs. Bailey. She owns this property, does she not?"

"Kahn, you are one damned fool," Gabriella said as Jonathan poked a microphone in her face. "No. I take that back. You're two damned fools. First you're a fool for saying that lying crap about Camilla, and then you're a fool for wasting your time on some story a poor old crazy gal told you over the phone." She pointed at Mrs. Boggs Bailey, who was dancing in front of the camera like a small child. "Meet my sister-in-law, Mitzi Boggs Bailey. Your news source."

"I'm Mitzi Boggs Bailey, the poet." The old woman looked up at Jonathan with a coy smile. "Are you all right?"

"Why sure, Mrs. Bailey, I'm just fine," said Jonathan. He gave a signal to the cameraman to focus on Mrs. Boggs Bailey as he brandished the microphone. "Do you remember talking to me on the phone when I called last night?"

"I sure do. I told you about my play." Mrs. Boggs Bailey beamed. "You stayed on the phone a long time. Much longer than old Obadiah does."

"And who is Obadiah? Is he involved in these murders, Mrs. Bailey?"

"Oh, I don't think so. He's kind of shy." Mrs. Boggs Bailey grabbed Jonathan's mike hand and moved closer to the camera. "Now that Joaquin—I wouldn't put anything past him. He murdered hundreds of folks, you know."

Jonathan put on his Walter Cronkite, serious-news face.

"Joaquin? Is he the head of this gang—these Viboras who have been suspected of Toby Roarke's murder?"

Mrs. Boggs Bailey let out a peal of laughter.

"Joaquin isn't the head of anything, silly. He doesn't have one. Captain Harry Love cut it off. Put it in a jar of booze and took it to San Francisco. That's why Joaquin's so mad."

"I don't understand, Mrs. Bailey. Are you talking about—?"

"She's talking about Joaquin Murrieta," said Gabriella. "The 1850s bandit. Mrs. Boggs Bailey talks to ghosts, Mr. Kahn." Gabriella's voice got slower and more deliberate. "She suffers from dementia. I'm sorry you had to travel from New York for nothing, but there's no story to report. The Sheriff has made no arrests at this time…"

Gabriella stopped mid-sentence as the crowd scattered and two uniformed Sheriff's deputies, headed by Detective

Fiscalini, filed into the room. Detective Fiscalini led them in a march down to the first row, where Jonathan and his entourage surrounded Gabriella and Mrs. Boggs Bailey. I felt almost relieved when I recognized one of them as D. Sorengaard, the nice deputy from the Solvang Sheriff's substation.

"Please," I said, rushing from the stage to Officer Sorengaard. "This is all just another one of Mrs. Boggs Bailey's phone calls causing trouble. She's been babbling nonsense to Jonathan, and as you know, she suffers from dementia. Please, you know Gabriella Moore didn't kill anybody."

The crowd pushed in as Detective Fiscalini stood in front of Gabriella, acting as if he'd never met her before, as he read her name from some document as "Gabriella Mora Boggs." He proceeded to arrest her for the murders of "Ernesto Jaime Cervantes" and "Tobias Patrick Roarke." Gabriella's face had drained of color, but she said nothing as a uniformed deputy recited her rights in English and Spanish and clapped her in handcuffs.

The Ralph Lauren woman looked as if she might attack Detective Fiscalini with her bare, be-ringed hands.

"That's ridiculous, officer. Don't you know who this is? Mrs. Betsy Pike from *Big Mountain*! She's an American icon."

"This is a goof, right?" said one of the smugsters, pushing his way in. "How did Kahn know this was going to happen?"

"Kahn has informants all over. And I'll bet he pays way more than a deputy sheriff makes in a month," somebody else said.

The red-faced Brit asked loudly why the officers repeated everything in Spanish when this was an English-speaking country. He then began regaling the crowd with his theories about "Mexican toy boys."

Meanwhile, Jonathan, with two cameramen behind him, intoned a running commentary into his microphone. At one point, a gallant Plantagenet tried to grab the mike and called

Jonathan several names that were probably intended to spoil the tape for basic cable TV, but Jonathan didn't miss a beat as he spoke into the microphone.

"Plantagenet Smith, I understand you've been implicated in the murder of your lover, Ernesto Cervantes. In fact, Miss Moore bailed you out of the county jail only a few hours ago. Tell me, did Miss Moore kill your lover, or did you?"

Plant pushed away the mike and lunged at the cameraman with a curse. One of the other crewmembers picked up a chair and gestured toward Plant as if he were taming a circus lion. The crowd pushed in closer.

"Oh, please," Plant said. "Are we breaking chairs now? What, are you going for the Jerry Springer demographic, Kahn?"

D. Sorengaard stomped onto the stage.

"Okay, folks," he said in a foghorn voice. "There's nothing more to see here today. Time to go home. Everybody who is not registered at this hotel is trespassing. Return to your vehicles and vacate the property."

Detective Fiscalini led Gabriella toward the exit as deputies started dispersing the crowd. But Jonathan held his ground, thrusting his mike in Plant's face. The lighting and camera men closed in.

I hovered, staring at Jonathan. He was once an idealistic newsman. How had he become this shameless monster?

Up on the stage, D. Sorengaard contended with Mrs. Boggs Bailey, who was attempting to get him to join her in a kind of Shirley Temple soft-shoe dance. The cameraman shifted focus and aimed at the stage.

Gabriella laid a cuffed hand on Detective Fiscalini's arm and turned to give me a pleading look.

I understood. I strode toward Jonathan and put the palm of my hand over the camera lens.

"That will be all. Jonathan," I said. "You heard Officer Sorengaard. You're not a guest at this hotel. The presentation is over. You're trespassing. Please leave."

Jonathan grabbed my hand and fixed me with his icy blue stare. A cameraman swiveled and moved in on me.

"Camilla Randall," Jonathan said. "I understand you found the body of Toby Roarke as well as that of Mr. Ernesto Cervantes? People keep losing their lives wherever you go, Camilla. Can you explain that?"

Jonathan's smile was as steely as his grip on my wrist. The microphone nearly touched my lips. I could smell his *Emporio Armani* — the scent that once made me melt with wanting him. But at this moment I felt nothing but disgust.

"There has been a lot of loss here — a lot of tragedy," I said finally, trying to present a composed look to the camera. "The world has lost a promising young writer. Gabriella Moore has lost her longtime companion. Mitzi Boggs Bailey has lost her mental faculties, and you, Jonathan Kahn, are about to lose whatever shreds of honor and integrity you have left. Can I explain it? No, I cannot."

Jonathan let go of my hand, lowered his microphone and signaled the cameraman to stop. He covered his mouth and shut his eyes.

"My God, Camilla!" Only when he dropped his hand did I see that he was laughing. "Do you have any idea how sexy you are when you turn on that Dr. Manners stuff? Babe, can we just talk — five minutes — off the record?"

"No! She can't 'just talk' with you, Kahn," said Plantagenet, pushing the formerly chair-wielding crewman aside with surprising force. "Nobody wants to talk to you on the record, off the record or — "

"No, wait!" said Gabriella. "Mr. Kahn, this is some kind of foul-up, and it will be cleared up in a few minutes at the station, I'm sure," She turned to Jonathan with surprising calm. "But please, for Mitzi's sake, don't air this. I'll give you an exclusive when I get back. You have my word on it. Don't air this footage, and when I get back from the Sheriff's station,

I talk to nobody but you. Is that a deal?"

"Do you want to take my picture again, Mr. Kahn?" said Mrs. Boggs Bailey, her voice loud and flat in the hushed room.

"No," said Jonathan, still apparently transfixed by Gabriella's serene stare. "I won't be taking any more pictures today, Mrs. Bailey." He handed his microphone to the chairman. "If you can put up my crew while we film some background, we have a deal, Gaby."

"Good. Alberto will give you a couple of cabins. Camilla, can you take him to the desk? Tell Alberto to give Paladin to Mr. Kahn. And the crew can have the Cisco Kid. The workshops can be relocated to the Fiesta Hall."

"Come along, Miss Moore," said Detective Fiscalini.

Gabriella turned and accompanied him with the dignity of a French aristocrat being led to the guillotine.

"Kahn, how do you sleep?" said Plantagenet, still tense with rage.

"Very well, thanks," Jonathan said. "I eat right, exercise and make sure I get my minimum daily requirement of alcohol." He turned and beamed a grin at me. "So where can a guy get a Jack Daniels around here?"

Chapter 29—Silver Foxes

ALBERTO WASN'T HIS USUAL efficient self as he presented me with the paperwork to register Jonathan and his crew. The poor man kept apologizing for some imagined transgression he seemed to think was the cause of Gabriella's arrest. I wasn't happy with the position of authority I seemed to have inherited in Gabriella's absence. I could only hope the arrest was a stupid mistake and she'd be back soon. Entertaining Jonathan and his people was not how I wanted to spend my evening. Why not Luci? Or Rick—wherever he was?

The lobby was filling up, and Alberto looked increasingly uncomfortable as we saw Miguel—the writer-waiter and sometime assistant concierge—hauling a load of luggage from the upper floor, at the head of a parade of guests. Everybody was going to try to check out at once.

"Where is Santiago?" said Alberto. "I asked him to help carry bags. Miguel, I need you to help me here."

Miguel put down the luggage. He muttered something under his breath in Spanish that contained the words "Santiago, Guatemala," and "loco."

"Please wait your turn," Alberto said to the crowd of guests trying to check out.

"I don't want Ronald Reagan anymore," said Mrs. Boggs Bailey. "I want Roy Rogers back. Mr. Kahn's going to be down at the cabins, so I want to be there. I need to show him my play. He can put it on TV, now that I'm famous. Mr. Kahn, did you know I was on TV? I stopped them from killing the squirrels."

Jonathan nodded, but his newsman's bland expression was beginning to crack.

"And I'm sure the squirrels are deeply grateful, Mrs. Bailey."

Mitzi pounded the desk in front of Alberto.

"Ronald Reagan has too many ghosts. My play got stolen. Give me Roy Rogers!"

The frazzled Alberto shot a questioning look at me, as if I had some way of channeling Gabriella's wishes.

"Isn't someone free to…spend some time with Mrs. Boggs Bailey?" I tried to be polite about the sudden elder-care duties. "Maybe one of the other faculty members?"

Alberto shook his head.

"Lucille Silverberg has gone to the Saloon with Mr. Montgomery. Captain Zukowski as well, I believe. We cannot locate Vondra DeHaviland or Herbert Frye; the greeting card lady has gone back to Fresno, and many are not staying here. They have gone home for the day. Nothing is scheduled tonight but dinner and Mr. Smith at seven o'clock." He gave a nod in Plantagenet's direction while he handed keys to Jonathan and his crew. "Miguel will take you to the cabins in a golf cart."

So Rick and Luci were out drinking with Walker Montgomery — having themselves a little party while chaos reigned at the Rancho. I could only pray that Luci wouldn't show the awful photo to Rick. And that Rick wouldn't believe the woman in the picture was me.

I turned to Miguel, as he hefted the luggage of Jonathan's crew.

"Is there someone who could watch Mrs. Boggs Bailey — maybe one of the maids? Someone who knows a little English? I'm sure there would be extra pay."

Miguel gave me a stiff smile.

"I will try. Much of the staff is calling in sick. We don't have enough legals..." he stopped himself, glancing at Jonathan and lowered his voice. "I can't explain now.Too many reporters."

The camera crew followed him, obviously eager for the refuge of the cabins, but Jonathan lingered. I tried to freeze him with my chilliest look, but he clapped a hand on Plant's shoulder as if they were old friends.

"How about that drink? Don't tell me there's no bar in this place?"

Plant gave me an apprehensive glance.

"Drinks are served in the Ponderosa Lounge only," Alberto said with clipped efficiency. "The Longhorn Room is a crime scene. No one is allowed until the investigators get their laboratory results."

"You can buy me a whiskey sour, Mr. Kahn," said Mrs. Boggs Bailey, taking Jonathan's arm. "I love a silver fox."

Jonathan's hair was indeed more silver than brown now — but still thick and impeccably cut. And he was obviously still working with his personal trainer.

Plantagenet gave me an eye roll. "I'll call my lawyer and tell him his firm has another client," he whispered. "Gaby is the one we should be worrying about right now."

The Ponderosa Lounge was already full by the time we arrived. All the conference-goers who had not yet checked out seemed to be there, still clutching manuscripts. They mobbed

Jonathan as soon as we walked in the door.

"Mr. Kahn can't talk," said Mrs. Boggs Bailey. "He and Gaby have a deal."

In the far corner of the Lounge, on the table that had once held only water pitchers and paper cups, a makeshift bar had been set up. Jonathan pushed his way through the crowd with a few affable jokes and made his way to the bar-table as Mrs. Boggs Bailey trailed behind him.

Plant whispered in my ear. "Why don't we go back to Gaby's apartment? We can leave Jonathan with Mitzi and his other adoring fans."

"Quick, before they catch us."

I grabbed Plant's hand and pulled him toward the door, but it was too late. Jonathan materialized behind us.

"They're out of Jack Daniels," he said. "I'll bet Toby Roarke kept a private stash. Mitzi tells me Gaby's got a private bar upstairs?"

I sighed. Part of me almost felt sorry for Jonathan. Whatever evil plans Luci had for that photograph, they would probably be even worse for Jonathan than for me.

Plant smiled a little too wide and squeezed my hand.

"Yes," he said. "We were just talking about going up there. I'm sure Gaby won't mind."

"Oh, she'll mind all right," said Mrs. Boggs Bailey. "But she can't stop us now. She shouldn't have made the ghosts mad. The Sheriff took that old cowgirl to the hoosegow, just like Joaquin said he would."

"Joaquin said Gaby would go to jail?" Plant looked into the old woman's eyes, as if he hoped to find something rational there.

"Oh, yes. Him and Obadiah. They told me."

"The ghosts talked to you about Gabriella — when?"

"On the night that boy died."

Chapter 30—Hello Trouble

MRS. BOGGS BAILEY BASKED IN Jonathan's attentions, obviously unable to comprehend the seriousness of Gabriella's troubles. Saying she was too tired to climb the stairs, the old woman triumphantly located a key to the secret elevator, stashed in a magnetic box stuck to the underside of the ice machine.

"This place is better than that Winchester Mystery House in San Jose," Jonathan said. "I wonder if Gaby would let me tape a whole show here?"

"This ranch is in pictures all the time," said Mrs. Boggs Bailey. "Back when I was a girl, this was the elevator they used for equipment like those great big lights. We used to catch heck for playing on it."

"Really?" Jonathan said. "Gaby and Toby built their house on a movie set?"

I felt tense standing so close to Jonathan in the tiny elevator. His scent and warmth were so familiar—but he'd become a dangerous stranger. I stood as close as I could to Plant and was relieved when the red leatherette doors opened into Gabriella's apartment.

Mrs. Boggs Bailey laughed and rushed to climb up on a bar stool.

"Not Gabriella and Toby, stupid. I told you before: this is my place. Me and my brother Hank. He bought this ranch after the Prohibition. He was a kid himself, but nobody wanted an old speakeasy, so he got it cheap. He rented it to the movie people. We had all the big stars here — Hoot Gibson, Buck Jones, Jonny Mack Brown. You ever see Buck in *Hello Trouble*? That was one of my favorites."

I looked around the apartment, and thought it looked a little messier than it had last night, although the investigators had been pretty neat, if they'd been through it. Toby's desk looked rifled. The Rolodex seemed to be missing. I couldn't tell what else.

Maybe they'd found evidence here that pointed at Gaby as the murderer.

Maybe she was actually guilty. I supposed it was possible.

I felt guilty sitting at Gabriella and Toby's bar with Toby dead and Gaby in jail. I wished Rick was here, even if he was an ex-gangster who was involved with another woman. His presence made me feel safer. I wondered if he even knew about Gabriella's arrest yet.

I sure would like to know what he and Gabriella had been arguing about.

As I looked at Jonathan, pumping Mrs. Boggs Bailey for dirt about Gaby while he pretended to be entranced by the ghost stories, I could imagine being angry enough to bonk a spouse on the head with a frying pan, if I happened to have one handy.

And Gaby had that office in the service wing — right near the kitchen. Didn't Rick say that's where Toby had been killed?

Jonathan poured himself a large whiskey from the array of bottles behind the bar.

"So tell me, Mitzi — you say you've got two cowboy ghosts here? Old Obadiah leaves you notes, and Joaquin Murrieta talks to you? How does he do that without his head? Is it an ESP kind of thing?"

"ESP? Oh, I don't believe in that crap." Mrs. Boggs Bailey grabbed a highball glass. "How about a whiskey sour? You know how to make a whiskey sour? My husband, Bob Bailey — rest his soul — now that man could make a whiskey sour. Couldn't make a decent living to save his soul, but he sure could make a mean cocktail."

Jonathan gave me a pleading look.

"I guess I'm the opposite," he said. "I make pretty good bucks, but I haven't got one cocktail in my repertoire. Just Jack on the rocks. Camilla, can you — ?"

I couldn't believe he was asking me to play waitress.

"Whiskey sour? Coming right up!" Plantagenet scooted behind the bar, a picture of efficient charm.

I sat in silence. Jonathan could make money all right, but he could spend even more. What about Luci's claim that Jonathan would never pay me the divorce settlement? Could he do that?

"So you believe in ghosts, but not ESP, Mitzi?" Jonathan said. "Ghosts who can talk even though they've got no head?"

"He had a head the other night, if you must know," Mrs. Boggs Bailey said. "He had that big collar on his coat pulled up to scare me. But I could tell it was Joaquin."

The collar of a coat. In the dark shadows of the cabins, that might have made a person look headless. Maybe that was what I'd seen last night. Could that be the same "apparition" as the Burberry woman?

The awful thought came to me that all these apparitions and ghosts could have been Gabriella herself.

"So this spirit came into your bedroom last night..."

Jonathan was gulping down whiskey in a way I'd never seen when we were married. "And he said, 'My name is Joaquin Murrieta and I'll be your ghost this evening'." His voice was thick with sarcasm as he put on a stagy gay-waiter voice. "'My warning tonight is that Gabriella Moore is going to be arrested.' Something like that?"

Plantagenet rolled his eyes at me as he pushed the button on the ancient blender he'd been filling with mysterious ingredients. It gave off a fierce roar.

"No. Nothing like that!" Mrs. Boggs Bailey shouted. "I didn't see the ghosts last night. But I know they were there because they left stuff and they signed it. Mr. Smith can show you the letter. It's signed Obadiah Wilke."

"Obadiah Wilke is the other ghost?" said Jonathan. "So how did you know it was Joaquin and not Obadiah talking about Gabriella going to the hoosegow?"

"Because he told me who he was, Mr. Smarty-Pants." Mrs. Boggs Bailey grabbed one of the glasses Plantagenet had filled with frothy liquid.

"He told you?" said Jonathan. "What? You asked him if he was Joaquin and he spoke to you?"

"Bingo." Mrs. Boggs Bailey blew a bit of whiskey-sour froth from her upper lip. "I saw the two ghosts over by the Zorro cabin where the dead boy was, after I went in to ask him to stop the disgusting noises and shooting his guns and all. When I got back to Roy Rogers, the tall ghost was in the bushes by my cabin with his collar up, making spooky noises."

I sipped whiskey sour, taking this in. Apparently this ghost act was a duet. Could they have been gang people? Maybe Fiscalini would go back to his gang theory if he heard about the two ghost-impersonators. I really needed to talk to Rick. He knew how policemen's minds worked. Maybe he could get Fiscalini to look into Mrs. Boggs Bailey's ghosts.

She went on with her tale:

"So I said 'Hey, Joaquin, is that you?' and asked him if he was all right. Then I said maybe he wasn't all right because he was a ghost and that meant he was dead. I guess that tickled him, because he laughed like crazy, and then he said, 'That's right, Mitzi Boggs. I'm a ghost, and if you tell anybody any different, you're going to get Gaby in a heap of trouble'."

So much for the Viboras theory. Gang people were unlikely to refer to Gabriella Moore as "Gaby".

As Jonathan interrogated Mrs. Boggs Bailey I pulled Plant aside and whispered in his ear.

"Do you think it's possible that Gaby is guilty?"

"Not a chance," he said. "They said her cowhide walls were splattered with paint. She'd never let that happen. Do you have any idea what they cost? And she couldn't lift one of those steer heads."

His phone chirped.

"I hope this is Silas. I'll tell him we've got another emergency here, even bigger than Oscar Wilde."

"Oscar Wilde?" Jonathan said as Plant gave his attention to the phone. "You've got the ghost of Oscar Wilde running around here, too? Hey, let's hear it for diversity!"

I couldn't stifle myself any longer.

"Jonathan, you'd be less of an embarrassment if you learned to listen a little more and drink a little less."

Plantagenet shot me a warning look, but I could see for myself that I'd gone too far. Jonathan's face changed as he grabbed the whisky bottle and refilled his glass to the brim.

"An embarrassment?" Jonathan's voice rose. "Yeah. I was always an embarrassment to you, wasn't I...?"

"Could I have a little less noise here?" Plant covered the phone and spoke over his shoulder as if he were speaking to a badly behaved child. Then he spoke to the phone again. "Silas, I'll see you at dinner here, then..."

"Who are you to tell me to shut up? You think an Academy Award makes you king of the world, Smith?" Jonathan slammed down his drink so hard the contents shot up and rained on my Chanel suit.

Urgent knocking on the outside door startled us all.

Chapter 31—The Donna Karan Girl

"MISS RANDALL! MISS RANDALL! where is Mrs. Boggs Bailey? Is she with you?"

I opened the door and saw Miguel the waiter-writer—looking harried, with his jacket off and shirtsleeves rolled up.

With him was, of all people, Toby's Donna Karan girl, looking like a schoolgirl in jeans and a skimpy tee-shirt, with her severe chignon unwound into a glossy pony tail. She even seemed to have washed off a few layers of make-up.

"My cousin can watch Mrs. Bailey and take her to Roy Rogers," Miguel said. "The maids are gone. They are afraid of the policemen." He started down the stairs. "Alberto says dinner is at six-thirty sharp."

I looked at my watch. It said five twenty-five.

"Can they feed all of us—Jonathan and his crew?"

"Many people are leaving. There is plenty. I must go. We

are very busy."

"I can see that." I glanced at Miguel's rolled-up sleeves.

Miguel suddenly looked nervous—or was it frightened? He took off, rolling down his shirtsleeves as he ran to the stairs, but not before I caught a glimpse of something on his arm: A long, black tattoo of a snake. A devil-headed snake. Just like Ernesto's—and the spray-painted image on the wall over Toby's body.

That meant Miguel was—or had been—a member of the Viboras.

I'd wondered why Miguel seemed so nonchalant about Ernesto stealing his story. Maybe that was because he'd already taken a terrible revenge.

Miguel could have led the Viboras to Ernesto so they could murder him. Toby, too. He had reasons to be angry with them both. Ernesto had stolen the story, and Toby gave it that harsh critique. A serious overreaction, but an unbalanced person might do that. Miguel didn't seem like a sociopath, but I'd so much rather believe he was a killer than Gabriella Moore.

"I'm Donna," said Miguel's cousin.

So the Donna Karan girl was really named Donna. I wondered if her devotion to the designer came from their shared name.

The girl shook my hand, but her eyes were fastened on Jonathan.

"Mrs. Bailey and I are friends. Right, Mitzi?" She waved at Mrs. Boggs Bailey, sitting on her bar stool swinging her legs like a small child, delighted with all the commotion. "I helped Miguel with her before," she said in my direction.

"Jonathan Kahn spilled his drink," Mrs. Boggs Bailey said.

"Fantastic to see you again, Mr. Kahn," Donna said, walking across to the bar like a Miss America contestant on the runway. "We met at a reception for the Governor. I used to date Duncan Fowler, you know—the commentator on Fox News? I love your work."

Jonathan basked, but Plant looked stunned.

"Duncan Fowler? You dated Duncan Fowler?" Plant covered his shock with a social smile. "Oh, yes. I suppose you met him here in town. I've heard he has a place somewhere around here?"

Jonathan used to refer to Duncan as "Crybaby Fowler" and a "fascist tool", but now he beamed at Donna as if she'd announced she recently discarded Leonardo DiCaprio.

"He lives in Los Olivos, right over that hill," Donna said to Plant, pointing out the window. She turned back to Jonathan. "The beach towns are so over. They keep, like, sliding into the ocean, don't they? To meet important Industry people, you've got to 'head for the hills' — that's what Toby used to say."

With the mention of Toby's name, I expected to see some of the grief Donna had shown earlier, but there wasn't a flicker of emotion on her pretty face.

"You're an actress?" Grabbing a bar towel, Jonathan wiped his spilled drink from the stool next to him and motioned for Donna to sit down.

Donna sat.

"Right now I'm a fragrance spokesmodel at Nordstrom in Santa Barbara, but I'm hoping my book will get me noticed in, like, the right places. I want to work in TV news." She leaned over to display the cleavage that had probably helped her pay for those expensive clothes.

Plantagenet rolled his eyes at me and shrugged.

"TV News? Really?" said Jonathan. "Will you have a whiskey sour, Donna?"

"None left!" Plantagenet emptied the last of what was in the blender into the sink. "But if you want to go down to your cabins — here!" He handed Jonathan the Jack Daniels bottle. "Why don't you take this to your people? I'm sure Gaby would want to include them in our happy hour."

He wiped the bar, like a bartender cleaning up for the night.

"Do you have any champagne?" Donna said. "I only drink champagne."

Plant opened the small fridge under the bar. "Just one sparkling wine in here. But it's been opened. Probably flat by now. He reached in and pulled out the bottle of *Blanc de Noir* from the night before. In the daylight, I could now see the number "14" scrawled across the label in red marker.

"Want to try a little, Donna?" Plant grabbed a champagne glass.

Donna stared at the bottle.

"No. No. I don't want...that."

She pushed the bottle away as if as if it were something that had just been dug up from the grave.

◊ ◊ ◊

Plant barely got the door closed behind them all before he let out a hoot of laughter.

"Camilla, darling, I hope Jonathan was good in the sack, because otherwise, life with him must have felt like being confined to one of the darker, hotter circles of Hell."

It felt good to be able to laugh. "It looks as if Jonathan may have met his match with that Donna creature. Did you hear her comment about Duncan Fowler? That wasn't name-dropping, it was name-hurling."

"What a crock," Plant said. "Everyone knows Duncan Fowler is an old queen." Plant rinsed out the blender. "More whiskey sours?"

"No thanks. I should try to keep a clear head, since people seem to expect me to be in charge of things around here." It felt so safe being alone with Plant. Part of me wanted to confide all my worries in him—the increasing number of things that were making me feel a little nuts.

1) The ghostly Burberry woman.
2) The headless ghost I saw with my own eyes.
3) That horrible, nonsensical photograph.
4) The scar on Rick's forearm that was shaped like the

Viboras tattoo.

But there wasn't time to talk this stuff out. I figured I'd better keep the mysteries to myself until I'd sorted them out a bit for myself. And I didn't need another man to give me that "you've had a shock, dear, have a drink," attitude I got from Rick last night.

Plantagenet sniffed at my sleeve.

"You'd better change before dinner, darling. Essence de Jack Daniels isn't a good fragrance for you. Don't want to start any new rumors about the Manners Doctor's bad habits. Let me help choose your ensemble, for old time's sake."

Chapter 32— Gay Caballeros

I COULDN'T TELL IF THE investigation team had been through my things. Nothing seemed to have been moved, but I hadn't been in a state to notice much when I left this morning.

I opened the top suitcase and found my speech notes— exactly where I'd put them. I took the folder with the mysterious *Newsbabes* manuscript out of my tote bag. I'd have to ask Alberto if somebody had reported a lost manuscript.

I understood how Rick might have thought the folder was mine when he found an unfamiliar manuscript in his room, but I couldn't figure out how it got there. It seemed odd that anybody would ask a policeman to critique a chick lit novel.

Plant chose a sexy little Valentino jacket dress in an aquamarine knit for me. Watching him choose my clothes transported me back to my debutante days, when Plant and I bonded over clothes, society gossip, and dishing every celebrity we met.

"So you know Duncan Fowler?" I said as I re-did my make-up for the paler outfit. "He's gay? Isn't that difficult for a right wing pundit?"

Plantagenet laughed. "There's always talk of outing him, especially now he's aligned himself with the gun-nut crazies. And it's weird—about his guns. You know the big cannon that they say killed Ernesto—the thing they found tossed on the floor of my Ferrari?"

"Of course. I'm the idiot who locked the car door after it got put in there. I'm afraid that's why the police suspected you."

I gave his arm a squeeze, hoping he knew how sorry I was about what he'd had to go through.

"I'm kind of an obvious suspect: the old fool with the frisky young lover—one of the ten basic plots." He gave a grim smile. "But what I was going to tell you is about that big Colt. It was reported stolen—the day of the murder—from Duncan Fowler. Odd coincidence."

"Odd indeed."

My brain started connecting dots. Duncan Fowler, who owned the gun, was the ex-boyfriend of Donna. So Donna had access to that gun. Donna was Miguel's cousin: Miguel—with the Viboras tattoo. Last night, alone at the front desk doing his substitute concierge duties, Miguel had had the perfect opportunity to kill Toby. Or let his cohorts inside to do the deed.

"That's it," I said out loud. "It's definitely Miguel! He's strong enough to lift that cow head."

Plant lifted an eyebrow.

"That waiter who was just here? Why on earth would you suspect him?" Plant was neatly tidying the room and putting things into my suitcases. Very helpful, since it wouldn't be right staying in Gaby's apartment, under the circumstances.

"Miguel has that tattoo. He was trying to cover it up."

"Plenty of fine people have tattoos, darling. The Manners Doctor needs to get a clue."

"The Manners Doctor has no problem with tattoos!" I hated it when Plant got all politically correct. "In fact she's written that a small one can be quite elegant. But Miguel's tattoo is the same devil snake design as Ernesto's — and the one on the wall over Toby's body."

Plant's expression changed.

"It was the same as Ernesto's gang tattoo? Are you sure?" His tone was businesslike. "You should tell the investigators."

His phone rang. "That will be Silas. I've got to meet him downstairs. I'm hoping he'll have some news about Gaby — and he ought to be able to help me figure out this Oscar Wilde mystery."

Oscar Wilde. I'd almost forgotten. How did he fit in?

◊◊◊

A few minutes after Plant left, I heard frantic knocking at the outside door of the apartment.

There was Donna, back in camera-ready make-up and Donna Karan evening wear. I searched her black-lined eyes, but saw no hint of nervousness that might indicate guilt. Of course, even if she'd stolen that gun, she could be ignorant of what it had been used for.

The only emotion she showed now was exasperation.

"You gotta help me with the old lady," she said. "She says she's got something to give you, and she won't leave that room until she gets rid of it." She gave an exaggerated shrug. "You gotta hurry, because I need to get her moved to her new cabin before dinner."

I followed along the upper-level porch and down the stairs to the old wing. As I walked behind her, the evening breeze wafted with her perfume — a familiar scent:

Patchouli, with a hint of tuberose and apricot.

I sped up and sniffed again. Yes. There it was — the same scent I smelled on Rick last night.

The phantom woman who crawled in his bed could have been Donna.

"Do you happen to own a Burberry coat?" I asked with what I hoped was nonchalance. "A belted trench in the signature fawn, cream and red plaid?"

Donna looked at me with scorn.

"Do I look like I'd wear plaid?"

The phone in her bag played the *Sex in the City* theme.

No. She wasn't anywhere near my height. Even with a wig, she couldn't be my Burberry phantom. But I was going to keep an eye on her — and her cousin Miguel.

As she chatted to someone about workplace issues, she led me to a door with a plaque that said "Ronald Reagan Suite."

She knocked on the door.

Mrs. Boggs Bailey's gray head poked through a crack. She'd styled her hair in a perfect 1950s pageboy and wore a red, white and blue bandanna around her neck.

"Are you all right?" The old woman opened the door a little wider. She was dressed in an amazing rhinestone-studded denim cowgirl outfit, complete with fringed white cowboy boots. "I got myself all gussied up for dinner, but I thought you'd skedaddled somewhere..."

She opened the door to reveal a large, rustically-decorated room that was a mess of open drawers and tossed-about pillows.

"I can't find my play. The ghosts took it." She looked at me with an expression of something between recognition and disgust. "You look like that Dr. Manners. I suppose you've come for the rest of the junk the ghosts left in my chifforobe?"

She pulled me away from the door and lowered her voice.

"Filthy stuff, if you ask me. But I guess you didn't. Neither did the ghosts."

"That's why we're here, Mitzi" said Donna with a bored sigh. "So you can give the stuff to Dr. Manners here and then you and me can move you down to a cabin near Jonathan

Kahn. So you wanna get a move-on? That Santiago guy has got a golf cart waiting. I don't know how long he'll wait. He doesn't speak much English or Spanish. Just some Guatemalan Indian dialect."

Mrs. Boggs Bailey looked confused for a moment.

"Now where did I put it? I don't want those maids seeing that filth when they pack my things." She bustled around the room. "I'm glad I won't be around Ronald Reagan any more. He stares at me."

She gestured to the end of the room where, above the stone fireplace hung a huge oil portrait of the late President, dressed in jeans and a plaid shirt, with an ax in his hand. A framed note beneath read: "There are no easy answers, but sometimes there are simple answers." It was signed "For Gabriella — Ronald Reagan, 1964."

I sincerely hoped there was a simple answer to all the questions swirling in my brain at the moment. Could someone actually have stolen the old woman's play and substituted some sort of "filth"? Like maybe the Burberry woman? The old woman could have been hallucinating, of course, but for us both to hallucinate the same apparition seemed unlikely.

When she was out of hearing range, Donna leaned in and whispered. "You're pretty tight with that L. A. cop, right?"

I had no idea how to describe my relationship with Rick at that moment, but I nodded anyway.

"I think I might have left something in his room last night. I really need it. It's the only copy I have, and I'm dying to show it to Jonathan Kahn."

She left something in Rick's room. And she wore that perfume. Maybe she wasn't Ms. Burberry, but she certainly seemed to be the failed seductress.

Now I could place that scent: Donna Karan's *Black Cashmere*.

"And what did you leave in Rick's bedroom?"

Donna looked embarrassed.

"It's the first three chapters of my chick lit novel, *Newsbabes*. Can you ask him to return it? I kind of went in his room by mistake last night. I wasn't hitting on him, I swear. I thought he was...somebody else. Somebody who promised to show the manuscript to that agent—Lucille Silverberg. I got so flustered when I realized I was in the wrong place that I left my folder."

Newsbabes. So Donna was Lourdes Donna Inez Carillos, who must have left the folder when she crept into Rick's room. The "someone else" had to be Toby.

He must have planned his assignations in the hotel's lousiest room—thinking it was sure to be unoccupied.

So Donna thought Rick was Toby—that room had no windows, so not even moonlight would have illuminated the darkness. She'd probably arrived to exchange sex for a recommendation to the great Luci. That explained Donna's revulsion at the sight of the sparkling wine bottle with the room number on it.

What a slug Toby had been.

Above us, Ronald Reagan's portrait did indeed seem to be staring as he wielded his ominous ax.

Mrs. Boggs Bailey emerged from the bedroom with yet another gold-colored conference folder.

"Here," she said, handing it to me. "Don't think I'm not on to you." She shoved the folder at me with tight-lipped disapproval.

"Santiago isn't going to wait all day," Donna said. "I had to flirt with him like crazy to get him to take us down to the cabins while he's supposed to be helping Miguel. Come on. Jonathan Kahn is down there. I gotta see him before he leaves."

As I made my way toward the dining room, I opened Mitzi's ghostly folder and stopped dead. Stuffed into the pockets of the folder were at least a dozen handwritten letters, on different kinds of stationery, all yellowed with age, the ink faded to a pale purple. I couldn't imagine what Mrs. Boggs Bailey thought they had to do with me. They were addressed to a man named Joaquin Montoya, at a Los Angeles address. I opened a fragile envelope and started to read the bold, masculine hand, but the words made my face flush.

It was a very explicit, homoerotic love letter.

But what was most shocking was the signature: "Will Sugarfoot Hutchins" — one of the old time TV stars whose picture graced the walls of the Hacienda's main corridor downstairs. As I made my way back to the apartment, I pulled a few more letters out of their fragile envelopes. The missives all seemed to be in the same blush-making vein, each one signed by famous and semi-famous stars of the nineteen-fifties and 'sixties. This Joaquin was quite the gay caballero.

Another letter from "Ty Hardin" was full of cowboy metaphors for some steamy sexual activity, and when I opened a third, I could barely breathe. Underneath all that homoerotica was the signature, "Ronald Reagan." The handwriting looked identical to that on the note I'd seen framed on the mantle of Mitzi's suite.

I tried to fit these into the other mysteries of the past three days, but it only hurt my head. Were they related to the Oscar Wilde book and Calamity Jane letter? Strange coincidences. But aside from the fact that they concerned gay men, these letters didn't have much to do with the Oscar Wilde find that I could see — separated as they were by nearly a hundred years.

I had to show them to Plantagenet. Immediately. I hoped I could get him alone before dinner was served.

As I put back the letters, I felt something sliding around behind the envelopes in one of the folder's pockets. A small photograph. I drew it out and my palms went clammy. There it was — another copy of Luci's horror — showing Jonathan's butt and the surgically-enhanced Manners Doctor in pearls.

◊ ◊ ◊

At dinner, Plant was surrounded by fans, so I couldn't sit

anywhere near his table, much less get him alone for a conversation. I could almost feel heat coming from those steamy letters in my tote bag.

I hoped Plant knew of some gay cowboy star named "Joaquin," so we could return the letters.

Rick seemed to be surgically attached to Luci. They were sitting at the center of another knot of eager students, and Rick was still wearing that damned jacket. I saw him reach under the sleeve to scratch his forearm — the forearm with the snaky scar. Maybe he and Luci deserved each other. She had to be mixed up in this somehow, since that photo was in the folder with the letters.

I sat with some memoirists who all agreed that Gabriella Moore was a national treasure and couldn't be guilty of anything, and they wouldn't be surprised if it was ghosts.

Everybody knew the place was haunted.

One of the ladies was sure she'd seen the ghost of an old cowboy last night, floating outside her window.

Donna and Mitzi arrived just as I was finishing my dinner.

I promised Donna I'd run right up and get her manuscript back. The girl was an idiot, but it wasn't her fault Toby died before he could deliver her a read from the great Luci. I'd feel terrible if I kept her from getting the opportunity to show it around. She was just an innocent bystander caught up in all this craziness.

At least mostly innocent. Of course, if her cousin Miguel was the murderer, maybe Donna had helped Miguel do it.

Or — the thought exploded in my brain — what if Gabriella killed Toby, then got Miguel and his gang to cover it up? A couple of tough young guys would have no trouble moving the body — and the steer head.

And Rick had that scar. If he'd once been a member of the gang, he might have helped them, too. And that's why he'd been wandering around that night.

There was awful logic to the theory.

But I did not want to believe any of them was guilty. Not Rick, in spite of his thing with Luci. And not Gabriella. Or Miguel and Donna. They'd all have to be very good actors if they were part of some murderous conspiracy.

Besides, Plant was right. Gabriella would not have authorized vandalism of her cowhide walls. It was going to cost a fortune to re-cover them.

Chapter 33—Double Trouble

WHEN I GOT BACK TO Gabriella's apartment, I was startled by a noise: something between a thump and a snap.

"Luci?" said a voice from inside. A voice I didn't recognize.

Maybe the investigators were back.

"Officer?" I called down the hall.

No answer.

I opened the door and gasped.

There she was—the Burberry woman: blonde, about my height and figure—maybe a bit taller, with considerably bigger breasts—wearing a vintage *prêt a porter* Chanel suit in a color and style I happened to own myself.

On her wrist was what looked like the Paloma Picasso diamond hugs and kisses bracelet Jonathan had given me for our tenth anniversary. Over her shoulder was a huge Fendi-style spybag—a knock-off of the very one I carried until a few months ago.

This was a caricature of my own last year's self—a Bizarro Camilla. Like a very bad dream. I grabbed the door jamb in an attempt to make contact with reality.

"Dr. Manners!" The woman's voice had a deep, whisky-and-cigarette rasp. "I thought you'd be at dinner." She laughed as if this were terribly funny. "Thank God it's you. I was afraid you were Luci Silverberg. That woman is the devil, you know that? Satan in support hose. She's over sixty. Did you know how much work she's had done?"

She eyed my shoes.

"Are those real Louboutin sandals? I love the bronzy cobra skin. If only he made them in my size…" She stepped from behind the bed, displaying astonishingly large feet.

I kept a firm grip on my shoes and spoke in my most intimidating Manners Doctor tone.

"Who are you, Madam, and what are you doing in my room?"

"Oooh, I just love that: 'Madam.' That is so classy."

The thief went back to ransacking my Vuitton suitcases, now open on the bed.

"That's your appeal. You just ooze class. That's why Dr. Manners is my trademark character. I used to do Martha Stewart, wearing the little apron, spanking them with a sweet little antique wooden bread paddle, but, well, Martha's so over, isn't she? After jail everything she does is boring. I do Sharon Stone—and Ann Coulter, of course, but once I started doing Dr. Manners, you wouldn't believe how my client list grew. And with this new press you're getting…"

She laughed again and went back to rummaging in my suitcases.

"How nice my humiliation has been good for somebody."

My head reeled with the implications of having a real dominatrix impersonate me.

"You haven't answered my question. What are you doing in my bedroom?"

She smoothed out my ravaged Dolce and Gabbana suit.

"I didn't know it was yours at first. Honestly. I came up here looking for some, um, property that Toby should have returned to me. When I was poking around, what should I find but all your gorgeous things! Couldn't resist a peek. Do you realize how much this means to a Dr. Manners impersonator? Mostly I base my wardrobe on magazine photos, but here—well, it's a treasure trove!" She picked up my Oscar de la Renta charmeuse chemise

I grabbed it and tossed it in the bag.

"You were going to steal my clothes?"

"Steal? Oh no, sweetie. I do not steal. Besides, they wouldn't fit me, would they? You're a little curvier around the hips than me and, well, my girls here—" She looked down at her gravity-defying breasts. "When I had them put in, I told the doc to just fill 'em up—give me a D cup. I wouldn't have if I'd realize how much harder it would be to fit into designer clothes. But it's not like I'd ever had breasts before."

"You're a transsexual?" That would explain the husky voice and thickish neck.

"Pre-op. I'm saving. That's why I do this." She opened my make-up case.

"This? Sneaking around people's apartments and not stealing things? Does that pay well?"

"Oh, sweetie, don't be hostile. I admire you so much. No—I only go where I'm invited. And you'd be amazed how many places that is. I work for a celebrity impersonator escort agency." She studied my tube of Lancôme Vintage Rose lipstick.

"You're a prostitute who pretends to be somebody famous? Like in the film *L.A. Confidential*?"

I could see Donna's manuscript folder lying on the dresser behind the intruder. I'd retrieve it, then go tell the investigators they had a new suspect. I took a deep breath, trying to keep my face calm.

"Right. Like *L.A. Confidential*. If you paid attention in that film, sweetie, you know that pretty much everybody in L.A. is a whore. But I don't sleep with my clients. I discipline them."

She dropped the lipstick back in my case.

"You're one of those people with the leather corsets and whips?"

She sighed, as if this conversation were too boring for words.

"Leather is so vanilla these days. That's all gone mainstream, hasn't it? So for us professionals, the secret is to come up with something fresh, like..."

"Like impersonating me?" I walked to the dresser, grabbed Donna's folder and slipped it into my tote bag. "Please leave. Now."

She eyed my tote bag. "You don't carry that fabulous Fendi spybag any more?"

"No." I was not going to admit I'd had to sell it.

"Too bad. I love mine, even though it's not the real McCoy. It's roomy enough for all my make-up and...well, you know, props."

I did not know about her "props." Nor did I want to. I wanted this creature to disappear from the galaxy.

But now he/she smiled broadly and grabbed my hand, uttering one incomprehensible word that sounded like "Marva."

"Marva?" I awkwardly shook the hand. It didn't let go.

"Used to be Marvin." With a sudden move he/she slipped my tote bag from my wrist as if it were the most normal action in the world. "Shows what sort of a childhood I had. What kind of parents name a kid Marvin?"

"What do you think you're doing?" I reached to retrieve my tote. "Give me that!"

Marva only smiled wider as she pulled out both gold pocket folders—Donna's and the one with the steamy letters and horrible photograph.

"Now what's this? Two folders, and they look just alike! Think of the confusion that could cause!" He/she tossed one folder back to me. "I've already seen this. Do you think a book about pundits in love will sell?"

I took Donna's folder and cringed as Marva opened the other.

"Oh, my, my." Marva flipped through the steamy letters. "These are good. No wonder Toby didn't want me to see them."

The time for manners was over. I lunged, reaching for the open folder. Marva's grip was firm, but I did get my hand in one of the pockets to grasp a couple of the envelopes, but the awful photo slid out with them and onto the floor. As she bent over to pick it up, I stuffed the few letters I'd grabbed into my tote. At least I'd have proof they existed.

"Here it is." She stood and studied the awful photograph of Jonathan with cool detachment. "So how did you get this stuff out of Toby? I've ransacked the place looking for this folder. Even Luci has never seen these letters — not that I know of."

"Luci is involved with those love letters, too?"

"Of course. She and Toby were partners. Did you kill Toby, you sly thing?"

"Of course not. Why would I do that?"

This was getting creepier by the minute.

"Maybe because you didn't want this photo all over the Internet? Blackmail is a powerful motive."

"Don't be ridiculous. That's not even me in the picture."

"Of course not. It's me." She gave a big laugh. "But who cares? By the time the word got out it was fake, Dr. Manners would be history. It only takes a few days to gerbil somebody these days."

I didn't know whether to be afraid of this person or laugh at her.

"You attack people with gerbils?"

She gave another throaty laugh.

"You of all people should know that nobody cares if a story is true; they only care if it's juicy. Like those old urban legends about the hottie of the hour having anatomically impossible sex with a gerbil. I'm sure certain Hollywood leading men would like to kill whoever started those gerbil-sex stories."

"I didn't kill anybody. Or molest any rodents. Besides, Luci has a copy of that photo. I'd have to kill her, too, wouldn't I?"

"No. Because she doesn't have it any more." Marva reached into her faux Fendi bag and pulled out a familiar little Lulu Guinness rose basket purse. "I switched it for a knock-off this afternoon when she was at the Maverick Saloon with that hunky L.A. cop."

The Maverick Saloon. So Marva did business there. That explained why my biker-chauffeur friend talked to me about "the Saloon" when we met in Santa Barbara. And why he thought I wanted to go there. He must be one of Marva's customers. Apparently a satisfied one.

Marva dangled Luci's stolen handbag from a sturdy finger. "It's cute, but I could never carry such a dinky thing, could you?" She lifted the fabric rose lid and pulled a second copy of the photo from the bottom of the purse. "Only two copies were printed, and the picture was deleted, so you're safe now, dear."

I did not feel the slightest bit safe.

"The person in the picture with you — it's really Jonathan?"

"Of course." Marva smiled. "The riding helmet was his idea. He says you ride English and hunt foxes and stuff? That is sooo old money. My riding is strictly Western. In fact I used to work cattle on this ranch when I was a boy. Working for Gaby was the best summer job in town."

I did not want to hear Marva reminisce while my head was about to explode. "Jonathan was in on this? He wanted a transvestite to…"

"Transsexual, sweetie. There's a difference."

"But Jonathan hired you to impersonate me and…"

"Spank his naughty bottom? Yes, he did. But if it makes you feel any better, he didn't like the fact that I'm trans."

"How could he accuse me, when he was the one who was getting kinky…?"

"Oh, don't get all judgmental on me. Remember what the Manners Doctor says, 'There is no place for judgmental behavior in a civilized society. If you believe you are morally or spiritually superior to another being, the only way to prove it is to be kind'."

"Do you think allowing this photograph to be taken was a kind thing to do?"

"No. But I don't claim to be superior to anybody. Besides, I didn't know about the pictures. Turns out my former boss hid cameras in the rooms. She called it 'business insurance.' But she made the mistake of shopping her memoirs to Luci. And Luci started approaching our clients—getting them to pay to keep the book off the market."

"Luci gets celebrities to pay her to keep her books from getting published?"

Marva nodded.

Things started to click into place. It sure explained Rick's book. It was full of dirt on thinly disguised A-listers.

And Luci wanted me to agree to a fake "memoir" so she could blackmail Jonathan.

There was an authoritative knock on the front door. We both froze.

"Cops," Marva said. "Nobody else knocks like that. I'm outta here." She rushed toward the hidden elevator. She must have done more than herd cattle around the place when she was a boy. She obviously knew its secrets.

"I'll send the elevator back up for you, sweetie." Marva blew a kiss just before the red leatherette doors clicked shut. "I'm sure you're better with cops than I am."

Chapter 34—Satan in Support Hose

THE KNOCKING ON THE DOOR to the apartment got louder as Marva vanished into the secret elevator.

"Camilla? Is that you in there?" Rick's voice. "Why did you leave the dining room so fast? We need to talk. Gaby...her arrest. You know she's not guilty, right? "

I was so relieved it wasn't Detective Fiscalini, I opened the door and threw my arms around Rick before I remembered I was angry with him.

I eyed the new leather jacket, and all my fury at Luci came pouring forth.

"Do you know what Marva said about Luci? She said she's the devil. Satan in support hose."

"Whoever Marva is, she's probably right," he said.

I started to explain. "Marva is..."

Did he just say I was right about Luci?

Rick put a finger over my lips. "You can tell me later. Don't you want to hear the keynote address by your friend the Oscar-winning screenwriter? I hoped you'd sit with me. I'm so sorry I missed your talk. Business with Luci."

"Right. Business," I said. "That involved a new leather blazer…"

He shook his head.

"Don't worry about Luci. Come on." He walked me toward the elevator. When he pushed the call button, the doors opened immediately. Marva had kept her word and sent it back up. He pulled me inside the tiny elevator and closed the door.

"You and Luci have been awfully cozy—are you sure she's just your agent."

"Luci is nothing to me. And she's no longer my agent." He was close enough that I could smell the leather of his jacket, and the warm scent of his Old Spice.

"She isn't? But your book…"

"Is trash. It sucks. Learning to write takes years. At least I know that now, so maybe this conference wasn't a total waste of my time. Gabriella and Toby set me up. At least Toby did. I don't know if Gaby was in on the scam or not. I'm sure she didn't kill anybody. But Toby and Luci were definitely pulling some sort of con. And Gaby defended them—even when I told her I suspected Luci was a fraud."

"Is that what you were fighting about—just before my talk?"

"Yeah. I'm so sorry I missed it. But I had to follow up on my hunch about Luci."

He leaned over me and pressed the button for the ground floor.

"So you and Luci aren't…anymore?" I looked up at his velvety dark eyes. His face was only inches from mine.

"Never were."

His mouth hovered over mine.

"Never?"

"Nope."

I could feel the elevator descending as he kissed me. I felt weightless — suspended in mid-air, mid-moment, mid-emotion. I didn't know what to think. Or feel. Except that I wanted the kiss to last forever.

◊◊◊

When I reached the Ponderosa Lounge, Rick by my side, I was surprised to see the stage empty and the remaining conference-goers gathered in ominously muttering clumps.

But a moment later, Plantagenet rushed down the aisle and leapt up to the stage.

Silas followed at a more dignified pace.

Conversation fell to an uneasy rumble as people moved to seat themselves in the rows of folding chairs.

As we sat in the front row, I was intensely aware of Gabriella's absence. The whole place seemed creepy and wrong: like a body without a head.

I felt Rick's arm slide around the back of my chair, and was grateful for the warmth and solidity of his body, although I wished I could stop thinking about that snaky scar on his arm. And how easily he and Miguel had chatted together in Spanish.

But I needed to trust him. Needed to be able to hang onto that lovely elevator moment for a few moments longer.

At least I seemed to have been wrong about his feelings for Luci. When she arrived in the room and sauntered down the aisle, every muscle in Rick's body went taut.

He was like a wary animal that sensed a predator had entered the scene.

Chapter 35—We May All Be in the Gutter

"THERE YOU ARE, DEAR!" Luci said to me, theatrically ignoring Rick. I tried not to be obvious about studying the flowerpot handbag. Marva may have told the truth. The satin petals of the roses looked a bit too orange.

Luci plunked herself into the chair on my other side. "Camilla, dear, you need to talk to that funny little man at the front desk. Not the intense young man who's always scribbling—the old Hobbity one: Alberto. He says he's been looking for you everywhere."

I hoped Alberto was going to assign me a new room—a place to organize my thoughts after all this chaos.

I hugged my tote bag, wondering what sense I could make of the letters inside—or of Marva. If anything about Marva did make sense. She did seem to dislike Luci. That was in her favor.

"What have you got in there, notes for your memoir?" Luci said, her eyes wide and fake-girly hands waving. "Or do you want to write it as a *roman à clef*? I'd love to see whatever you've got."

I looked over at Rick for moral support, but he was chatting with somebody in the row behind, apparently avoiding any eye contact with Luci.

I was going to have to do this by myself. "I am sorry, Ms. Silverberg. I thought I'd made myself clear. I am not writing a memoir, or a novel, or anything else. Just a weekly column."

I started to stuff the folder back in my tote when it came to me. Donna's book. I could give it to Luci right now, which was what Donna wanted in the first place. I could relax in my new room instead of trying to find Donna and I would know I'd made one of Toby's wrongs right.

Something needed to go right for somebody this weekend.

I turned to Luci with a smile. "A young woman named Donna Carillos has written a novel that I'm sure is much steamier than any narrative I could write, and I have it right here..."

But I couldn't continue with my little mission of mercy because the audience went suddenly quiet.

Plant stepped to the lectern and began to speak on his chosen topic — "Prospecting for Stories: How to Mine History Books for Blockbuster Plots."

I was impressed. He talked about how he'd put together the stories of Calamity Jane and Oscar Wilde after discovering they'd been in San Francisco at the same time, and how he'd invented a whole new storyline for them both, using real historical details.

He also made the writers who had stayed on feel like heroes. He said his own and Gabriella's arrests were simply "routine police procedure," and assured them he expected Gabriella to be released "any minute now."

"Camilla, dear," Luci whispered in my ear. "Plantagenet is

so gorgeous. I hope you'll include a few chapters about your, um, romantic history with him."

I tried to silence her with raised eyebrow, but she was unstoppable.

"And if you've got any stories about Jonathan with him — or other guys, I can get even more for your book."

"I am not writing any books!" I whispered back at her.

"That's fine, dear. I can get you a ghost." Luci whispered back, leaning close to my ear. "A ghost who makes deadlines better than poor old Toby. All I want is a true story about life with Jonathan Kahn. It couldn't have been easy for you, dear, with his, um, unusual tastes..." She eyed my sandals. "Ten thousand dollars will buy some very nice shoes." She patted my knee. "And I'd hate to see you lose your little home..." She reached for my bag.

Her hand collided with the buckle and broke off one of her talons. She looked at me with thinly disguised fury.

"I'm sorry I ruined your manicure, but here..." I handed her Donna's folder. "I believe this could be a real blockbuster."

This seemed to calm her for the moment. In fact, the manuscript must have begun pretty well, to judge from her sharp intake of breath after she opened the folder.

But a moment later she was at it again. She leaned close to my ear and murmured.

"My, my, my. You're more of a businesswoman than I thought. Any more where this came from?"

"Talk to Donna Carillos." I kept my eyes on the stage.

Plant enchanted the audience with the story of Mrs. Boggs Bailey's literary discovery in the chifforobe of the Ronald Reagan suite. Storyteller that he was, he entertained them with tales of the Rancho ghosts and suggested the book and letters might have been lying around the Hacienda for a hundred years — resurfacing with some sort of "supernatural" aid at Gabriella's time of need.

At his mention of the ghosts, there arose an "Oh, pu-leeze" from the back row. I turned and saw the alpha smugster lounging on his chair like a high school bad-boy, flanked by his cohorts. He smirked at me and rolled his eyes.

As I tried to avoid acknowledging his rudeness, I caught sight of a tall figure behind him, leaning by the back doors: Walker Montgomery, glowering at us all.

I turned back as Plant introduced Silas, who read a passage from the note that seemed to have been written to Calamity Jane by Oscar Wilde after their first meeting in San Francisco in March of 1882 —

"Please accept my thanks for your rescue of my poor person as the admiring hordes knocked me from the sidewalk in the Chinese District yesterday. You are right, I suppose, in saying that in this city, everyone ends up in the gutter sooner or later. However, though we may all be in the gutter, Miss Canary, some of us are looking at the stars."

I recognized that line. It was the "high falutin'" quote from Ernesto's title for Miguel's story. The exact quote: "We *may* all be in the gutter" — the words Ernesto had originally read. It didn't say "we *are* all" as Toby had insisted was the correct quote. Could Toby have been wrong? He had been so arrogant in his certainty — even to the fact that the line came from the third act of *Lady Windemere's Fan.* Was it possible that Ernesto did not get his quote from *Lady Windemere's Fan,* but from this letter?

This could mean Ernesto had seen the letter. Maybe even got killed for it

"If it's authentic, this material could fetch as much as fifty thousand dollars," Silas said. "Maybe more."

The audience made suitable "Antiques Roadshow" sounds as they moved toward the stage to get a closer look.

Plant opened up questions to the floor.

The Englishman called out, "Where did this tomfoolery really come from? Don't give us any more hogwash about ghosts." His cell phone rang in his pocket. He flipped it open. "No. I'm not doing anything…"

"Well then—thanks so much…" Plant said, trying to wind things up as the Brit babbled on, apparently convinced that, since he wasn't paying attention to us, we couldn't hear him.

There was a reason the Manners Doctor did not like cell phones.

"Dude!" The head smugster lolled back in his chair. "You don't honestly believe Oscar would have screwed a dog like Calamity Jane, do you? Martha Jane Canary was pure Gainsburger. Even Bill Hickok had to get liquored up to do her."

"Have you ever seen a picture of the real James Butler Hickok?" said Plant, with a "can we dish" smile. "Talk about the kennel club. Reality is always such a disappointment. But to answer both questions—who cares? I don't know if this is tomfoolery or not. I'm not claiming the existence of ghosts, or that Calamity Jane looked like Gwyneth Paltrow—and certainly not the authenticity of this material. That's not the point. The point is selling fiction. Which is almost impossible without buzz. And let's face it, controversy creates buzz. These things, forgeries or not, are cool for me, since they surfaced the week before my film comes out in DVD. So everybody, go out and buy yourself one."

He waved the DVD like a flag of surrender.

It was time to wrap things up. Without Gaby, the audience wasn't picking up on its cues. Hands waved. People shouted clueless questions.

I stood and clapped loudly. But before Plant and Silas could descend from the stage, the Englishman and most of the smugsters got them cornered. The volume of the Brit's aristocratic speech escalated as the smugsters' California slang rose even higher.

"Looks like Plant could use a little help," Rick said, taking off in their direction.

I turned to pick up my tote bag, expecting another barrage of nonsense from Luci. But the chair next to me was empty.

Luci was gone.

Fine. She wouldn't be missed.

I wondered how soon she'd discover her flowerpot bag was bogus — and the photo was gone. I had to be grateful to Marva for that. Major crisis averted.

Although I still didn't have a clue about how those strange letters related to Marva — or Luci or Toby. I wondered if Marva had figured out I'd salvaged a few. As soon as Plant was free of his fans, I'd get him to look at them. I wondered which letters I'd managed to save. I opened my bag.

But it was empty. The letters were gone.

Chapter 36—A Damp Trap

I SEARCHED MY TOTE BAG three times before I had to admit to myself that I must have shoved the gay cowboy letters into Donna's folder after my tug of war with Marva.

And that meant I had delivered them into the hands of Luci Silverberg—the devil herself. Luci was probably already off drafting her extortion letter.

I had to find her before she did any damage with them. I hated to think what I'd just let loose.

I found a service door along a side wall—the most likely way to make an exit from the Ponderosa Lounge without being noticed. The door opened on a narrow passageway, lit only by a bare bulb. It probably led to the kitchen. I thought I heard Luci's mincing footsteps ahead. I hoped those stiff new cowboy boots would slow her down.

Following the passage, I looked for something familiar, but as I climbed several stairs, then descended some more, I realized I was lost again. My mind went to creepy places as I thought about last night's ghostly intruder into my cabin.

I still hadn't figured that out.

Could it have been Marva?

Or Donna?

What if it had been somebody from Miguel's gang?

Whoever or whatever had broken into the Roy Rogers cabin was still at large. And it was probably involved in murder. But I had no idea why he/she/it had chosen my cabin. Maybe someone thought I was the one who had seen something incriminating — not Mitzi. I hadn't even let myself think about that.

Could I be next on some hit list?

Now I was in panic mode. I started to run. At the end of a dimly lit hallway, I found a small doorway I was pretty sure led in the direction of the kitchen. I opened it, feeling around for a light switch, but encountered a step down I hadn't expected. I fell against a wall as the door swung shut behind me.

I reached for the knob in the darkness. But there was no knob on the inside. I tried to push it open.

It didn't budge.

I couldn't feel a light switch on the wall. Maybe there was an old fashioned pull light. I reached ahead, waving my hands in the blackness, hoping to feel a chain or a string. But the dark was empty and getting scarier by the minute. I told myself to breathe, but the place smelled awful and stale. Maybe it wasn't a passage at all. I took a step ahead, but with a clatter and a shot of pain, I felt something clamp onto my foot. I was caught in a trap. A damp trap.

And nobody knew where I was.

Except maybe the murderer.

◊ ◊ ◊

A few minutes later, I heard footsteps outside the stuck door. I had no idea if I should call out for help, or if I'd be safer in hiding.

But the air was foul and my foot hurt.

Finally, I knocked tentatively on the door.

The door burst open. There stood Rick, stifling laughter.

"What are you doing in the broom closet, Camilla? When Luci said Alberto wanted to talk to you, I don't think it was about volunteering for clean-up duty."

"I'm, um, looking for Luci." I wished he'd act more sympathetic. "I didn't know where she went, so…"

"So you thought this was just the moment to run down here and stick your foot in a mop wringer?" Rick bent down to study the contraption clamped around my ankle. "Doesn't that hurt?"

I tried to smile, but it did hurt: enough to make my eyes tear. I had stepped into an old-fashioned bucket designed to wring out a string mop. A number of mops, in various stages of decay, hung on hooks around me. I pretended to study them, trying not to let Rick see my childish tears.

Rick clicked something on the bucket, and the pressure on my ankle released.

"Thank goodness Plant saw you take off through the service exit. Nothing broken, I think." He massaged my ankle. "Do you feel okay?"

"If feeling like a complete idiot is okay, yes, then I'm okay."

I didn't even want to see what damage had been done to the Christian Louboutin cobra skin.

"Why did you take off like that? Was it something I said?" He stood and examined my face. "You're crying. Crying doesn't say okay to me. Do we need to get you to a doctor?"

"No. No! It's Luci. I have to find her. She has some things…" How was I going to explain what Luci had, and how she came by them?

"I have a feeling Luci won't be around this place much longer." Rick's dark eyes looked directly into mine, which made my knees feel as unsteady as my ankle.

"Luci's leaving? What about your book? The advance, everything, you're really going to let it go?"

Rick sighed. "There never was going to be a book—and that wasn't an advance. What she paid me for was a lot of dirt about the celebrity busts we've kept quiet over the years. She was going to use the threat of publishing the book to blackmail the celebrities. She's just a scammer. Somebody should have shot me with a clue gun. I can't believe I fell for her crap."

He bent down on one knee and looked at my ankle again.

"Can you walk on that?"

I gave it a try. A little wobbly, but I was okay.

"It's not your fault you were taken in. Luci has a huge reputation."

"Based on a few sales a very long time ago. Now, she's just a crook. A lot of things didn't smell right about this deal from the beginning, but it was Gaby who hooked us up, so I wanted to believe. Plus, I wanted something in my life to be going right."

He offered his arm for me to lean on.

"I wasn't a total doofus. I did ask my detectives to check her out. She's had a lot of complaints against her, but nobody's been able to prove anything. In fact, I still don't have enough solid evidence to take to a prosecutor, and last time I checked, Gaby wouldn't hear a word against her. I guess I got a little angry when I found out. But these murders have something to do with Luci. I can smell it."

All I could smell was old mops, but as I leaned into the warmth of Rick's body, I realized I was the one who'd been a doofus. If the recipient of those letters—"Joaquin Montoya"— was alive, Luci was about to ruin his life. And it was all my fault.

A voice came from the end of the hallway.

"Captain! I have been looking everywhere for you. I also

need to speak with Miss Randall, but she is nowhere..."

The small, sturdy figure of Alberto rushed toward us. He looked terrified.

Chapter 37—Sharpshooters

"MISS RANDALL IS HERE! I am relieved to find you. Captain, I must speak with you!"

Alberto spoke in a whisper, as if he feared being overheard, even here in this ridiculous broom closet.

"I prefer to speak to you—not Detective Fiscalini, Captain. And Miss Randall, you must hear me too. You will know how to speak with Miss Moore—to tell her about this."

He clutched a gold pocket folder to his chest.

Was there anybody here who didn't have a manuscript to sell?

"Please." Alberto's voice sounded desperate as he pressed the folder to his heart. "It is urgent. I can wait no longer."

"I'd be glad to do whatever I can to help."

I smoothed my hair as I exited the broom closet as gracefully as I could.

"But first I have to speak to Luci Silverberg."

I tottered on my left shoe as I shook water from my right one. My hose felt clammy on my wet foot.

"Miss Silverberg is not to be disturbed," said Alberto, offering an arm for balance. "She has a headache and will see no one."

"When did she tell you this?"

What was Luci up to now?

"Miss Silverberg spoke to me a few minutes ago. She say— 'no calls; no visitors; no exceptions'. Come. We go this way."

His fingers gripped my arm with urgency.

"I told you Luci wouldn't be a problem anymore, Camilla," Rick said with a grim smile. "She's probably locked herself away until her flight home. She'll have a hard time explaining why I turned down her offer."

He offered me his shoulder as I put my shoe back on.

Alberto led us down the hall and pushed on a wall panel that sprang open—another of the Rancho's hidden doors. He stepped into darkness.

"Come," he said again.

Soon we were hurrying down the service corridor I recognized as the one where Miguel had led me to the secret Hole in the Wall room. But Alberto didn't stop. He opened another panel a little further down the hallway that revealed a narrow staircase that looked freshly scrubbed and smelled of bleach.

"Servants' stairway," he said simply. "They are somewhat steep."

As he made his way up the narrow stairs, I realized Alberto was probably older than he looked. His dark hair was only flecked with gray, and he could have been anywhere between forty and seventy.

The stairs stopped at a corner landing where a cracked-open door showed a small balcony, festooned with yellow caution tape—and French doors that led to what looked like an office that must have been Gaby's.

But Alberto led us down a smaller passageway and unlocked a simple wooden door that looked as if it might lead to a linen closet.

When he switched on a light, I could see it was a studio apartment, complete with a small stove and refrigerator, a monastic bed, a table with two wooden chairs and chest of drawers. A framed picture of the Virgin of Guadalupe above the bed was the only decoration.

"Please, sit." He waved at the chairs and put the folder he carried on the table. He opened the top drawer of the chest and pulled out several more of the gold folders.

"What a pleasant little studio apartment," I said, to try to fill the tense silence. "And so private. You'd never guess it was here, tucked away in this little corner."

"Yes." Alberto gave a sad smile as he looked around the room. "My little home. I moved in here after the old housekeeper died. I have worked at the Rancho most of my life. I was only thirteen when Mr. Boggs gave me my first job, in the kitchen." His face contorted and he looked as if he might burst into tears. "I was a little wet-back child. No papers. No English. Mr. Boggs and Miss Gabriella — they were so kind, so good to me, and this — this is how I have repaid them."

He threw the folders on the table.

"What is this?" Rick opened one to reveal a neat stack of papers.

"Lies! Betrayals! My crimes." Alberto waved at the papers as if he were waving away fumes from raw sewage.

"And here —" He pointed at the folder he'd been clutching. "Here is ruin. Utter ruin. I should not have listened to Toby. I believed he would make the money back from the grapes. I thought it would save the Rancho. There was so much debt. But that was before..." He handed me one of the papers. "Read it."

I gave Rick a look of apprehension after glancing at the document.

"What is this? Some sort of government report?"

"Yes. It is the report that came in last Friday. I showed it to Toby and told him he must tell Gabriella everything. She must be told there is no longer any hope. They are here. They will destroy us. No one can fight them. Miss Randall, you must help me tell Gabriella."

He turned to Rick. "Captain, you must arrest me."

"What?" I said. "Who is it you think you can't fight?" I wondered if Alberto was talking gangs or ghosts, or whether he was talking sense at all.

"Sharpshooters," Alberto said, hissing the word like a curse. "Sharpshooters. We have been sent sharpshooters. The Rancho is doomed."

Chapter 38—The Badman

AS RICK STUDIED ALBERTO'S folders, I tried to soothe the sad-eyed concierge, who had collapsed again in tears. "I'm sure it's not as bad as it seems," I said. "I can't believe anyone would send armed gunmen to collect a debt. Not with all these people here..."

Alberto looked as if I were speaking a foreign language.

"What gunmen? There are no gunmen. I said sharpshooters. Glassy-winged sharpshooters."

"Fairy gunfighters?" Now I was really confused.

Rick let out a belly laugh.

"These are bugs. They lay their eggs in grapevines and carry Pierce's disease. It rots the vines down to their roots. Wipes out whole vineyards. There's no cure."

"They sent them in the last shipment," Alberto said. "Toby should not have ordered vines from the cheap supplier. Now we must destroy all our vines before the eggs hatch. It is ruin."

Alberto could barely get the words out as his eyes teared.

"The Rancho is lost. It is my fault. I signed the loan papers." He held his hands out to Rick as if he expected him to keep handcuffs hidden somewhere about his person at all times. "Please. You are a policeman. You must arrest me. And Miss Randall, you must take the news to Miss Moore—that I have confessed. That it is my fault."

Rick put a hand gently on Alberto's shoulder.

"Bad investing isn't a crime, Alberto, no matter how guilty you feel."

"No, but forgery is! Don't you see? Mitzi's signature is on all these papers! I am a criminal! You must arrest me!"

I glanced at the contents of the folder.

"These are loan papers, aren't they? Why would Mrs. Boggs Bailey sign Gabriella's loan papers?"

Alberto sighed.

"Mr. Boggs, in his will, left his sister half-interest in the Rancho Grande. Gabriella still had plenty of money coming in from television residuals—so he never thought she would have money worries. But he was afraid Mitzi's no-good husband would die and leave her with nothing. And he was right. But it has been difficult. She never wants to sign anything—especially not in the last few years since she has become more ill."

"You're saying Mitzi didn't sign this?"

Rick was all business as he examined the signatures.

"No. She has never seen those papers. And Gabriella—she was not told either. Toby signed for her and I signed for Mitzi." Alberto pointed to a wooden carousel that housed a collection of old pens. "I forged her signature. I have some training as a calligrapher, so Toby asked me…"

"Forgery's a serious offence," Rick said.

"I know." Alberto collapsed into the chair. "This is why I must go to jail. Toby made me believe it was necessary. The money was to plant the new vineyards. This conference loses money every year. Gabriella signs people to speak—famous people like Jackie Collins. Then Toby cancels them because he cannot pay. Gabriella—she must have had temporary insanity. But the fault—it was mine. That is why she killed him—don't you see?" Alberto covered his eyes.

Rick leaned back against the bureau.

"Alberto, calm down. You don't really believe Gabriella killed Toby? Not over some loan papers—or canceling Jackie Collins?"

Alberto looked up, his hands shaking.

"But she did kill him. I found the blood. It was on the balcony outside her office—and down the servant's stairs—all the way to the bar."

"Gaby's office is the one next door—above the kitchen?"

"Yes. You can reach it from a private stair from the utility yard, and also from the hall outside this room."

"And those stairs we came up lead to the Longhorn Room?"

"Yes," Alberto said. "The blood was not so much, but I saw the trail of drops. It is my job to notice..." He buried his face in his hands.

Rick's face was unreadable. "You saw blood you believed was Toby's and you removed it?"

Alberto looked up again, his lip quivering.

"Yes. I cleaned it with bleach, so no one would see what she had done. But the ghosts know. They have been here. The ghosts, they have left me a message..."

He stood and picked up a wooden carousel of old pens.

"You see! They took the pens and now they are returned!" He thrust the carousel into Rick's hands and started to pace. "It is not Gabriella's fault. It is mine. I should have told her. Now, Miss Randall, you must tell her I am sorry. You can do it in a way that is kind. And Captain, you must take me to jail."

"Are you sure?" I tried to make some sense of Alberto's story. "About the blood? Maybe the stains were old. Or red wine or something."

Rick nodded. "You're mistaken, Alberto. I think Fiscalini's dead wrong on this. Gaby didn't do it."

I wondered if I should tell him about my gangbanger-accomplice theory about Miguel.

"Plant says Gaby couldn't be responsible for the spray painting," I said. "Think what it's going to cost to replace that wall covering. It's fur, for goodness's sake. And she could never lift that cow head."

Rick gave me a surprised look and nodded.

Alberto just looked pained.

"I know what blood looks like," he said with a sniff. "Anger can make a person strong. Toby had been with Ernesto. Perhaps she was jealous. Toby was always with the students — boys, girls, he did not care. He would make a rendezvous in one of the empty rooms. He would write the room number on a bottle of champagne and tape a key on the bottle. I was furious he was always losing keys. Everybody knew he stole those keys."

"That's the problem with that scenario, Alberto. Everybody knew," Rick said. "Even my mother-in-law. She told me how Gaby's been putting up with Toby's tomcatting for decades. Why would Gaby kill one kid Toby was hooking up with, when there were dozens?"

Urgent knocking made Alberto go ridgid.

Rick opened the door.

I heard Miguel's voice and had a chilling thought.

He knew about the secret staircase just as well as Gabriella did. He could have waited for Toby in the servant's hallway, ambushed him at his front door, then dragged him down to the bar.

"She is gone." Miguel's voice was breathless. "Mrs. Boggs Bailey is has disappeared again."

Chapter 39—Spirited Away

"I AM VERY ANGRY WITH Donna," Miguel said. He looked more terrified than angry. "She left Mrs. Boggs Bailey at the cabins, while she came to the Hacienda to look for Ms. Silverberg."

He shifted from foot to foot as if he were still running.

"Mr. Kahn and his people are gone, too. They called many times demanding room service from the bar, but we do not have the staff."

"Don't panic," I said, as much to myself as anybody. "Jonathan's probably out looking for excitement, and Mrs. Boggs Bailey might have insisted on tagging along. Isn't there a casino around here where he could drink and gamble?"

Miguel shook his head. "No drinking is allowed at the Indian casino, except in the five-star restaurant. Perhaps the saloon in Santa Ynez. Miss Moore forbids Mrs. Boggs Bailey to go there." He stopped for breath, then started back down the stairs. "I must go. Only Santiago is at the desk…"

"You have left Santiago at the desk?" Alberto became the efficient concierge again. "He speaks no English. Go! Go!"

As he closed the door, he looked at me with pleading eyes.

"Can you get Mrs. Boggs Bailey? If she is with Mr. Kahn, she will get into terrible trouble. She always finds trouble…"

"I'm afraid I don't have a car." I could not go searching the watering holes of the Santa Ynez Valley for my drunken ex-husband. I had to find Luci—and retrieve those letters. I'd worry about Miguel and his gang later. At least he was too busy at the moment to murder anybody else.

But Rick seemed all too eager to go on a hunt.

"I'll drive," he said. "Don't worry. We'll find Mitzi."

He folded the loan documents and put them in his pocket.

"But Alberto, Detective Fiscalini's team is going to have to see these." He took another look at the carousel of pens. "What were you saying about these? They went missing and then turned up again? You used them for the forgeries?"

"Yes," said Alberto. "Obadiah started to take them a few months ago. One at a time. I was upset. I thought Ernesto had taken them. They were given to me by Wu Lin, who was housekeeper here when I was just a kitchen boy. He taught me the art of calligraphy, and I was passing it on to Ernesto. Toby asked me to teach him. Ernesto had just finished making new labels for the photographs in the gallery on the ground floor. He could copy every one of those autographs. He had a gift— not like Miguel. He has ten thumbs."

"Ernesto…he copied those autographs?" I found this very interesting. Ty Hardin, Will "Sugarfoot" Hutchins—the autographs on the pictures downstairs—they were also the signatures on the Joaquin letters. They had to be forgeries, too.

And it looked as if Ernesto was the resident forger.

Glancing at my watch I tried to think of a polite way to make my escape. I had to get those forged letters away from Luci, now.

Rick saw me looking at my watch.

"Give me a minute, Camilla. I have an obligation to report this cover-up right away." He turned back to Alberto. "You thought Ernesto took the pens, but now you say the perpetrator was a ghost?"

"I suspected Ernesto, but my supply of old scrap paper disappeared, too—just writing paper—yellow and old, of no use to anybody. And some old ink. But they were locked in my supply cabinet—only Toby and Gabriella had the key. They said the thief must be Old Obadiah, but I didn't believe—until the pens all reappeared—here in the carousel. In my locked room. The day after Ernesto died. It was a sign."

"The room was locked?" Rick examined the door. "Who else has a key?"

"Only Gabriella and Toby."

"The writing paper—did it reappear, too?"

I knew the answer before Alberto shook his head. Of course the paper wasn't returned. The gay cowboy letters had been written on it. Toby must have stolen the paper for Ernesto to use. Which meant they were working some scam together—planning to do some gerbilling, as Marva called it.

Marva. How did she fit in?

She'd known about the letters. And she wanted them desperately enough to burglarize the Rancho. She also had just as much access to the murder scenes as Miguel, and a lot more motive. She said she'd worked at the Rancho as a kid, and obviously she knew her way around. She could easily have been the one to lie in wait and bonk Toby on the head—or follow Ernesto to Plant's cabin and shoot him. And in spite of whatever hormones she was taking, Marva looked strong enough to have pulled that steer head from the wall.

Rick laughed with forced cheer.

"Old Obadiah is a real generous ghost, isn't he—first he gives those Oscar Wilde things to Plant Smith, and he then returns your pens?"

"It is not something to laugh about," said Alberto. "It was a message—the ghosts took the pens because I was using them for crime. And now people have died. That is why I knew I had to turn myself in."

Rick patted Alberto's shoulder.

"You did the right thing to tell me about it. Detective Fiscalini needs to hear your story. Right away." He ushered Alberto toward the door. "I hope you know that tampering with the crime scene was a really bad idea—not just because it's aiding and abetting. You did Gabriella a lot more harm than good. Now it's going to be much harder to find the real killer—who is still out there, my friend. I'm sure of it."

I followed them both down the stairs, wondering how to explain to Rick that the killer was probably a transgender dominatrix who looked a lot like me.

Chapter 40—Rampaging Writers

CHAOS HAD DESCENDED ON THE lobby in Alberto's absence. Now that Plantagenet's talk was over, and Luci seemed to have disappeared, everyone left seemed to be in a frenzy to vacate the premises.

Guests mobbed the desk, shouting at Miguel and Santiago. Miguel clutched the phone to his chest, as Donna tried to wrest it from his arms. Santiago stood at attention beside them, looking at the crowd with an authoritative scowl, but real fear shone through his eyes.

"Call a taxi!" the Englishman shouted. "Phone a taxi to take me to Santa Barbara. I don't care how much it bloody costs!" He pounded the desk in front of Santiago.

"Call a taxi," Santiago said, his accent thick. He earnestly pounded the desk in imitation of the Englishman.

I had to stifle a laugh.

Rick pushed through the crowd, saying something in

Spanish that involved the word "Fiscalini."

Miguel looked at Rick and shook his head as Donna clawed at his shirt sleeve, still trying to get at the telephone.

"Okay, then you ring her room." Donna fairly shrieked the words. "I told you she phoned my cell and asked me to meet her. Right now. But she won't open her damned door. Tell her I'm coming up."

"Lucille Silverberg is not to be disturbed. Orders of Alberto. How many times do you want me to say it? She will not talk to anybody."

Miguel shook her off. But I had to admit he didn't really look like a double murderer. He looked like a little boy about to cry.

"Except me," Donna screamed. "She phoned me! She read *Newsbabes*. She's all—I'm 'a genius of a businesswoman.' That's totally what she said. Then she told me to come up to her room ASAP and we'd talk money. Miguel, stop being such a pain! This is my chance of a lifetime! I'll ring her room if you won't. She's not answering her cell."

As Rick pushed through the crowd toward the desk, the phone in Miguel's arms rang. He picked up the receiver and Donna pulled the rest of the phone from his grasp.

"No. Nobody can talk to *Entertainment Tonight*," Miguel said to the caller. "Unless they send a taxi..." He shook his head at Rick again. "The Sheriff's men have left. I have heard nothing."

"Are you calling a taxi?" said a memoirist, grabbing the phone from Donna. "My cell can't get a signal. We need a taxi. We are not spending another night here, with all these gangsters and ghosts and dead homosexuals running around. Why is there no limousine? We came in a limousine."

Everyone screamed at once:

"Why isn't anybody here to carry my suitcases!"

"Where are the bellboys?"

"I want my bill!"

"Give me that telephone!"

The Englishman tried to wrestle the phone from the memoirist.

"Somebody call the bloody airport! Isn't there an airport in this town? What about those hot air balloons? I'll take one of those if they haven't got anything else. "

"Enough!" Alberto's voice rang over the turmoil. As he strode toward the desk, the crowd parted to let him enter his domain. "Give me that!" he commanded, as all parties relinquished their respective grips on the phone.

He barked something at Santiago, who emerged from behind the desk and started picking up luggage.

"Alberto, old chum, can you get me a taxi?" said the Englishman. The crowd closed in, calling for bills and bellboys and transportation.

"I'd say we got here just in time," Rick said into my ear. "I'll call in the forgery information to Fiscalini after Alberto processes these people so they can go home. I don't think the poor guy is going anywhere, and nobody benefits from keeping a hysterical crowd like this hanging around."

I tried to lighten things up. "I can see the headlines now: 'RAMPAGING WRITERS WRECK RANCHO!"

I figured Rick's plan was to sit on the evidence against Gabriella while he did some sleuthing on his own. I wondered if he had the same worry I did that Miguel and his gang might have helped Gaby cover up the murder. At the moment, he seemed absorbed with watching Santiago carry more suitcases than appeared to be humanly possible. He was small but solid, and must have built up a lot of muscles washing all those pots and pans.

"There you are, you two!" said Donna as she made her way over to us. "You are so, like, totally cool!" Flinging her arms around us both, she planted a patchouli-scented kiss on my left cheek, and then one on Rick's right.

"Thank y ou. Thank you! Thank you for getting my

manuscript to Luci. I knew she'd totally love it when she read it. I'm sorry I got in bed with Rick, but swear to God, I thought he was Toby!" She flashed a smile at Rick, then turned back to me. "I did not know about Toby being, like, dead down in the bar. I was way late, and I thought Toby had been waiting all that time—and he'd be all mad at me." She squeezed my hand. "I wouldn't do that to you, honestly. The Captain isn't even my type."

Rick raised an eyebrow.

Donna tossed back her hair.

"I like more Anglo types, you know? You could be my uncle or something." She grabbed his arm. "It's not like you're old and flabby like Toby or anything. But—it was so dark. You kept going on about your headache, and then I realized the voice was wrong, so I got the hell out...I tried the other room fourteen, but the key didn't work. So I put the champagne back in the ice machine. It wasn't until then I realized I left my manuscript on the nightstand."

She kept playing with her hair and glancing over at Miguel and Alberto at the desk. I wondered what she was up to.

She went on. "I figured I could come back and get it in the morning, but I slept late and the maid had already packed up the room. I was, like, practically suicidal. That's the only hard copy. My printer cartridge ran out of ink right before I left home."

So that's what the girl had been looking tragic about—her lost manuscript. Not Toby.

She smiled prettily. "Anyway, it finally got to Luci and that's what's important!" She kept watching Miguel, who was now fending off five romance writers who had shared a suite but wanted separate checks.

"I told you so," I whispered to Rick. "It wasn't me giving you that headache."

Rick gave an apologetic shrug.

"But, Donna," I said, trying to put this new piece of

information into the puzzle. "What about earlier? Were you looking for Toby in the cabins earlier? Did you come into my cabin—the Roy Rogers cabin? Did I throw a shoe at you?"

Donna kept watching Miguel.

"Why would I throw a shoe at you? Do you know what these shoes cost?"

"No. I threw a shoe at you."

"Whatever!" She gave me a scornful look. "I gotta go!"

"What do you suppose that was about?" Rick gave me a bemused smile. "Aside from the fact it seems we both nearly got lucky with Donna last night?"

I shrugged. I needed to get to Luci's room before Donna did. Luci had probably contacted Donna right after she snuck out of Plant's talk. She probably thought Donna had some kind of blackmail thing going herself with those letters. Who knew how she'd treat a girl she believed was poaching on her territory?

I wondered if I should tell Rick about the letters. I needed to be careful. If he told Detective Fiscalini, people's lives could be ruined. And I didn't know for sure the letters were related to the murders. The person I needed to talk to first was Plantagenet. He could help me figure out what to do.

I asked Rick where he was.

"He and Silas Ryder left for San Luis Obispo right after the talk. They were going to compare their Oscar Wilde find with a book Silas has in his store up there."

I had a sudden feeling of abandonment. I wished they hadn't gone off on their wild goose chase without telling me. With all this forgery going on, the whole Oscar Wilde thing had to be a hoax, too. I could have saved them some trouble. Of course, I hadn't been that available—what with getting stuck in broom closets and listening to concierge confessions.

"So, shall we go?" Rick said.

"I don't think so. San Luis Obispo is over an hour away... "

"I meant to go looking for Mitzi. Do you really think she's

hanging with your ex? That can't be safe. We'd better go look for her. Have you had the pleasure of visiting the Maverick Saloon?"

I tried to think of how I might get out of revisiting the haunt of my biker friend, when there was a howl from the top of the stairs.

Donna clutched the banister above and screamed at us.

"She's gone! They took her! Oh my god, I saw the ghost—it flew right off the balcony!"

Donna slowly descended, looking as if she might faint. She clutched what looked like her manuscript in her arms. Its crumpled pages dripped with red.

"My manuscript—it's covered in blood!"

Chapter 41—Always Wild

PANICKED GASPS CAME FROM the guests as they ran toward the stairs.

Rick pushed the crowd aside and climbed toward Donna.

"Who's gone, Donna? What's happened?"

"Luci! I went in her room. I'm sorry. I know I shouldn't have but...look. It's all dripping blood!" She waved her red-stained folder at Rick.

He gave her a quick glance but his attention was on the hallway above. He looked like a coiled spring. I could see him feel for his weapon.

"Have you been hurt?" he said.

She shook her head.

"How about Luci?" Rick's voice was metallic, efficient.

"How should I know? She's gone."

Rick ran up the stairs in the direction of Luci's room.

Donna continued to wail. "Luci must have been reading my

manuscript, because the pages were scattered all over..." A typed sheet escaped her grasp and sailed part way down the stairs. "Somebody get that!" she screamed "It's the only copy I've got with me! My printer ran out of ink..." She reached for it and stumbled, sliding down the stairs to the landing.

I ran up to where she lay, covered in her crumpled, red-stained pages, still clutching the much dog-eared gold folder.

Miguel followed right behind me. He ran up to her and felt her forehead.

Donna came to life, pushing him away. "Do not touch me!" She started collecting the scattered pages and stuffing them into the folder and looked up at Miguel and me with disgust. "Can you guys do something useful and help me with this?"

Miguel looked at the pages but didn't move. He spoke in a sharp voice.

"Donna, I told you not to disturb Mrs. Silverberg. How did you get into the room?"

"Maybe I kind of found the housekeeping key in the desk while you were busy helping those ladies." She looked up at him with some stagy little-girl eyelash batting. "But it's not like I knew everything would be all — totally — blood."

Somebody screamed for help into a cell phone. People started to gather around the bottom of the stairs. A couple of smugsters tried to push past us and climb the stairs. Miguel pushed them back and stood on the bottom stair, blocking them as best he could.

The Englishman shouted, "So what, now the Sheriff's people aren't here? Why is law enforcement never around when you need them?"

Donna whimpered as a corner of a page tore.

Santiago rushed past me and gave Donna one of his odd little bows, presenting her with a fresh gold folder. He crouched beside her, picking up pages, murmuring something in a language I'd never heard before.

I leaned over and picked up a few pages. Some of the slimy

red stuff got on my fingers. It didn't look like blood. Or smell like it. But I recognized it immediately. Not my color, but I knew it well.

"Donna, this isn't blood. It's nail polish. Revlon Always Wild, I believe. Luci broke a nail earlier. She was probably repairing it." Maybe Donna's smelling faculties had been numbed by spraying perfume at people every day. "Couldn't Luci simply have gone out for a walk or something? Maybe she went to the Saloon. I don't think we have to assume anything criminal or supernatural is involved."

Donna looked up at me with fury. "I know what I saw. It was a ghost. Out on the balcony. It was huge—like nine feet tall. With no head."

More screams from below. Donna was good with the dramatics. If she knew how to put that kind of drama on the page, her book would be a best-seller.

"Donna, can you stand up? Did you break anything?" Miguel said over his shoulder while he kept watch on the crowd.

Santiago helped her to her feet, but Donna shook him off.

"I'm fine. It's Luci that's not fine. We have to find her. Who knows what they've done to her—if she's still alive."

Below us, the cat woman screamed hysterically into her cell phone, as did the Ralph Lauren woman and a number of memoirists. I searched the lobby for someone who looked competent to help with crowd control.

Where were Vondra and Herb Frye?

Santiago methodically collected Donna's pages. As he handed them to her, I saw his eyes were full of hopeless longing. Miguel barked something at him, and he rushed down to pick up a load of bags, but he could hardly take his eyes off Donna. Poor boy. He was crazy in love.

Donna smoothed the pages and put them carefully into the folder.

"Why do you think something's happened to Luci?" I

asked her. "She might have gone out—for a drink or something. Maybe shopping. She obviously likes that billionaire cowgirl look."

Donna looked up at me as if I were intellectually deficient.

"She just took off shopping? Without a car? Or her purse? In the middle of doing her nails? I don't think so. She even left those fancy cowboy boots."

"The nail polish bottle—it was open?" The girl had a point. Luci might have gone out with a different bag, but she would not leave in the middle of doing her nails. She would have closed the bottle if she'd finished the last coat.

If anything had happened to the woman, it was my fault. It sounded as if somebody had searched her room. That somebody had to be searching for the letters. My prime suspect would be Marva. I had to tell Rick when he came down from Luci's room. I knew she wanted those letters enough to break and enter, and she seemed to know all the secret passageways of this place.

Miguel managed to herd most of the people back toward the desk.

"Everything is okay," he said in a loud, if not entirely convincing voice.

Rick reappeared at the top of the stairs. He spoke with calm authority:

"Luci's suite looks as if somebody's been searching in there, but we don't know she wasn't doing the searching herself. I don't see any sign of foul play. She's probably gone for a walk." He looked at the crowd below. "Anybody here see Ms. Silverberg after the presentation this evening?"

A couple of people shouted about hearing her tell Alberto that she didn't want to be disturbed.

"She didn't go for a damn walk," Donna said. "She got taken by a ghost. Swear to God. I saw it."

Rick gave me a quick look, then turned to Donna and asked her to tell the full story.

Obviously relishing the spotlight, Donna stood on the landing and spoke in a strong voice, as if she were on stage.

"Okay, so when I let myself into the suite, I heard someone in the bedroom. I thought it was Luci, and I was pissed off because she'd tossed my manuscript all over the place. I ran in the bedroom to give her a piece of my mind, but she was gone. Instead, I saw this thing: it had on a long coat—and no head. It went behind the curtains and out the window. There's a balcony, but it would have had to fly, because that room is on the second floor."

The crowd murmured and gasped.

Donna went on. "And after that—the room was empty. Spooky and empty. And the room was trashed. Totally."

She looked at Rick's impassive face with obvious exasperation. "So are you going to call that detective, or what?"

Rick gave her his calm-down-now-ma'am look.

"We can't waste Detective Fiscalini's time until we know there's a problem. He's the only full time investigating officer in this Valley. He's got two murders on his hands. A guest leaving a hotel room in a mess isn't exactly a crime."

Donna moved toward him, wincing dramatically as she put weight on her ankle.

"Luci's been taken away by those ghosts everybody talks about," she said in dramatic tones. "I know what I saw."

The crowd pushed around us as Rick and I helped Donna down the stairs. I didn't believe her about the ghosts, but I did have a bad feeling about Luci. If Marva had murdered Ernesto and Toby—and ransacked Luci's room and taken her somewhere—Luci was in terrible danger.

If she wasn't dead already.

Chapter 42—Mustang Country

RICK ASKED ALBERTO TO AN ambulance for Donna.

"No way!" Donna turned to me. "Don't let him. Do you have any idea what an ambulance costs? I don't have insurance!"

"Okay, call a cab then." Rick said.

Alberto shook his head. "Every taxi in the valley is taking people to the airport."

Donna whimpered as she sat on a couch across from some disapproving memoirists.

I hovered, not sure what to do next. I had to get Rick alone to tell him about Marva. And the letters. He needed to know.

So did Detective Fiscalini. Or maybe I should go up and look at the room first. If by any chance the letters were still there, this had nothing to do with Marva and I could relax. A little.

It was creepy the way Santiago kept staring at Donna. I could see Rick had noticed the lovesick stares too. He pulled the boy aside and spoke with him in Spanish. I wondered what the two had to talk about.

"Drive faster!" one of the memoirists said into her phone. "You should see this girl. I think she's on drugs. She fell down the stairs. She's all cut up and bleeding."

"You'd fall too if you saw what I saw." Donna gave a reproachful look before noticing some Always Wild had spilled on her arm. From a distance it did look like a nasty cut. She tried to scrape it off with her fingernail.

I handed her one of my travel nail polish wipes.

I had to ask, "This ghost you saw — could it have been, um, female — sort of? With blonde hair in a long bob? Who looked kind of like me, only a little bigger in…places?"

"Duh. How would I know if it was blonde when it had no head? It flew off the balcony. That's all I can tell you."

Donna handed me back the dirty wipe, as if I were the maid, and resumed putting her pages in numerical order.

"I'd worry about poor old Mitzi, if I were you. She's out there somewhere and you know how she likes to hang with those ghosts."

Alberto called from the desk.

"We must find Mrs. Boggs Bailey. This is more important than Miss Silverberg's room."

"Whatever!" said Donna. "You're all going to be sorry when Luci shows up dead."

"Have you called the Maverick Saloon to see if Mitzi's there?" Rick stood by the desk and spoke in a calm voice. His presence seemed to calm people down. "I'll bet Luci is there, too."

Miguel responded in a strained voice. "No one answers. I

have called three times. There is nothing more I can do."

"What about Jonathan Kahn?" said Rick. "Does anybody have his cell number? He's probably drinking with them too."

"Mr. Kahn has not returned my call, not him or his people," said Alberto. "Do you want me to ring Mr. Ryder?"

Rick shook his head.

"He'll be in to San Luis Obispo by now."

Donna stood up and started toward the desk, clutching her manuscript.

"Did you say Mitzi went to the Saloon with Jonathan Kahn? Miguel, you gotta let me borrow your car to go find her," she said.

"You are not taking my car to the Maverick Saloon," Miguel said to Donna in a stern voice. "You are underage, and if you get in trouble, your mother will..."

Donna's face contorted in pain as her ankle gave way and she fell against a couple of elderly men in cowboy hats.

They helped her back to the couch as she cried, "Oh my god," over and over. "It's broken. My ankle must be broken. I guess I need to go to the hospital after all."

Miguel looked up at me from his calculator.

"Perhaps you can drive Donna to the hospital, Ms. Randall. I'm sorry. You could stop on your way back at the Saloon. I would go myself, but you see—everybody needs their bills..."

An impatient smugster leaned on the desk waving his credit card.

"I'm afraid I don't have a car," I said. "I came by...other transportation." I needed to stay and talk to Rick about Marva and the letters. Somebody else could play chauffeur to Donna.

"What about Vondra DeHaviland or Herb Fry? Or Walker Montgomery? He seems to know the area."

Miguel shook his head. "Miss DeHaviland and Mr. Fry have been gone all day, and I have not seen Mr. Montgomery since Mr. Smith's talk in the Ponderosa Lounge. His car is no longer in the parking lot."

Rick laughed. "Montgomery's gone? That probably explains where Luci is. That old dude was acting like a stalker with her all day. He seems to have a serious crush on her." He looked at Alberto. "Do you have Walker's cell phone number?"

"He is not a guest," Alberto said with a sniff. "We have no contact information. Mr. Montgomery was Mr. Roarke's client. This is all I know."

It was obvious he had no fondness for Mr. Montgomery.

Donna moaned from the couch.

Rick pulled me aside. "You can take my car. It looks as if I should stay here to keep people calmed down. Alberto can't handle this on his own. And I need to tell Fiscalini about him as soon as the place is cleared. I can't put off reporting his confession much longer—although I've got another theory about Toby's murder..." He squeezed my hand. "Gaby didn't do it. I'm gonna find out who did."

He lowered his voice to a whisper as a group of memoirists walked by, followed by the stoic Santiago, hauling another impossible load of luggage.

Rick pulled a set of keys from his pocket, pulled off a car key and handed it to me. "There's a hospital in Solvang. You know my Saturn."

I made one more attempt to stay.

"I'm a New Yorker. I'm not that good at country driving."

Rick gave my shoulders a squeeze. "I know you'll do just fine."

I sighed, gave him what I hoped was a gracious smile, and fastened the key to my own keychain.

I brought the car up to the front door and Santiago and Rick helped the moaning Donna to the car. As I drove off into the darkness, I saw Rick turn away with a smile as if we were going off for a routine errand. Nothing about this felt routine to me.

As I drove the slow curves down the road from the

Hacienda, Donna seemed to perk up. She pulled out a lighted compact and started redo-ing her elaborate make-up, complete with Amy Winehouse black eye-wings.

We'd reached the cabin area and the gate that led to the main road. I realized I had no idea where to go.

"Do you know how to get to the hospital?"

"Just turn left and we'll be fine."

"Turn left? Are you sure?" I thought I remembered coming from the other direction when Rick had retrieved me from the custody of D. Sorengaard.

"I'm sure." Donna gave a laugh as her pink hobo bag began playing her phone's *Sex and the City* theme. She fished the phone from her bag

"Work." She shrugged. "My supervisor probably wants me to work for somebody tomorrow. Like I could just run back to Santa Barbara when I haven't even had one nibble on my book. I am sooo going to love telling her to piss off when I get an agent. I told Luci I'm looking for at least a hundred thou for my advance." Donna tossed her phone back in her bag. "That would, like, pay off my cards and give me spending money until I get a movie deal."

So. She'd quoted a figure to Luci. No doubt Luci had thought it was for the letters. What would Luci's next move be — rounding up victims? A moneyed partner maybe? I wish I knew if Luci had really left on her own.

I turned to Donna. "Why were you so sure Luci was taken away? Was it anything besides the bag and the nail polish?"

"Well, duh, her phone. Who smashes their own cell, I'd like to know?"

My neck went cold. I slowed the car to a crawl.

"A smashed phone? There was a smashed phone in Luci's room? Did it look stomped-on or hit with a hammer?"

"Yeah. And it was definitely Luci's — a silver iPhone."

My head roared. A stomped-on cell phone, just like Ernesto's: signature of Captain Road Rage.

What if the killer was Rick?

He could have killed them both. Or all three, if Luci was dead. Rick certainly had been angry with Luci. Could he have killed her and disposed of the body between Plant's talk and when he found me in the broom closet? I had no idea how much time elapsed there—a half hour at most. But Luci was tiny. Her body wouldn't be so hard to hide. And Rick had a gun.

But there was the problem of Donna's ghost. Rick had been down in the lobby with me when Donna saw whatever she thought she saw.

Of course, it could be Rick had gangbanger accomplices— which would work with my earlier theory about a ghost-impersonating gang. No wonder he didn't want to "bother" Detective Fiscalini. And here I was driving down a dark, winding mountain road in Rick's car. Probably aiding and abetting.

I was actually glad of the bright headlights that followed close behind. Normally I would have thought such closeness more than a bit rude, but now company seemed to help. I didn't know what was out there, but none of it felt friendly.

I was relieved when we finally saw the lights of a small town ahead. After I got Donna to the hospital, maybe I should find that sheriff's substation and talk to D. Sorengaard and company. If Rick really was a rage-aholic killer, everybody left at the Rancho could be in danger.

"Turn left," said Donna.

The car behind turned, too. With a chill I realized I'd seen it before.

"Is that an old Mustang following us? That big old 1970's battleship?" I might be imagining things, but it looked a lot like the one that sped away from my cabin last night: Mrs. Boggs Bailey's orange Mustang.

"Yeah. Probably Walker Montgomery."

"Walker Montgomery drives a vintage Mustang? Is it

orange?"

"Duh, it's red. It's the car from his old TV show. But it can't, like, swim and stuff. That was all special effects. So cheesy in those days. Turn right. Here!"

I made a quick right while my brain processed this information. A red car could very well have looked orange under those security lights. I didn't know for sure the Mustang was related to anything, but it had been around when both murders happened. Walker Montgomery could very well be involved. He had threatened Toby. I'd heard that with my own ears.

I recognized the cowboy-kitch streets of the village of Santa Ynez. I was surprised when Donna ordered me to park in a small dirt-covered lot to our left.

We seemed to be in the parking lot of the Maverick Saloon.

"Where's the hospital?"

"Duh. It's like, in Solvang." Donna made another quick check in her mirror.

"I can stop here on the way back to look for Mrs. Boggs Bailey. But first we have to get you to the hospital."

Donna looked at me as if I had dementia, too.

"Look, I have to connect with Jonathan Kahn and show him this manuscript. Do you know how much my outfits for this conference cost me? And I haven't made one important contact." She opened the car door with a healthy shove. "When I heard you say Jonathan was down here, I figured faking the ankle thing was the easiest way to get you to bring me. Miguel is such a Nazi about me going to a bar when I'm under age. It's not like I don't have a fake ID."

She jumped out of the car headed toward the buildings without a hint of a limp.

"Look for Mrs. Boggs Bailey!" I shouted at the devious little creature, but knew it was futile. I'd have to go look for the old woman myself. But I dreaded dealing with whatever might be inside: a drunken Jonathan, Luci, Marva, and/or my former biker chauffeur.

I especially didn't want to run into Marva. If Rick hadn't committed those murders in fits of rage, I was pretty sure Marva was the killer.

An awful thought came to me: What if Marva didn't realize Luci got those letters from me? What if she believed they were Donna's the way Luci did? And she thought Donna had more? The silly girl could be walking into something pretty icky.

I locked up the car and took a breath for courage. Up on the road, I saw the Mustang, stopped on the shoulder—and the tall, thin figure of Walker Montgomery, silhouetted in the moonlight. I even sort of recognized the car now—it did look like the one from his old TV show. He was doing something with the trunk. I wondered if he was having car trouble. Should I offer to help? I waved.

He hesitated a moment, then waved back—a "don't worry, I'm fine" kind of wave. I was glad I didn't have to deal with him.

Something about the man gave me the creepy-crawlies.

Chapter 43—Cowboy Poet

I SAW NO SIGN OF MARVA in the dim light of the Maverick Saloon. Jonathan, either. I tried not to look as paranoid as I felt, although it was hard with the awful suspicions of Rick bouncing around in my brain.

The inside of the place was almost too wild-west to be true. Entering its scruffy, pine-paneled barroom felt like walking into an old movie. But I could see that the cowboys at the bar were the real thing—as real as the whiff of stable-droppings coming from the boots of the red-faced cowboy zeroing in on Donna.

I could see why Jonathan might be attracted to the place. Besides authentic western charm, and of course, the booze, its ceiling was pasted all over with money—mostly dollar bills, but also British pounds, Japanese yen, and obsolete European currency. What fastened them to the old wooden ceiling was something I probably did not want to know.

"I can't see Jonathan in the bar," Donna said, abandoning her odiferous admirer. "But he might be in the dance hall." She pointed at a glass-windowed door which led to a bigger room, where patrons sat at small tables around a dance floor. "There's a cover. You got money? I left my bag in the car."

I sighed and reached for my wallet.

When I handed a five dollar bill to the burly man at the door to the bigger room, he eyed both of us suspiciously.

"Doctor, I got no quarrel with you, but we eighty-sixed your party tonight for a reason. You gotta take your L.A. friends somewheres else. Those people run our staff into the ground and they don't tip diddly squat."

"You are such a liar!" Donna turned on me with fury. "You got thrown out of this dump, like, tonight? And you pretended you didn't know how to get here!"

I didn't have time to explain the existence of my doppelganger. But I was interested to hear that Marva had been here tonight—and with company. Was it Luci?

I beamed a Manners Doctor smile at the burly man.

"We're looking for Mitzi Boggs Bailey. Is she here?"

"Sure is," The man relaxed a little "She's getting ready to do her number right now."

"Her number?" Donna rolled her eyes. "Please tell me Mitzi's not going to sing?"

"Not singin'. It's cowboy poetry night." The man put my bill in a cash box and took out a rubber stamp. He tried to grab Donna's hand, but she resisted.

"No way," she said. "You have to get, like, dermabrasion to clean that stuff off. We're just looking for our friends." She turned to me. "Do you see Jonathan in there?"

"Can't get back in without the stamp," the man said. "And you can't buy drinks in there. Gotta get them from the bar."

"We're only going to be a minute," Donna said. "I'm a spokesmodel. I can't go to work with some gross inky thing on the back of my hand."

Finally the man let us through door, unstamped.

From the look of the high, vaulted ceiling of the big room, it could have once been a barn or a stable. Mrs. Boggs Bailey, alive and well, whooped it up at a crowded table down near the stage. She'd acquired a large cowboy hat and was sitting on the lap of a man less than half her age.

At other tables sat tourists in polo shirts, media people in rumpled suits, plus a few bedraggled protesters in anti-grape tee shirts.

But no Jonathan. Or Luci.

On the stage, a bearded man spoke into a microphone.

"And now, as a special treat tonight, we've got a lady who's been crankin' out cowboy poetry since most of us were sleepin' in our Roy Rogers jammies. You're on, Mitzi, darlin' — "

"Jesus," Donna hissed in my ear. "I can't take this. I don't see Jonathan, but Walker Montgomery just showed up." She turned and waved at Mr. Montgomery, standing in the doorway.

He displayed the same grin-and-bear-it faux smile he'd given the woman who stopped him in the lobby on that first night.

Donna lowered her voice. "He's totally geezeroid, but maybe he could give my book to somebody important. I don't suppose you thought of bringing in my manuscript?"

The woman's sense of entitlement was epic.

"My manuscript," Donna said again. "I suppose you just, like, left it in the car? What do you think I came in here for?"

"I don't know, Donna, but I'm here to get Mrs. Boggs Bailey and take her home, since your ankle seems to be just fine."

I had an urge to say something really unkind as I dug into my bag for Rick's key, but I kept my temper.

"Lock the car and bring the key right back. We're leaving as soon as Mitzi has finished her performance."

Leaving. The words were out of my mouth before I realized

I wasn't at all sure where we should go. Would it be safe to go back to the Rancho? If Rick had done something to Luci in a fit of phone rage, or whatever it was that came over him, things could be dangerous back there.

I hated to face it, but I was going to have to ask Jonathan for help. At least he could get a hotel room for Mitzi until everything got sorted out at the Rancho.

Donna was impervious to my tone of disapproval. "That key chain is so cool. Is it Kate Spade?" She fingered the pink and green leather of the elegant little wallet-keychain I still adored although it was years old.

The bearded man on stage shouted, "Ladies and Gentlemen, our own Mitzi Boggs Bailey!" Someone helped the old woman onto the stage.

"Are you all right?" she asked, staring at his beard.

"I sure am, Mitzi." The man handed her the microphone. "I'm just fine. And I bet all the folks out there are fine too."

Mitzi took the mike and turned to address the crowd.

"Are you folks all right?"

The audience clapped and stomped. Mrs. Boggs Bailey took off the cowboy hat, fanned herself, and gave everybody a huge grin.

"I can't remember how I got myself here tonight, folks. But I guess what I should do is tell you the real story of Bill Bailey and why that old cowboy never did come home. You may have heard a song or two about that old man, but I'm the one who can tell you the true story, on account of that outlaw was my own father-in-law..."

Mitzi Boggs Bailey plunked the cowboy hat back on, adjusted the mike stand, and for the next twenty minutes, that microphone, and the entire room, belonged to her.

Disease or injury might have destroyed her short-term memory, but her distant memory banks were perfectly intact. Without hesitating on a word, Mitzi Boggs Bailey recited, in rhyming iambic pentameter, the tallest tall tale of the Wild

West I had ever heard. It was the sort of verse where "poem" rhymed with "roam" and the images were as predictable as the outcome of the story, but that, I realized, was the point.

This was an ancient folk-art form, and Mitzi Boggs Bailey the Poet was mistress of her craft.

By the time she finished and took her bows to a storm of applause, my eyes were moist with tears for this amazing woman — for her current triumph and her irretrievable loss.

Even Donna — hovering by the exit — applauded with what looked like enthusiasm. Walker Montgomery seemed less impressed. He had one gnarled hand clamped onto Donna's shoulder while the other clutched the folder with her battered manuscript inside. Did he actually think it might be good?

As the applause died down, the bearded M.C. jumped back onto the stage, the house lights came up, and someone offered Mrs. Boggs Bailey a hand down. But as she started toward the audience, a look of terror crossed her face. She pointed in the direction of Donna and Walker Montgomery.

"Wacky," she said. "It's wacky."

Her expression was one of pure terror.

Chapter 44—Joaquin

THE M.C. TOOK THE MIKE from the terrified Mitzi Boggs Bailey and looked where she was pointing.

"What's that, Mitzi? Is something out there wacky? Well, look who's here! Not wacky: Walker. Folks, we got us a real cowboy star here tonight!"

He signaled the lighting man to shine the spot on Walker and Donna.

"There he is, folks, Walker Montgomery: the TV star. Otherwise known as Stetson McGee, *The Brazos Kid*. Anybody here remember that show? Or, for you youngsters under fifty — how about Thomas Colt, *Eye On the Beach*?"

Walker waved at the stage with the gold folder, but he did not move from Donna's side, or release his grip on her. There was another round of applause.

Mrs. Boggs Bailey's eyes darted around the room, as if she were looking for an escape route. Her eyes focused on me.

"Dr. Manners! Are you all right?" She made her unsteady way down from the stage. "Do you know what Jonathan Kahn said about you?"

I pushed toward her.

"You talked with Jonathan? Here? Tonight?"

"Jonathan Kahn is the one who brought me here, silly."

I'd feel better once I found Jonathan. He might be a lot of things, but I was pretty sure he wasn't a murderer.

Mrs. Boggs Bailey grabbed my arm and pulled me toward the door to the bar.

"Is Jonathan in there?" I followed through the crowded bar. "Where we going?"

"The biffy." She pointed to the sign that said "GALS" at the far end of the room. "I gotta go like crazy."

Not having much choice, I followed her from the dance hall through the crowd around the bar area and past some intense pool players. I searched for Jonathan but didn't see him or any of his entourage. Mitzi must have been muddled about seeing him here. We finally reached a line of women waiting their turn to use the facilities.

I looked at my watch. It was after ten. Wherever Jonathan was, I'd have to sober him up. If only Plantagenet were here.

The women in the line crowded around Mrs. Boggs Bailey.

"You are poet!" said a European tourist wearing a white cowboy hat and a Disneyland tee shirt. "Please to autograph my hat?"

Mrs. Boggs Bailey was delighted to sign the hat, plus several cocktail napkins and a Chamber of Commerce tourist map of the wineries of the Santa Ynez Valley.

When the business in the GALS room was finished, Mrs. Boggs Bailey wanted to go back to the dance hall.

"What were you going to tell me?" I asked as she pushed through the crowd. "Do you remember? When you were up on the stage? About what Jonathan Kahn said? "

"I was on the stage?" Her eyes were opaque in the dim light.

"Hey, Doctor," said a voice behind us. It was the odiferous cowboy. "That hottie that was with you. Is she—really a she? Or is she, you know, like you?"

As much as I wanted to dispel the confusion of myself with Marva, I couldn't ignore his bigotry.

"Like me?" I said. "You mean—she's a fan of cowboy poetry?"

"Oh, I love cowboy poetry!" Mrs. Boggs Bailey beamed as she pulled me back to the door to the dance hall and displayed her stamped hand. "Come on; it'll be fun."

But as I tried to follow, a man at the door stopped me with a heavy hand on my arm. "Two-fifty cover," he said.

"But I already paid." I looked around for the burly man, but he'd disappeared.

"Nobody gets in without a stamp," said the man.

I turned around to give the smelly cowboy my best smile.

"Donna, the hottie you were talking about. She's in there. She has my wallet. Could you talk your friend into letting me get her?"

The cowboy laughed.

"Good one, Doctor, but I happen to know you're lyin'. I saw her and him take off a few minutes ago."

"Who? When?"

"Her and that old-time TV star. What's his name? Mitzi, what was that old dude's name? They took off right after your number. A couple of bats out of hell."

Mrs. Boggs Bailey ignored us as she peered through the door to see what was happening on the stage.

"Walker Montgomery is his name," I said. "And you must be mistaken, Donna wouldn't have left. She has my car keys and my money. Mrs. Boggs Bailey, do you see them in there? Donna or Walker Montgomery?"

"I don't know any Walker Montgomery," said Mrs. Boggs Bailey.

The cowboy laughed. "Sure you do, Mitzi. You called to him from the stage. He used to be a big TV star."

"That man is no TV star," said Mrs. Boggs Bailey with a laugh. "That's Joaquin."

"Joaquin?" My mind was spinning. "Walker is—Joaquin? He's the ghost? The headless ghost of the Rancho Grande?"

Mrs. Boggs Bailey gave me a look of amused scorn.

"Of course not, silly. Sometimes he pretends to be a ghost, to scare me—but he's just Joaquin. Joaquin Montoya. He used to work on the ranch, in the old days. When I was a girl. Oh, I did have a crush on that boy. But you know, I don't think he really liked girls, if you know what I mean. There was scuttlebutt around town that he was kinda light in his boots..."

Joaquin. The cowboy all those gay letters were addressed to—he was Walker Montgomery.

Chapter 45—An Old Friend

JOAQUIN MONTOYA, GHOST and gay cowboy, was Walker Montgomery, gun-toting poster boy for right-wing machismo.

What a secret that man had been keeping.

Those letters could destroy Walker's life, forged or not. Even a hint he was gay—no matter how bogus—would alienate his whole fan base.

Another example of "gerbilling."

Random incidents started falling into place with obvious and terrifying logic.

Walker/Joaquin must have been searching the Rancho looking for those letters—disguising himself as a ghost. Scaring Mrs. Boggs Bailey.

And me, of course. He was my headless ghost—tall, with that big collar on his coat turned up. He must have thought the letters were in my cabin, although I couldn't imagine why.

And then he'd driven off in his red Mustang, which looked

orange under those lights.

Mrs. Boggs Bailey said he'd worked on the Rancho when she was a girl. So he'd know all the passageways and tunnels. That's probably how he'd "flown out the window" with Luci.

If he knew Luci had those letters, he had a motive to take her. Even kill her. He'd been stalking her all day, somebody said. And I'd seen him be pretty fierce with her. He might have followed her up to her room after Plant's presentation.

Those letters would have given him a motive to kill Ernesto, too, if he knew Ernesto was the forger.

I'd heard him threaten Toby myself—in that phone message:

"Toby Roarke, if you don't have that stuff for me tonight, you are a dead man!"

That "stuff" wasn't some ghostwritten memoir. It was the forged letters. Which had somehow traveled from Toby's desk to Mrs. Boggs Bailey's chifforobe, and then to me—and I'd stupidly given them to Luci in Donna's folder.

Which meant Donna Carillos was off pitching her book to a murderer.

And it was my fault.

I needed to call the Sheriff's department. And hope it wasn't too late.

Mrs. Boggs Bailey pushed past the bouncer and made a bee-line for the cowboy with the lap. She seemed safe enough there. I needed to call Detective Fiscalini. Now.

I made my way back through the bar crowd and was relieved to spot an ancient pay phone in a dark corner near the entrance. But as I fought my way through the incoming patrons, I thought about the actual facts I had to substantiate my fears:

1) Luci Silverberg left the hotel without putting the cap on her nail polish.

2) Walker Montgomery used to be called "Joaquin," owned a red Mustang, and used exaggerated language in a telephone

message.

3) Alberto's calligraphy pens went temporarily AWOL and came back again.

4) Ernesto Cervantes liked to copy old movie star's autographs.

5) I'd seen some ersatz gay cowboy letters that had been stolen by an ersatz Manners Doctor.

They'd probably call the paramedics to pump me with Thorazine if I took that stuff to the sheriff.

No. The person I needed to talk with was Rick. I'd let him try to get through to Detective Fiscalini.

Was that safe? I still felt pinpricks of fear on my neck when I thought about that stomped cell phone.

But if Walker was the killer, Rick wasn't. Simple as that. I could not see those two in league with each other. There had to be another explanation for the stomped cell phones.

Okay, I'd call Rick at the Rancho.

I finally made it to the phone, but when I picked up the receiver, I realized I had no credit cards on me—not even a couple of quarters.

I tried to fight the panic that rose in my throat as I realized how helpless Donna had left me. I pretended to study the ceiling, where matchbooks and business cards were glued among the bills. It was so low that I could almost reach a bill and pull it down. Would they miss just a dollar?

"Hello, Darlin'!"

I cringed as a bear hug from behind nearly knocked me over. I could smell the familiar breath of a certain motorcycle rider.

"You need change for that, darlin'?" the biker said, dropping several coins into the slot. "Long distance or local?"

I gave him as grateful a smile as I could muster as I heard a dial tone buzz.

The biker planted a kiss on the back of my neck.

"Just calling the Rancho Grande," I said as I dialed, trying to figure out how to dismiss him politely.

"You ain't calling that TV dude you've been hanging with, are you?" he said. "I hate that guy." He scrutinized my body, stopping to stare at my breasts. "What—doesn't Mr. Obnoxious TV star like big tits? I didn't know those were falsies before, but I kinda like you without 'em. Looks better with your shape. I've always been more of a leg man."

I gave him a tight smile and pulled my jacket across my chest as I listened to the phone ring at the other end of the line. At least the call seemed to be going through.

The biker's words finally filtered into my brain—the TV star he was talking about had to be Jonathan.

"The obnoxious TV star. Are you talking about Jonathan Kahn—the host of *The Real Story*?"

"That's the one." The biker grinned. "I'm glad he got eighty-sixed. If I was you, I wouldn't put up with his crap no matter how much he paid, but that's just me. I'm gonna get another beer. You want something?"

I shook my head. So Jonathan had been in here. With Marva, of all people—and they'd been asked to leave the bar. What was Marva up to? Did she know about Walker Montgomery and his ghost impersonations? She had to know Walker was the Joaquin of those letters. So she must be some kind of blackmailer, in competition with Luci. Maybe she was blackmailing Jonathan, too. I held the phone to my ear, listening to it ring at the Hacienda. Why wasn't anybody picking up?

"Well if it isn't the Manners Doctor!"

I turned just as a camera flashed. A reporter. I recognized him from the crowd that had surrounded me at the Rancho last night. He gave me a mean grin.

A photo of the Manners Doctor at the Maverick Saloon would probably be a marketable commodity, given my current position in the news cycle . I tried to hide my face, but he moved in for a closer shot.

A voice finally came on the phone. Miguel.

After I'd outlined our situation, he shouted over loud noise in the lobby.

"Donna pretended her ankle was broken? Ambition can make her stupid."

I thought I heard somebody screaming in the background. Miguel shouted in Spanish.

"Can you put Rick Zukowski on the phone?" I blocked my face with my purse as the reporter moved in on me. The camera kept flashing. The reporter asked something about my "secret life as a hooker." I tried to shoo him away.

"Can't you see the lady is making a phone call?" said a shrill voice. "You people make me barf. You've got real news going on here—hundreds of people protesting the destruction of our habitat—and what do you report? Some trash-TV guy's ex-wife makes a phone call!" I recognized the Stomp out Grapes tee-shirt. He pushed the photographer aside and gave me a grin.

I've never been so happy to see blonde dreadlocks.

I strained to hear Miguel's voice over the din.

"I cannot leave the desk. Some guests are still waiting for their rides. I will tell Alberto you have found Mrs. Boggs Bailey." He lowered his voice to a whisper I could barely hear. What he said sounded like, "Santiago has gone crazy. He wants to kill himself. He has a knife."

Someone in the background in the lobby shouted again.

I heard Rick's voice from far away.

Then Alberto's.

Then...dead air.

I clung to the phone, clicking the cradle. I finally got a dial tone and hung up, confused and defeated. Santiago had chosen a really bad moment for a nervous breakdown.

Behind me, the crowd was turning ugly. The protester and the reporter were exchanging unpleasant words.

I heard a familiar voice.

"Are you folks all right? Where are your manners?"

Mrs. Boggs Bailey's small body pushed through the crowd toward the bar.

"Let a lady sit, for goodness' sake." She swept a cowboy off his stool. "Barkeep, let's have a whiskey sour."

The pay phone rang. I rushed to pick up the receiver, hoping Miguel might have called back. But all I heard was someone shouting in Spanish. I was about to call for the bartender, until I realized I understood some of the words. They sounded like "Jonathan Kahn" and "television." The voice could have been Santiago's.

"Hello?" I said. "You want Jonathan Kahn? He's not here, but..."

Another voice came on—Alberto's. Or what sounded like a robot impersonating Alberto.

"Please put Jonathan Kahn on the phone," he said. "A young man here wishes to speak to the media."

"It's me, Alberto," I told him. "Camilla. Jonathan's not here. I don't know where he is. I'm alone with Mrs. Boggs Bailey. And no car keys. Are you still having trouble getting taxis? I can tell you've got a crisis there, but things aren't good here either. We really need a cab..."

I heard only silence. Then in the distance, I heard someone scream. I pressed the phone closer to my ear. I could just make out Alberto's terrified voice whispering:

"Captain Zukowski. He is in the gang—the Viboras!"

Chapter 46—Big Trouble at the Maverick Saloon

I STOOD IN STUNNED SILENCE as the phone went dead. Rick. One of the Viboras. I was right about that damned scar. What was happening at the Rancho? Were the Viboras there? Was Rick helping them?

I clung to the receiver, wondering if I should call 911. I looked around for the biker. I'd have to beg more change.

But someone grabbed the phone from my hand—a pony-tailed man wearing a Ted Nugent tee shirt that said Guns Rock!

"Tourist bitch," he said, elbowing me out of his way as he dropped coins into the phone. The crowd shoved me toward the bar, nearly into the lap of Mrs. Boggs Bailey.

"Are you all right? I could call 911," she said, reaching into her pocket. She pulled out her rhinestone-studded phone case.

I had forgotten about her phone.

"Mrs. Boggs Bailey, you're a life-saver!" I grabbed it and wriggled through the crowd, trying to get a signal.

"Oughta be a law against those things," said a grizzled cowboy, peering over my shoulder. "Looky there. Rhinestones. 'Mitzi' it says. Is that you, Miss Wine Snot?"

"Who are you calling a wine snot?" said a large woman with light-up, grape-cluster earrings.

Somebody by the pool table started chanting "Stomp out grapes."

Then a pool player hit a wine taster with his cue. The woman with the earrings slapped a woman in a cowboy hat, who screamed at a chanting man in a tie-dyed tee-shirt.

Trying to make myself as small as possible, I tried to get back to Mrs. Boggs Bailey, but I bumped into Tie Dye, who said something that sent a couple of old cowboys into a frenzy of flying fists. I ducked to avoid the blow, but it landed on a passing tourist.

"Hells Bells!" Mrs. Boggs Bailey grabbed me. "These guys are bad news. Let's go!"

We pushed though the crowd, but the tourist was now lashing out at everyone, swinging his camera case as a weapon.

The case hit Ted Nugent, who was still chatting on the phone.

Ted Nugent retaliated by hitting Tie Dye.

The burly man emerged from the crowd and grabbed Tie Dye and Ted Nugent and shouted that all fighters were eighty-sixed.

The seething crowd, now being herded toward the door, blocked my escape route.

Just as I was about to despair, a familiar, ragged grin appeared, as my biker friend grabbed each of us by the wrist.

"Come on, ladies. Let's get you out of here!" He used his bulk to make a path and managed to pull us both to the exit.

When we finally got outside, I stood in the parking lot,

panting for breath.

"That was very kind," I said to our rescuer. "I don't know how to thank you." I offered him my hand. He grabbed it and pulled me to him. He gave me a kiss, mercifully short.

"Sorry, sweet thing, but I gotta run. Wish I had time for some fun." He smacked my derriere.

"Is that man all right?" Mrs. Boggs Bailey, watched the biker mount his Harley.

I shivered in the cold night air as I watched the big man take off on his bike.

"Yes, he's all right."

"Well, his breath isn't."

The Saturn was parked where I'd left it. I tried the doors, hoping Donna had left it unlocked.

"Let's get in the car," said Mrs. Boggs Bailey. "I'm freezing."

"We can't. Donna went off with Walker Montgomery and took the car key."

Mrs. Boggs Bailey eyed the eighty-sixed fighters, several of whom were now lighting up cigarettes outside the entrance.

"We should call Jonathan Kahn. He said I should call him if any bad news guys started to bother me."

"You've got Jonathan's cell number? Call him!" I handed over the phone.

I never thought I'd wish for Jonathan's company again, but right now, my ex seemed to be the only person in this whole surreal place I could trust.

"He put his number on my phone list," said Mrs. Boggs Bailey. "I didn't go to the casino because Gaby gets real mad when I gamble."

"Jonathan went to the Indian Casino?"

"He said I just have to push this button." Mrs. Boggs Bailey pressed a key and put the phone to her ear. "I'm Mitzi Boggs Bailey. Are you all right?" she said loudly as she leaned on the Saturn. "There are bad news guys at the Maverick Saloon.

And that Donna went off with Walker Montgomery and took the Manners Doctor's car keys."

Now the fight was resuming outside.

The earring woman yelled at the smoking cowboys.

Ted Nugent punched Tie Dye in the mouth.

I grabbed the phone.

"Jonathan, this is Camilla. Please come get us right now. Donna has taken the car keys and gone off with Walker Montgomery. I think she's in danger. There's a huge brawl at the Maverick Saloon, and the Rancho seems to have been taken over by gangsters, and Luci's disappeared and...Jonathan, can you hear me?"

The phone was dead.

"I think that was the wrong number," Mrs. Boggs Bailey said. "That didn't sound like Jonathan Kahn. I don't always remember which button to push."

More fight spilled out into the parking lot.

Giddy with desperation, I again tried each of the locked handles of the Saturn. One of the windows was cracked open. If I could find a coat hanger, maybe I could break in. But I couldn't start it.

"Mrs. Boggs Bailey, I don't suppose you can hotwire a car?"

"Nope, but I sure can ride a horse." The old woman pointed at the pair of Arabians tied up at the sidewalk railing.

I fought panic as a van painted with rain forest scenes and smiling whales pulled into the parking lot. It was followed by two wine-tour limousines.

Reinforcements. This could be nasty.

"Come on, slowpoke!" Mrs. Boggs Bailey called from the wooden railing where the horses were tied. With sudden, surprising energy, she raised the toe of her boot and stuck it in the stirrup of the saddle of a bay gelding. "Ride 'em cowgirl!" She vaulted herself up on the animal with creaky, but practiced flair.

"You can't take somebody's horse!" I ran toward her.

But Mrs. Boggs Bailey was off down the road at a healthy trot. I stood by the remaining horse, a sorrel mare, who looked away from me as if even she could tell I was a loser.

"Hey, yuppie scum. You stay away from those horses!" yelled one of the cowboys.

I looked at the mare. I'd never ridden western, but it was supposed to be an easier seat than English. The fight was getting noisier. And bloodier.

Mrs. Boggs Bailey was halfway down the street.

As I attempted to mount, someone grabbed me from behind.

"You stay away from that animal, Miss Wine Snot," said a boozy voice. It was Ted Nugent. "Or should I say Mister? I heard you're some kind of a tranny pervert."

I aimed an elbow at his gut.

"You leave her alone," said another voice. "She's a published author!"

Something made an awful thud.

I turned to see Ted Nugent on the ground, with Herb Frye the Sci-Fi guy standing over him, brandishing a tire iron. "Come on Dr. Manners," said Herb. "Over there. Get in the car!"

He pointed at a PT cruiser—a bright custom pink, idling in the middle of the road. At the wheel, Vondra DeHaviland called to me.

"Jump in, Dr. Manners!"

I ran and opened the door to the back seat. But it wasn't there. The whole car, except for the front seat, was stacked with books.

"No room back there," said Vondra, who was wearing a silvery pink cowboy hat. "It's my new book, *Love on the Range*. I've been hitting the malls."

Ted Nugent, still lying on the ground, gave a roar and grabbed Herb's trouser leg.

Herb kicked him away.

"Come on!" he said, as he ran to the car and jumped in the front seat. "Come on, Dr. Manners, there's room for all of us."

There wasn't.

But Ted Nugent was getting to his feet now. I perched myself on Herb's lap and pulled the door shut just as Nugent, followed by three cowboys and a tourist started moving toward the PT Cruiser. Vondra took off with a squeal.

"Where are we going?" she said.

I pointed at Mrs. Boggs Bailey, now several blocks ahead.

"Follow that horse!" I said.

Chapter 47—Indian Territory

VONDRA ASSURED ME THE casino was only a few streets over from the Saloon, and we should have no trouble finding Mitzi once we got there. I was grateful for the rescue, but would have been happier if Herb Frye hadn't put his hands in such awkward places as I balanced on his lap—and if Vondra had paid more attention to the road and less to Herb's shirt collar, which had been torn in the fight.

Vondra seemed to have trouble comprehending what I was trying to tell them about the recent events at the Rancho Grande.

"Luci Silverberg was killed by ghosts?" Vondra said.

"No. Weren't you listening?" Herb said. "It was a gang. She heard them over the phone. Gangbangers right there in the Hacienda." He grabbed me tighter. "Do you think Luci Silverberg was murdered?"

I shifted my weight on his bony knees.

"Nobody knows," I said. "We don't even know if she's actually missing. She could have gone for a walk. All I know for sure is that Alberto sounded terrified on the phone. It's lucky most of the guests have left. He's the only sane person in the place."

"The guests have—left?" Herb stopped, mid-grope. "The conference isn't supposed to end until tomorrow. Is this going to be on the news?"

Vondra's voice went shrill.

"These gangsters—are they looting the place? Where's the sheriff? What about that policeman friend of yours? Isn't he doing something? Oh, my lord, I hope they're not burglarizing our rooms. I have some very nice matching luggage."

I tried to sound calm.

"All I know is that it didn't sound safe—and Alberto said the sheriff's people are busy at the vineyard protest. I'm sure they'll get up there soon, but this probably isn't the best moment to go back up to the ranch."

I didn't want to alarm them with my worries about stomped phone stories, or Rick's murky gang connections, or suicidal dishwashers, but I had to warn them not to walk into the middle of something nasty.

Herb seemed obsessed with the possibility of media coverage.

"If the conference is over early, people will know! I'll be expected home tonight. Tomorrow at the latest."

"Expected home?" Vondra said. She slowed the car to glacial speed. "By whom?"

"My wife!" Herb said in a panicked voice. "I'll never hear the end of it."

"You have a wife?" Vondra's voice was pure ice.

A car behind us honked.

"I never said I didn't," said Herb.

"You said you loved me!" said Vondra, a sob escaping from her hot pink lips. "You sleaze!" She pulled the car over on the shoulder. "You lying, low-life sleaze!"

"I did not lie!"

I could see the entrance to the parking lot of the Chumash Casino ahead. When the car came to a full stop, I opened the door and escaped. I could still hear Herb and Vondra shouting when I was well down the drive.

When I reached the main casino building, I saw no sign of Mrs. Boggs Bailey or the horse. In fact, I found it hard to believe I was only a few blocks from the Maverick Saloon. I felt as if I'd been transported to an elegant urban club. The entrance was graced with gorgeous fountains and crowds of people dressed in evening wear.

As I glided up the waterfall-flanked escalator to the main casino, a hand on my back startled me.

"Now you mind your P's and Q's, Dr. Manners."

I turned to see Mrs. Boggs Bailey — looking a bit the worse for wear, but as determined as ever.

"These Indian fellas have their own police. They don't allow any hanky panky. And no drinking except at the Willows Fine Dining Restaurant. Come on Dr. Manners. Don't be such a slowpoke."

She sprinted up the last few steps of the escalator like someone a third her age.

I was afraid to ask what had happened to the horse.

The huge, multi-storied room was packed with flashing, beeping gambling machines — and people smoking. I coughed as the acrid air hit my lungs.

"You can smoke here, but you can't drink," said Mrs. Boggs Bailey. "Jonathan Kahn said that was a crazy-ass rule."

"Do you see Jonathan?" I wondered if I'd been naive to pin my hopes on him. There was a very good chance he might not believe me about Walker Montgomery. In recent years, he seemed to have had a compulsion to tell me I was wrong about pretty much everything.

"Gaby calls this room the morgue," Mrs. Boggs Bailey said

with a chuckle. "Full of dead people."

Some of the gamblers did look dead. Others seemed to be hooked up to the gambling machines as if they were life-support systems, with thick coiled wires hooking credit card-like things from chest pockets to the gambling machines. Only the ubiquitous Indian security guards showed signs of life, smiling and talking together as they eyed the gamers, like cowboys keeping an eye on a restless herd.

"There he is!" said Mrs. Boggs Bailey.

Jonathan was plugged into a machine like the rest of them, his eyes reflecting an unearthly glow from the machine's lights. And beside him was Marva.

What a party.

Marva waved happily at me, balancing precariously on her stiletto heels. I had to fight my sense of revulsion at the sight of her. She did look a little like me—if I'd been a little meaner, tartier, and a lot drunker. It was like looking at my own dark side.

I hoped she didn't have anything to do with the murders or Luci's disappearance—or Walker Montgomery. If she got into the media, it would pretty much end what was left of my career.

What was she doing with Jonathan? A little blackmail of her own?

Mrs. Boggs Bailey walked up to Jonathan and tapped him on the shoulder.

"I had to come to the Casino. Those fellas at the Saloon weren't all right."

Jonathan merely grunted at her over his shoulder. His crew people said nothing, and neither did Marva—all playing their own solitary games—their gazes never wavering from the blinking lights.

"Did you hear me, Mr. Kahn?" said Mrs. Boggs Bailey. "I couldn't get you on the phone, so I had to borrow a horse. I told them in the parking lot that I was with you."

"I warned you, didn't I, Mitzi?" Jonathan said with a fixed, impatient grin. "You should have come with us in the first place."

He shifted focus from his video poker as the machine blinked "Game Over" and finally saw me.

"Well, well. The former Mrs. Kahn. What are you doing here? So far from your police protection! Poor bastard."

Jonathan's glazed eyes and clumsy movements suggested he was seriously inebriated.

His machine beeped and boinked. He swore at it.

"Rick isn't protecting anybody right now, except maybe some gang. Awful things have been going on at the Rancho Grande, and what's worse, Donna has gone..."

Jonathan swore at his machine again.

"Jonathan, Luci is..."

"Yeah, yeah. Marva told me all about Luci." He dismissed the subject with a wave, never looking up from his machine.

"I know Luci showed you that damned photo. The whole thing's a scam. You'll never see more than a fraction of that money she's promising. She just wants to get you under contract to write a memoir, and then she plans to blackmail me into paying to keep it from being published. She's not a literary agent at all. Hasn't been for years. Nobody in the business will have anything to do with her."

"I know that. But you need to listen..."

"No, Camilla." As Jonathan's machine boinked again, he turned to me for a moment. "You listen to me. Listen very carefully."

He spoke slowly, as if I were a learning-disabled child.

"Luci had a scam going with Toby Roarke. It went like this: he posed as a ghostwriter for a celebrity memoir, got a bunch of dirt on the celebrity's friends, and then the friends got a visit from Luci, offering to keep the book off the shelves—for a fee. Sweet, huh?" He clicked a button on his beeping machine. "Damn!" he said, clicking again.

"Jonathan, I kind of figured that out. But Luci..."

"But Luci's greedy," Jonathan said, his focus all on the machine now. "She and Toby were getting low on actual dirt, so they started to manufacture it. That's when they contacted Marva's employer. A photo with a hooker is ho-hum these days, but a photo of some poor jerk getting spanked by the Manners Doctor: that's page one stuff. Nobody cares if it's faked. They retract it a month later on page thirteen. So they were getting big bucks from poor shmucks like me. Marva calls it 'gerbilling'."

He finally looked up at me and his glazed eyes came to life for a moment.

"It's like my stupid joke about how being married to you was so kinky—S/M, bestiality, necrophilia and all that. Of course they didn't print the damned punchline—when I said how my wife would torture me by cuddling with the dog when I wanted sex, and when I did finally get her alone, it was like doing a dead person. Okay, the joke sucked, but that reporter bitch was trying to get me to admit to all kinds of crazy stuff—maybe she'd heard I'd been visiting Marva's club—so I said it to shut her up. I didn't think she'd take a few words out of context and print them."

So that's what happened.

My life had been ruined by a bad joke.

Ronald Reagan was right: there might not be any easy answers, but sometimes there were simple answers: Jonathan didn't hate me—he'd just said something stupid.

He always was jealous of Barkley. Big old fuzzy face. I still missed him.

Still, the words stung.

"I was that bad in bed?"

"Not as bad as that one." Jonathan pointed at Marva with a rough laugh. "It was a joke, Camilla. A lousy goddam joke." He glanced around the room like a guilty child and pulled a pint bottle of Jack Daniels from his pocket and downed a furtive slug.

Marva shook her head and pointed at a surveillance camera above us.

"You!" said Mrs. Boggs Bailey, after staring at Marva, then me, and back at Marva again. "Are you two all right? There shouldn't be two Manners Doctors." She glared at Marva. "Your boobs are too big."

"Calm down, Mitzi," said Marva. "Now don't call 911 again, okay?"

"I don't like your kind." Mrs. Boggs Bailey turned back to Jonathan. "Mr. Kahn, what are you doing with a pervert that looks like Dr. Manners?"

Jonathan put away the bottle.

"That, Mitzi, is a very long, complicated story."

"No it isn't." Marva rolled her eyes. "After Luci contacted Jonathan on Monday about "your upcoming book," Jonathan hired me to get the photo back. So I did. End of story."

Monday. The day Gabriella phoned me. Toby and Luci must have put her up to it. They already had plans for me. Probably because of the *Post* article.

"By 'hired' Marva means she blackmailed me," Jonathan said.

"Luci was the blackmailer. I just did some retrieval. For a finder's fee." Marva said. "Sorry, folks, I've got to go to the little girl's room. I'm about to explode."

"Whatever," Jonathan said. "But she asked a whole lot less than Luci did for your damned book." He gave me a scowl before turning back to his machine.

"There is no book! Luci never talked to me until the conference." Jonathan's rudeness was infuriating. "It was much worse for Rick. He actually wrote a book for Luci..."

I stopped, remembering Alberto's fear and panic. Rick was one of them. The Viboras. I had to face the fact that Rick might be the worst villain of all.

Of course Jonathan wasn't listening to a word.

Mrs. Boggs Bailey stared at the lights on Marva's machine.

"If she's not gonna finish this game, can I play it?" She pressed a button and the machine gave a boink.

I left her playing Marva's machine, hoping she'd be safe for a few minutes.

Marva had those letters. She must be planning to use them to do a double-blackmail deal with Walker the way she had Jonathan — she'd stolen them back for a "finder's fee."

But how had she known I had possession of them, when I didn't even know what they were myself? I seriously doubted that Mrs. Boggs Bailey knew either. She'd simply found them in her chifforobe — a gift from "ghosts."

Meanwhile, Walker was probably trying to get them out of the clueless Donna. Whatever Donna's flaws, she didn't deserve to be hurt for Luci and Toby's sins.

Or Marva's.

Chapter 48—Horse Thief

THE BATHROOM WAS EMPTY except for the tell-tale size twelve pumps under the door of one of the stalls. Of course if I was wrong about Walker Montgomery, and Rick wasn't some enraged phone-stomping gangbanger-killer, that meant I was alone with a murderer.

But I was the one who'd got Donna in this mess, so I had to get her out.

"Where are those letters you took from me, Marva?" I said to the bathroom stall door, trying to sound calm. "Luci's missing. Somebody ransacked her room looking for those letters. Now he's got Donna, too…"

"Whoa! Back up now! Luci Silverberg is missing? Are you sure?"

"She disappeared from her room at the Hacienda and somebody tore it up looking for something. She had some of the letters, so I'm sure they were looking for the rest. Luci doesn't have a car, and nobody saw her leave. Plus she took off without her bag—and she left the top off her nail polish. I think Walker might have done something to her—kidnapped her or even killed her. And now Donna's gone off with Walker, trying to pitch him her book. Luci thought Donna had the letters, and maybe Walker does too…"

Marva emerged from the stall, adjusting her pantyhose.

"Slow down a minute. Did you say Luci left the top off her nail polish?"

I nodded.

"Doesn't sound like she took off for a leisurely stroll. And who else is missing?"

"Donna Carillos. She's…"

"Duncan Fowler's arm candy. Or she used to be." Marva rummaged in her bag for a lipstick. "Yeah. I know who Donna is. What does that little media whore have to do with the Joaquin letters? Luci never got hold of the letters. I still have them." She pulled out the familiar gold pocket folder and opened it. "Yup. Right here."

"But some are missing." I looked at the yellowed bits of paper. They really did look old. Ernesto had been a gifted forger. "I kind of hung on to a few. And they've been, uh, floating around. Now Donna is trying to pitch her novel to Walker Montgomery, and I'm afraid he may hurt her. He used to be called Joaquin, like the person in the gay letters, and if he thinks Donna's got them…"

Marva arched a carefully plucked eyebrow.

"You know about Walker—that he's the Joaquin in the letters?" She looked into my eyes as I nodded. "Okay. But why would he think Donna had the letters?"

I sighed. "I put the letters in the folder with Donna's novel by mistake."

"What—are you going for the nitwit of the year award or something?" Marva applied lip color from a Chanel *Camélias* lip palette identical to mine. "Didn't you listen when I told you Luci was evil?"

She blotted her lips and looked pensive for a moment.

"Okay. We don't have to go all drama queen about it. For one thing, Donna can't be with Walker. He left for his house in Malibu a couple of hours ago. He's flying to Australia tomorrow morning."

I shook my head. "I just saw him at the Maverick Saloon. He followed us from the Rancho—after he searched Luci's room, while posing as a ghost. I'm pretty sure that had to be him. And Luci thought Donna had more letters, because Donna asked a hundred thousand dollars for them—well, she thought she was asking the money for her novel, but... well, it's complicated."

"Whoa!" Marva turned and gave me a fierce stare. "Walker believes Donna has those letters? And she's with him right now? She dropped her makeup in her bag and banged open the door. "Come on. We gotta find that girl." She grabbed my arm and pulled me out, nearly colliding with a group of overfed ladies in sparkly sweat suits.

"Damn!" Marva stopped dead.

At the end of the aisle, Jonathan was being led away by uniformed guards. Two more guards had Mrs. Boggs Bailey.

"What's going on?" I said to a sweatsuit lady, trying to sound off-hand.

"Probably drinking," the woman said. "I saw that silver-haired guy with a flask."

"Somebody said they were horse thieves," said another sweatsuit.

A third lit up a Virginia Slim. "When I came in, the tribal police were looking for some drunk celebrity who stole a horse from over at the Maverick Saloon."

"Miss Manners," said sweatshirt number one. "That's who they're looking for now. Miss Manners, drunk as a skunk,"

Marva pulled me down another aisle and out of sight of Jonathan. "You stole a horse?" she hissed. "And expected to get away with it? In this town?"

"I didn't steal it. Mrs. Boggs Bailey did."

Now the uniformed men were marching Jonathan and the old woman toward the Casino entrance. Marva pulled me in the opposite direction.

"I can't leave," I told her. "Mrs. Boggs Bailey is my responsibility. I've got to explain things to those tribal security people."

Marva tightened her grip on my arm.

"No way. Jonathan and Mitzi may be uncomfortable for a bit, but they'll live. But from what you tell me, Donna might not make it through the night. We need to stay out of jail so we can find her. Now. Come on."

Chapter 49—Head for the Hills

CLICKING ALONG AT AN impressive pace in her gigantic heels, Marva led me to the parking garage. When we got to level three, she stopped at a black rental Taurus.

"Here." She tossed me the keys. "You'd better drive. That ex of yours sure is generous with his Jack. I usually don't drink. I used to have a little problem with the booze before I got on the right track, gender-wise. Used to steal whatever I could from the Longhorn Room after hours when I worked in the kitchen."

"You used to sneak down that back staircase?" I took the keys, but this new information didn't make me terribly enthusiastic about getting in the car with her. "Those stairs. That's how Toby's body got to the Longhorn Room."

The words were out of my mouth before I realized how stupid I was to say them if Marva had killed Toby after all. She looked strong enough to move a body down the stairs.

And certainly strong enough to overpower me.

But she showed no reaction, so I decided to go on.

"Toby was killed on the porch outside his apartment and all that gruesome gang stuff was added post mortem. Alberto said there was a trail of blood all the way down the hall."

Marva only laughed. "Poor Alberto. He must have gone bonkers when he found bloodstains all over his nice floor."

"He thought Gabriella must have killed Toby."

Marva snorted. "How dumb is that? You knew it wasn't her, didn't you?"

I still gripped the keys. Should I say it?

"Actually, I thought maybe it was you."

"And that's why you're standing there looking like you don't know what car keys are for?" Marva laughed again. "Unlock the door, sweetie. I'm sure you've got trust issues after being married to Jonathan, but you gotta let them go right now. Otherwise that dimbulb little Valley Girl might get herself smoked, you know?"

I got in.

Marva slid in beside me, clutching her faux Fendi spybag.

"Now you've got me paranoid," she said, "Walker made such a big deal about how he had to drive to Malibu tonight. To pack for some big-deal trip to Australia. But I suppose he doesn't want to leave with all these…loose ends hanging around." She patted her bag. "My finder's fee is only twenty thou. I'm not greedy. I just need money for my operation."

I drove out of the garage as I put the pieces together in my head. "But how was Walker supposed to pay you if he was on his way to Australia?"

Marva didn't answer except to say, "Turn right up there. Don't get on the freeway."

I was tired of the cloak and dagger stuff, and the dark road ahead did not look inviting.

"Where, exactly are we going? I don't have a clue where Walker might have taken Donna. Why do you think he'd be somewhere in these mountains?"

"Because his boyfriend, Duncan Fowler, lives in these mountains, that's why. Duncan is the one who hired me. He was supposed to meet me at the Maverick Saloon earlier to buy the letters." She stroked her bag like a favorite pet. "He didn't want Walker to know, because Walker already paid Toby for them, and he's furious. But Duncan didn't show, so I figured he'd decided to let Walker deal with it. But after what you told me about Luci having some of the letters and trying to sell them... damn, he probably thought I was bluffing and Luci had them all along. Turn here."

"Duncan Fowler is Walker's boyfriend?"

Could she possibly be right? Walker Montgomery really was gay? I had to let that sit in my brain for a moment.

"I thought you said those letters were forgeries—now you're saying he's gay after all?"

The winding dirt road ahead looked as shadowy as Marva's schemes.

"That's why the forgery scam was so sweet. Those three latched on to just enough truth to scare the piss out of people."

"Those three—you mean Luci, Toby and Ernesto? Gabriella—did she know?"

"I doubt it. Luci did not like to share. That's where she and I ran into trouble."

"You and Luci—you'd been, uh, doing business together for a while?" I didn't know a tactful way to inquire if someone was part of a crime ring.

"No way. I only met La Luci last week, when she was putting the screws on Jonathan. He contacted me about the photo, and I tried to negotiate with Luci and Toby to get it back—you know, for a finder's fee. Toby actually offered me more—he wanted us to get a regular gig going with those photos. Ernesto was getting cocky—trying to branch out on his own with his literary forgeries—so Toby couldn't count on him. But Luci nixed the deal with me. She didn't want to cut anybody else in. Greedy bitch."

"You should be glad you didn't join their little crime family," I said, trying to fight my revulsion at this confession. "It's been a bit hazardous to their health. They all get dead."

"Yeah. Which sure points a finger at everybody's favorite gun industry spokesmodel as the murderer, doesn't it? He was their number one mark. Turn here."

I shivered in the cold night air, thinking the facts could equally well point to Marva herself—especially the frying pan murder

"Why wouldn't a gun person like Walker shoot Toby like the others?" I blurted out. "And why all the gang stuff? None of that sounds like Walker Montgomery to me, but maybe you know something I don't know…"

I stopped myself before I got in bigger trouble. At least I hadn't told Marva about Rick, or his gang friends who might be at the Hacienda. I did not need to tell her how friendless I was at the moment.

"Who knows? Walker's a loose cannon. He threatened to kill Toby if he didn't turn over the letters. Then he threatened Luci, after the letters disappeared the night Ernesto died."

"What did happen to those letters that night?" I kept my eyes on the road.

"I have a feeling Ernesto took them from Toby out of revenge. Maybe he was going to blow the whistle on the whole deal. Confess to Plant Smith or something. He and Toby had a big fight that night. The kid had his own scam going—trying to sell Plantagenet Smith some forgery he was doing on his own—and Toby went ballistic when he found out—and confiscated all Ernie's stuff. That night, the folder with all the blackmail evidence—Ernie's forgery, the Joaquin letters, plus that photo of me—disappeared from Toby's desk. Toby was pretty sure Ernesto stole it. He called me to warn me the kid might have the copy of my photo with Jonathan. I was pretty annoyed. But not as annoyed as Walker. He'd already paid Toby his blackmail money, so technically, the letters belong to Walker."

I peered through the dark as my brain sorted through this. Maybe Ernesto did steal the letters, but that didn't explain how they got to Mrs. Boggs Bailey — or how the Viboras figured in.

Marva fished in her bag for something.

"Slow down and take a hard right."

After I made the treacherous turn onto what was clearly marked a "private drive," I glanced over to see that Marva was efficiently inserting a clip into a small, rather elegant silver and onyx pistol.

I clutched the wheel and tried to keep my voice calm.

"Please, let's not shoot anybody. They may not know we're on to them. Can't we just talk Donna into coming back with us? I can say we've set up an interview with Jonathan for her. I don't think she even knows about the letters. Walker Montgomery sort of seems to like me, so..."

Marva clicked something on the gun.

"Don't be taken in by his aw-shucks act. He can be a vindictive bitch. Of course, he's always had it in for me because of my relationship with Duncan."

"You're involved with Duncan Fowler?"

This was getting more and more surreal. I was not relishing the idea of engaging in a shoot-out with Mr. Heavily-Armed Testosterone and Mr. Right-Wing Pundit, whether they were gay or not.

"Was," Marva said. "Long time ago. When I was...somebody else. But I know my way around his place. My parents had a little ranch just over the next hill. Sold out to a big winery a few years back." She pointed ahead. "Drive all the way past the stables and park just this side of the helicopter pad."

I negotiated the winding drive through the oaks up to the

sprawling, mission-style ranch house on the hilltop. I heard a horse whinny into the night. It sounded spooked. I could sympathize. As I rounded a curve, I saw the helicopter, silhouetted in the moonlight, perched like some monster insect in a clearing a few hundred yards ahead.

"Park here," Marva said. "They can't see us with that big old chopper in the way. Then you need to change out of those clothes. We have to be absolutely quiet once we get in the house. I've got a couple of pairs of flats and some jackets in the trunk. You can't do this in couture and heels, sweetie."

Chapter 50—NewsFowl

A FEW MINUTES LATER, wearing a gray hoodie and shoes that looked like they used to belong to somebody named Bozo, I followed Marva as she glided, cat-like, toward Duncan Fowler's ranch house, clad in a black satin trench coat, Gucci scarf and jeweled satin ballerinas. Trying desperately not to trip over the borrowed size twelve Adidas, I plodded behind, past the helicopter pad and onto to a path that led past the stables to a driveway that ran along the side of the house.

Once we reached the house, Marva sneaked behind the famous Mustang and a Lexus with vanity plates that said NEWSFOWL. She led me toward a fenced-off area full of trash bins.

"Uh-oh. Company," Marva whispered. She pointed at a car parked further down the drive.

It was a Ferrari 360 Spider convertible.

"Plant!" I said. "That's Plantagenet Smith's car!" What could he possibly be doing here?

Marva held her gun ready as she kept an eye on the house.

"Plantagenet Smith, the screenwriter? Cool. He's a friend of yours?"

I nodded.

"Fabulous," said Marva. "This will work great. Go up to the front door and ask for Mr. Smith and distract them. I'll sneak in the kitchen and find our little media whore and do my best to get her out safe. Meet me back at my car in ten minutes."

I checked my watch

"Distract them? It's nearly eleven o clock at night. Why do I say I'm here?"

"Say you're looking for your ex. Or Mitzi. You'll think of something."

Marva disappeared into the dark.

I clomped up to the massive carved doors of Duncan Fowler's house and shivered as terrible questions ricocheted around my brain. If Walker Montgomery had already murdered three people, was Donna was even alive? What if he'd killed Plant, too? My panic rose. It didn't make much sense to me that Plant would be visiting an arch-conservative pundit — gay or not — at this time of night.

Duncan Fowler himself came to the door. He looked old and tired without his TV make-up and his signature crew cut was more gray than blond. He pulled the door partly shut behind him and spoke in a fierce whisper.

"Marva, it's too late. We know you lied about having those letters, and we're about to leave…" His eyes rested on my chest. "Oh, excuse me. You're not Marva…"

"No. I'm Camilla Randall — the Manners Doctor. I'm staying at the Rancho Grande. I'm a friend of Plantagenet Smith. Is he here?"

I hoped my polite, clueless smile covered my inner terror.

The thought came to me that Marva might be a liar—or crazy. And this could be a horrible trap. But at this moment, I had no choice but to keep my smile pasted on and step into Duncan Fowler's lair.

"Camilla! Darling, what are you doing here?" Plantagenet appeared at the door behind Duncan. "Is something wrong?"

I quieted him with a friendly hug as I whispered in his ear. "The shoes are borrowed. I'll explain later…"

Duncan ushered us into a faux-rustic sitting room, where Silas rose to greet me.

"Duncan, you didn't tell me you and Dr. Manners were friends," Silas said. "But of course, with her ex-husband in the business…"

"Yes, Jonathan Kahn and I have met." Duncan Fowler's gracious-host mask betrayed nothing as he ushered me into the room. He poked the remains of a fire that glowed in the stone fireplace.

Plant didn't sit.

"Darling, we were just leaving. Duncan's taking off for Australia in the morning. He's taking his helicopter to LAX. Nice way to avoid the traffic."

I had to avoid Plant's eyes as I forced a laugh. I looked at my watch. I just had to keep them all occupied for ten minutes. I plunked myself down in a distressed leather easy chair, ignoring Plant's disapproving glance.

"Are things okay at the Rancho?" Duncan's eyes showed anger, but his voice was polite. "Any news about Gabriella? I hope she has a good lawyer. It's such a tragedy about her…"

"I don't have any news about Gabriella, but…" I put on a dramatic expression. "Mitzi Boggs Bailey has been arrested."

A small truth rather than a big lie. The Manners Doctor always said it was the best route out of a difficult situation.

"Oh my. What has that poor old girl done now?" Duncan said.

"She and Jonathan Kahn have been detained by the

Chumash security people. Something about stealing a horse. And things at the Rancho seemed, um, a bit chaotic when I spoke with Alberto."

I hoped my voice didn't sound as phony to them as it did to me.

"Mitzi was arrested for horse thieving?" Duncan laughed. "I'm not surprised. That husband of hers was an old horse thief, too. "Gaby Moore has been a saint to put up with her all these years. Maybe that's one of the reasons she snapped."

"Gaby didn't snap," Silas said with a sharp tone. "I'm sure she'll be released as soon as the Sheriff does some homework." He pulled a phone from his pocket. "I'll try the Rancho again. If Gaby hasn't been released yet, we'll head back to my house. The Rancho will be a zoo with the investigation going on."

He paced the room, trying to get a signal.

"I can't believe Gaby relies on that prehistoric phone system," Plantagenet said. "We haven't been able to get through to anybody all evening." He turned to me. "At one point your policeman friend answered, but we were cut off. He told Silas there's been a kidnapping, but for some reason, the Sheriff had been delayed…"

"I can't get a signal in here," Silas said. He took the phone out to the hallway.

"How did you find out we were here, darling?" Plant said. "Did you call Silas's store? I should have given you my cell number. Not that you can get any kind of reception in these mountains. Trying to have a conversation on the way up here from Santa Barbara was comical…driving my Ferrari forty miles an hour so I could hang onto a tenuous phone connection before the next curve in the road cut me off entirely."

A look of shock flashed on Duncan Fowler's face.

"You? You drove over the San Marcos pass last Friday—in a Ferrari?" With a nervous laugh, he turned to poke the fire again. "They're so unreliable. I like my Lexus."

Plantagenet stood beside my chair. "I guess Silas's manager told you his Wilde first edition has been stolen? Duncan was the last customer who looked at it, so..."

"He wanted to make sure I hadn't nicked it." Duncan gave a stiff smile.

Plant looked hurt. "Of course we didn't suspect you. But Silas thought somebody might have tried to sell it to you, before it made its mysterious reappearance at the Rancho, since you're a Wilde collector..."

"So the book Mrs. Boggs Bailey gave you—it's not a forgery?" I found this odd news. "Are you sure? What about the letter?"

"That's the strange thing." Silas called from the hallway, pacing as he pushed buttons on his phone. "The handwriting is identical to what's on my book's flyleaf."

"But that's the problem." Plant perched on the arm of my chair. "It's precisely the same. Usually a person's handwriting changes over the years."

Duncan cleared his throat. "Don't feel you have to stay. I'm sure you'll be in a hurry to rescue poor Mitzi..."

Silas stood in the doorway. "As soon as I check with the Rancho, we'll be on our way. I need to know if we should stay at the Rancho or go back to San Luis."

I glanced at my watch again. I needed to stall at least another five minutes.

"So that book Mrs. Boggs Bailey found was stolen from Silas's store? Didn't Ernesto Cervantes work in one of his stores? Isn't it likely he's the one who stole it—and stashed it in Mrs. Boggs Bailey's room for some reason?"

"You think Ernesto stole from Silas?" Plant's eyebrows went up. He looked in Silas's direction, but Silas finally seemed to have reached someone. He was listening intently as he paced the hall.

I wondered if he'd reached the Rancho, and what he'd

found there.

Duncan's eyes had sharpened as he glanced from Plant to me.

"Are you talking about that boy who was killed? He was in a street gang, wasn't he? I think I heard that on the news. I don't know why Silas would have let him work around valuable books. I hate to say it, but you just can't help these people. They don't want to work, and they'll steal you blind."

Plantagenet's lips went tight.

"Ernie loved Silas like a father. I refuse to believe he would steal from him." He stood and tried to get Silas's attention. "We all should go. We've stayed way too long. Duncan, I'm sorry we barged in at this hour." He shook Duncan's hand with stiff politeness and gave me a significant look.

But I stayed put. I had to keep them here a few more minutes while Marva searched for Donna.

"I think Ernesto may have intended to return that book. He might have sort of borrowed it to copy the handwriting from the inscription—so he could forge that Calamity Jane letter. I think he might have been the one who wrote it. And I think he intended to sell it to you, Plant."

I was getting dangerously close to showing my hand, but I had to do something.

"Sort of borrowed? You think Ernie robbed Silas to scam me?"

Plant turned back to me—not angry, but surprised.

"All the hero-worship—you think that was fake? Some con game?" He gave me a look that seemed oddly like relief.

We heard a loud hello from Silas in the hallway. I thought it was directed into his phone until Walker Montgomery strode into the room—all six foot four of him, still wearing his ankle-length leather riding coat.

My throat constricted. I tried to smile.

"Hello, Dr. Manners," he said. "Did you get bored with the entertainment at the Maverick Saloon? Cowboy poetry not your thing?"

His too-white teeth gleamed in the firelight like fangs.

Chapter 51—A Killer Confesses

SILAS CAME BACK INTO the room, dropping his phone in his pocket.

"I've got great news! Gabriella's going to be released. They finally know who's responsible for those terrible murders."

I tried to keep my face composed.

Walker gave a stagey chuckle. "Fiscalini caught the maniacs who've been murdering Gaby's hotel guests? Pretty dramatic stuff for this little town. It was that Mexican gang—right? The whole north county—we're infested with them."

To my surprise, Silas nodded. "Yes. The gang problem is terrible." He gave a smile. "But I guess they've had a confession and the Sheriff's people are on their way."

I sat in silent confusion. This seemed to mean that Walker was innocent, at least of the murders—and if I'd understood Alberto right, the guilty one was Rick after all.

I had so much not wanted to believe that.

"A confession? Who confessed?" Plant said.

"Some Guatemalan dishwasher. He confessed to bashing Toby with a frying pan," Silas said.

"Santiago?" I half-laughed his name. Partly because I was relieved to hear it was not Rick, and partly because it was so absurd. Miguel said Santiago was threatening suicide, and I could believe that. The boy was so intense. But I could not see him murdering anybody.

"Alberto didn't have time for details." Silas said. "He told me this kid had given a confession to Rick Zukowski but the Sheriff hadn't arrived yet. Unfortunately all available law enforcement is either dealing with the anti-grape people, or some crowd control problem down at the Maverick Saloon."

"Rick got the killer to confess?" I took a long, deep breath. Rick didn't join the gang-bangers; he communicated with them. So that's what Alberto had been talking about when we spoke on the phone at the Saloon: Maybe Rick got the gangster to confess by bringing up his own gang past. And the gangster was apparently Santiago. Which didn't sound right to me. The kid really was a dork.

But Rick was all right, as Mrs. Boggs Bailey would say. That was nice to hear.

Maybe Silas was wrong about the Guatemala part.

"Mean crowd at the Saloon tonight," Walker said. "Good you got out of there, Dr. Manners. You and that little Mexican girl."

Walker's smile didn't look so menacing now. Maybe he hadn't taken Donna after all—and Walker and Duncan were just two innocent old gay men. Donna might be back at the Rancho right now, safe and sound.

Why had I believed a self-confessed blackmailer like Marva rather than these two polite, well-respected gentlemen?

"Walker and I need to get on the road ourselves," Duncan said as he moved us toward the door. "We have a plane to catch."

I followed Plant and Silas out to the porch.

"Are you going back to the Rancho now?" I asked. All I wanted now was to get out. If Duncan and Walker were innocent, the last thing I wanted was to rendezvous with the armed and dangerous Marva. "I'd, um, love a ride. I haven't had a real drive in the new Ferrari."

Plant gave me an indulgent smile. "I'll give you a ride tomorrow, darling, after we've got Gaby out of jail, safe and sound, I promise. I think we should go to the county jail and make sure she's being released."

Silas opened the passenger door. "It's a two seater anyway—a tough squeeze for just me. And you'd have to come back for your own car..."

He got in and closed the door with a thunk.

I gave Walker and Duncan a careful smile. "I'll be off now, too. Have a wonderful trip!" I started on the path toward the helipad.

"Quite a hike back down to your car at the Maverick Saloon." Walker's voice was deep and menacing. "And I think you'll probably need these..."

I turned to see him holding my pink and green Kate Spade keychain wallet—dangling it like a hypnotist's pendulum.

Down in the road, the Ferrari lights faded from sight.

"My keys!" I gave a silly grin, trying to keep up the clueless façade. "Did Donna give them to you? I don't think she knew my ID and cards were in there. She can be kind of scatterbrained..." I ran back to the porch and reached for the wallet

But Walker put it in his pocket. "Where are those letters, Doctor? Your little friend wouldn't tell me, in spite of my, um, persuasion."

My spine went cold.

"Donna—is she okay?"

Walker's smile looked even more feral in the moonlight.

"Well, Dr. Manners, I guess that depends on your

definition of okay."

I glanced at the path along the house that led to the helipad and Marva's car, trying not to think about what Walker might have done to Donna.

If I made a dash, would I be able to run in these stupid shoes?

I'd have to try. If I could make it past the tennis courts and the barn, I'd be out of sight of the house. If Walker went inside to get a gun, I might have a chance. And if he tackled me, I could probably fight him. He was big and mean, but I was a whole lot younger.

I wasn't afraid of Duncan, standing over there under the porch light, looking as if he might burst into tears.

"Walker," he said. "Do we have to do this? I think..."

"No, Duncan. You don't think. You never do. That's why we're in this mess."

"Me? You think this is my fault?"

"You. It's always about you, isn't it?" Walker turned on Duncan in fury.

I didn't wait to hear any more. As the argument escalated, I ran along the path as fast as I could clomp. When I got past the stables, I saw a car out on the road, its lights off, moving slowly toward the house.

I ducked through a horse fence and onto the road. Running toward the dark car, I waved my arms wildly.

I had to pray it was Marva. Marva and her gun.

Chapter 52—Two-Gun Cowgirl

THE CAR MOVED TOWARDS ME and the door swung open.

"Inside!" Marva hissed "Where hell have you been? I've got to get these letters to Duncan before he takes off."

I jumped in. I could hear moans coming from the back seat. I turned and saw Donna, her mouth and hands bound with duct tape. No signs of injury except that her clouds of perfume had been replaced by the incongruous smell of bleach.

"Untie the poor girl, will you?" Marva said. "I couldn't take a chance on her making any noise until I got her out of that house. Is Walker still up there with Duncan? Duncan doesn't want Walker to know he's buying the letters from me."

"They're up there arguing. You're going to deal with those monsters?"

"How else am I going to get my money? Damn. Duncan made a big thing about not letting Walker know. But it can't be helped. I'm not going to be able to get him alone."

I reached between the seats and pulled the tape off Donna's face.

"Are you hurt?"

Donna wailed.

"I'd be fine if you hadn't just taken off a layer of my skin." She felt her face. "I kept telling that old guy I didn't know anything about any letters. He's a total psycho."

"I'm so sorry." I reached through to pull off the tape that bound her wrists. "This is my fault, I'm afraid. I gave those letters to Luci with your manuscript by mistake."

Donna wailed again. "Bitch! Then you should have been the one back there with a psycho geezer waving a gun in your face."

She reached through the seats as if she was going to slap me.

"Sit down and be quiet, for God's sake," said Marva, "Or I'll duct tape both of you. Keep out of sight until I finish my business with Duncan. Walker's a guy to shoot first and ask questions afterwards, and I'm pretty sure he killed Toby and that kid. Luci too, for all I know. If he sees Donna, he could kill us all before he lets me explain I'm the one who's got the goddam letters."

"You've go them? So you're the bitch! Screw you."

I couldn't blame Donna. She wasn't at fault in any of this.

"You're really going back up to that house?" I said. "When you know Walker's a murderer?"

I couldn't believe Marva had rescued Donna only to put her in danger again. Not to mention the two of us.

Marva gave a dramatic sigh.

"Of course I'm going back to the house. Duncan owes me twenty thousand dollars for these things and he's leaving for Australia for like, a month. So scooch down on the floor and stay there. Once I've got my money, we're gone."

"I'm so glad Marva found you," I said to Donna as we slid down on the car floor. "What about Luci? Did either of you see Luci?"

"No sign of her," Marva said. "I looked all over that house. Walker had Donna locked in the laundry room.

"I think there was bleach spilled on that floor. The place stank of it," Donna said with a loud sniff.

There was a terrible crack, and the car thudded to snail-pace.

My body went cold as I watched Marva take her gun from her pocket.

Walker Montgomery's voice boomed outside. "Come on out, Marvin. I know you're in there with your little girlfriends."

In the back seat, Donna babbled loudly in Spanish, I supposed to some saint. I hoped it was a powerful one. We needed all the help we could get.

Marva flicked on her lights and floored the gas pedal, swerving wildly. I hung onto the door handle as I tried to maintain my crouch.

Another shot blasted the car. Above, I could hear the windshield shatter. Marva slumped over the wheel. The car skidded to a stop.

We were trapped.

"Okay ladies. Out."

Walker Montgomery opened the door and yanked me out of the car. He shoved me toward Duncan, who was standing by the hood, holding Walker's big gun.

"Get your hands off me, prune-face!" Donna kicked at Walker as he pulled her from the back seat. She looked okay, except for the white splotches on the seat of her Donna Karan from the bleach. Poor thing.

But when Walker opened the driver's door, Marva lay slumped over the wheel. Walker pulled on her arm, and she didn't move. He gave another heave and she fell from the car, landing on her side, lifeless. The hugs and kisses bracelet glinted in the moonlight.

"Oh, my God, you killed her!" Donna screamed.

Marva, dead. It was too horrible.

I could hardly breathe as I stood by the car and stared at the deathly still body, looking more male than female now in spite of her satin trench coat and sparkling flats. Donna whimpered and ran to Duncan.

"Duncan, honey, how could you let him do that? I thought we were going to stay friends. That's what you said when we broke up. You wanted to be friends. You're such a liar."

Walker was down on the ground examining Marva's body. I saw a sudden flash of silver. In an instant, Marva came to life, all kicking legs and flashing gun. I heard a pop. Now it was Walker Montgomery who slumped — clutching his arm as he fell against the hood.

Ignoring Walker's cry of pain, Marva strode over to Duncan, lowering her gun as she approached.

"Sorry I had to shoot him, Duncan, but you saw what a brat he was being."

She opened up her tote bag and pulled out the folder.

"Here, sweetie."

She waved the letters in front of Duncan. As he grabbed for them, she casually clamped her hand on his wrist and wrestled him for the big gun.

"Duncan, you moron..." Walker screamed.

Marva turned, grinning as she brandished both guns.

"We don't need guns now, Walker," said Duncan. "We've got the letters. It's all over. You can let Luci go, too." He moved toward the house and leafed through the letters under the porch light. "Thank you, Marva. Walker's been beside himself.... Oh, my God, do you suppose this is true about President Reagan?"

Walker leaned on the car, clutching his wounded arm.

"Marvin, you pervert bastard! You had those letters all along? Luci said she was getting them from somebody — it was you?"

Marva dismissed him with a cold look and turned back to Duncan.

"Duncan, baby, don't let Miss Thing over there give you any more crap. Those are yours. Bought and paid for. You do whatever you want with them. Give me my twenty thou and we're done. A deal's a deal."

"A deal?" Walker exploded. "You're going to pay this blackmailing drag queen for stuff I already paid for? I told you I'd take care of it."

"Oh, sure. You took care of it." Marva kept both guns trained on Walker. "You didn't even bother to get the letters from Toby after you killed him."

"I did not kill Toby Roarke!"

Walker's voice boomed as he supported himself on the car's hood.

"I own over a hundred guns. Why would I kill somebody with a sissy frying pan? Besides, Duncan will tell you — I was here all last night."

"That's right," Duncan said. "We had a little dinner party with some of the network news crew who were here for the grape protest. Walker was here the whole time. Marva, can we go inside and be civilized? I'll get your money."

Duncan took Donna's arm and eyed her ruined dress.

"I'm sorry about your dress, honey. Walker can be so awful, can't he?"

Marva motioned for everybody to go back to the house.

I hated to go back into the house I'd just escaped from. But Marva had the power right now.

"Yes. Walker is awful," Marva said, menacing the men with the big Colt. "He's also a liar." She ushered us into the den. "So Walker — where the hell is Luci? Did you kill her too?"

Walker collapsed in the big chair, clutching his arm.

"Marvin, I did not kill anybody. That bitch Luci said she was in contact with somebody who had the letters. She wanted two hundred thousand. No way was I going to let her extort that after I'd already paid once. For totally bogus crap. I've never seen those letters before. They've got to be some kind of crazy forgery."

"And that's why you killed her?"

"Would anyone like a quick cup of coffee before you go?" said Duncan, putting on an absurd perfect-host smile.

"Totally!" said Donna. "Can I have mine with nonfat milk?"

"No, we wouldn't like a cup of anything," Marva said, stifling her with a look. "And we wouldn't like you to go call the cops or get more guns. Just show me the money, Duncan. Sorry, Walker. He wanted to keep it a secret from you. He said you wouldn't pay one more penny after what you gave Toby."

She stood by the doorway, wielding a gun in each hand— looking like an old-time, two-gun cowboy, except, of course, for her extraordinary cleavage and the purse in the crook of her elbow.

"I don't care how many network flunkies you hired to provide an alibi, we all know Walker killed Toby."

Walker sprang to his feet.

"I did not kill anybody!"

Something about his wounded pride convinced me the man was telling the truth. At least about Toby and Ernesto.

But that didn't mean he wouldn't kill us if Marva let down her guard.

Chapter 53—Shell Game

WALKER TOOK TWO STEPS toward Marva and laughed, in spite of the guns she had aimed at him.

Marvin, you've always been such a drama queen. I didn't kill anybody. In fact, they've got the real murderer in custody, over at the Rancho."

Marva snorted. "And if you believe that one, I'd love to sell you some nice real estate on the moon..."

We did not need the confrontation between these two to escalate.

"Believe it or not," I said in a perky voice. "Walker's actually telling the truth. Silas Ryder was just on the phone with Alberto. Apparently they have a confession. It was one of those Viboras after all."

"Oh, right," Donna said, plopping down on the couch. "Some gang kids walk into a fancy-ass resort, without anybody noticing, and murder Ernesto. And instead of tagging the place, they get all cute and make it look like a suicide. Then they sneak in the next night and bonk some geezer with a frying pan, even though they've all got, like, guns up the wazoo. And the third night they break into Luci's locked hotel room and kidnap her—and don't ask for ransom! And they don't touch that bitch's brand new two-thousand dollar boots or the collectible handbag. But they take the time to go through my manuscript and throw it all over the room. Oh, yeah. Gangbangers do that stuff all the time. They don't give a damn about money."

Marva laughed.

"Right. So why don't you admit it, Walker? You killed all of them. You knew that hotel inside and out. All its weird little secret passages. Because you worked for Hank Boggs way back when. I'm sure you learned how to sneak in and out of that place just like I did. So why don't you tell us where you dumped Luci's remains?"

Walker gave a raspy laugh.

"You always did live in fantasyland, Marvin." His grin looked grotesque in the firelight. "And Luci's fine—sort of. She shouldn't have lied and told me she had all the damned letters when she only had three. I only wanted to search the room. It would have been slick, since there's that door from the servant's wing that leads onto her balcony. I could have just sneaked in and out. But she sat in that room forever, painting her damned fingernails. I only found the three letters and she wouldn't tell me where the rest were."

"But she didn't know, because I had them." Marva smiled, obviously savoring it. "I promised Duncan I'd get them and I did."

"Well, the one thing I know about Luci is she lies a lot. So I brought her here for a little persuasion."

Walker gave an evil chuckle. I wondered where the poor woman was.

"Then she lied again and told me Donna had the letters and

was asking a hundred thousand for them."

Donna wailed. "Liar is right! She is such a bitch. I told her I wanted a hundred thousand for my novel advance, not for some stupid letters. I told her I don't even know about any letters."

Duncan harrumphed.

"But it's all over now!" he said. "Everything is fine. It's time to forgive and forget." He opened the folder Marva had given him, took out a letter, crumpled it and tossed it into the fire. "The important thing is the Sheriff has somebody in custody for both deaths, and Luci will be fine. This little episode is over."

Walker clutched his wounded arm. Marva stood in the doorway, her guns trained on him. Nothing seemed fine to those two.

"I couldn't care less about Luci," Marva said, "But if she's still alive, I suggest you keep her that way, because nobody's going to believe that gangbangers fairy story two times in a row."

Duncan threw another batch of letters into the fireplace. We all watched the flames in silence.

"What about those other folders you found in that cabin when you were nosing around, Walker?" he said. "Do they have forged nonsense in them, too? Let's get rid of everything and have done with this whole nasty business."

Walker opened an ancient roll-top desk and took out two more gold folders.

"You want to burn *Under Deadwood* by Mitzi Boggs Bailey? Or *Blue Rage*, a novel by M. J. Zukowski?" He started to toss them in the fire.

"No!" I sprang to save the manuscripts. "Mrs. Boggs Bailey's play? And Rick's book! You stole them — why?"

Walker lasered me with an angry glare.

"You know perfectly well, Miss Oh-So-Innocent. You're the one who had the fake letters all along. You gave them to Mitzi

313

Boggs when she came to Plant Smith's cabin the night that kid got shot. That's why they weren't there when I broke in pretending to be one of her ghosts."

"Mr. Smith's cabin? The Zorro cabin? You broke in?" Marva said. "Was that when you killed Ernie?"

"Of course not," Walker said. "I didn't go in until after the coroner had been there. But the letters should have been there. Ernie stole them that night to give to Smith and get back at Toby. But I searched that place from top to bottom the next night after the cops left. All I found was poor old Mitzi's cowboy play. Dr. Manners here must have switched them the night the kid died, because the cops were there the rest of the time. I don't know why, but I know she did it."

He tossed the folders to me with a sneer.

Truth dawned as I flipped through my memories of that night. Plant trying to zip his trousers. Mitzi coming over with her play and then taking it back.

I must have given her the wrong folder. There must have been two: one with her play and the other with Ernesto's forgeries and all the other blackmail stuff he'd stolen from Toby.

Maybe he had intended to confess to Plant. It was so tragic.

"I didn't do it on purpose! All the folders look alike." I stared helplessly at the yellowed pages of Mrs. Boggs Bailey's play as I realized what had happened. "Detective Fiscalini kept accusing me of violating his crime scene, but that was you looking for Toby's folder, wasn't it? Then you snuck into my cabin, pretending to be headless—still looking for the letters?"

Walker glared at the fire.

"Yeah. I broke in and took the folder. I tried to look like a headless ghost for Mitzi's benefit. I thought it was her asleep in that cabin—it had been hers the night before. But all I got for my trouble was that drivel written by Captain Road Rage. Plus a bump on my head from a flying shoe."

He gingerly touched the bruise on his forehead.

"You thought putting up your collar and slinking around would make me believe you were a dead bandito?"

I was not going to let him know his ridiculous ploy almost worked.

"It was Mitzi's cabin, for God's sake," Walker said. "The collar thing had worked on her before. But why the shell game, Dr. Manners?"

He moved closer to me. I could see blood dripping from the sleeve of his wounded arm. He wasn't clutching it now. In fact, his good hand hung limply at his side. Was something wrong with that one, too?

"Have you and Marvin been working together all along?" He took another step toward my chair.

"Of course not. I only met her when she broke into my room and started rummaging in my luggage..." I turned to Marva. "How did you know I had the folder? Mitzi only gave it to me right before dinner."

"Don't I know it! I was hiding under the old lady's bed the whole damned time. I knew the letters must be in her room, because she had Ernesto's Oscar Wilde stuff that had been in the same folder. I heard about her giving the Oscar Wilde forgery to Plant Smith. The maids must have packed that folder in with her stuff when they moved her from the cabin up to the Hacienda."

"So you were Mitzi's ghost that last time—the one she thought put the folder in her chifforobe?"

Donna sighed. "Can we stop talking about ghosts? I'm tired of the stupid ghosts."

Marva ignored her.

"Yeah. I was there to steal the folder. But she gave it to you. Mitzi moving around from room to room sure did make for one crazy shell game."

"And you have a Burberry coat? In the fawn plaid?"

"Of course. Just like you wore at that fundraiser when you

had that photo in *People* Magazine." Marva turned to Duncan. "Hon, you want to get a move-on with my twenty thou? I want to get the hell out of Dodge."

Walker seemed to be moving closer to me. I wanted to get out of there too. The man terrified me more than any ghost.

Marva waved her gun at him. "Walker, why don't you help Duncan get my money. After that, you can deal with these two idiots any way you want."

I felt my throat close. Marva was going to take the money and run.

And leave us here. With a couple of dangerous lunatics.

Chapter 54—Dead Women Tell No Tales

I TRIED TO KEEP MY expression calm as I watched Duncan unlock a drawer of the old desk and pull out a fat envelope that looked stuffed with cash. Keeping her guns on Walker, Marva indicated to Duncan that he should drop the money into her faux Fendi spybag.

"You're just going to leave us here? I don't think so." Donna jumped up and exploded in fury at Marva. "Do you know how much I paid for this dress? I deserve a cut of that."

She lunged at Marva, trying to take the envelope from her purse.

Marva elbowed Donna in the stomach, flinging her back toward the couch.

Donna grunted and Marva looked the tiniest bit apologetic. "You do not ever want to come at me like that, girlfriend. Special Forces training."

That was when Walker made his move. He had a dagger-shaped letter opener in his good hand. He grabbed Marva from behind, with the dagger-point at her throat. Blood dripped from his gunshot wound, but he had the strength to grip her, pinning her arms.

"Drop the weapons, Marvin. Drop them on the floor now."

The guns made an awful clatter as they dropped on the slate floor.

"Pick them up, Duncan, for God's sake," Walker said. "Do something useful for once in your life."

Duncan picked them up slowly, keeping clear of Marva's big feet. He hung onto the bigger gun and handed the other to Walker.

Walker let go of Marva, weighing the little silver and black gun in his good hand as he pointed it at Marva.

"A Kimber Eclipse. Nice little weapon, Marvin." He turned to Duncan with a condescending smile. "Now this is the kind of handgun you should have bought, Duncan. Not a big cannon like that King Cobra."

"I liked that gun!" Duncan said. "I don't know why you had to throw it inside Plant Smith's car. Nobody was going to believe he'd own a gun like that."

"You threw a gun into Plant's car?" I said. Just when things started to make sense, they fell apart again. "Why would anybody do that?"

Walker turned on Duncan in fury.

"You see what you've done, you moron? You just told them. You told them what you did. Now we'll have to kill them."

Marva stood by the door, rubbing her throat, her expression unreadable. Donna glared at the door, as if expecting to guilt-trip it into producing a *deus ex machina*.

Donna turned to Duncan with a bratty whine.

"Come on guys, I don't have a clue what anybody did to anybody, and I don't know thing one about guns. Let me call a cab. That rental car of Marva's isn't going anywhere with your damned bullet holes in the tires."

Duncan gave a sort of whimper.

"See. They don't know anything."

Walker looked at me and then at Marva.

"These two—they'll figure it out. Why would you try to incriminate Plant Smith if you didn't do anything, huh?"

Donna was still trying.

"So why don't you take us down to the Saloon?" she said. "We've got a car down there, if you'll give me back those keys you stole. We'll forget all about this. What happens in gay-cowboy-land stays in gay-cowboy-land, okay? I'm cool with that."

Walker just growled. His arm wound was obviously giving him a lot of pain.

"About that keychain, Donna," I couldn't let this pass. "How could you walk away with it? You knew my cash and cards were in there." I clutched the manuscripts to my chest, trying to sound calm.

"I didn't steal your keys on purpose, for God's sake," Donna said. "You think I wanted to come up here? Like I'd choose to hook up with a useless geezer when I had a chance to make it with Jonathan Kahn? Do you have any idea what one spot on *The Real Story* could do for my career? Walker said he had a gun and he'd shoot me if I didn't go with him."

"Don't count on Kahn," said Marva. "You'd think in all those years, the Doctor would have taught him some manners, but from what I can see, he doesn't have any."

She gave me a thin smile.

"Some men just need discipline."

"That's it!" Walker shouted. "Everybody into the kitchen." He stuck the gun in Marva's ribs. "Now! Come on, Dr. Manners." He grabbed my shoulder with his bloody hand.

Duncan whimpered. "Don't! Walker, please. You know I hate violence."

"You should have thought about that before you shot that

Mexican boy's head off, Duncan. Nobody would have to die if you had just kept your road rage under control." Walker herded us down a hallway hung with gorgeous Navaho weavings.

The room went dead quiet. Marva turned on Duncan.

"You?" she said. "You killed Ernesto, Duncan? It wasn't Walker?"

Duncan looked exasperated.

"I did not mean to kill that boy. I thought he was the guy driving a Ferrari forty miles an hour while he gabbed on the damned cell phone. A goddam kid. Owning a car like that, and not even appreciating it. When I saw him get out of that Ferrari, I just saw red. It's illegal you know, driving with one of those infernal telephones."

"Yeah, but I don't think it's a death penalty offense." Marva said.

"Especially when the wrong guy got executed." Walker gave a surreal chuckle as he ushered us down the hall. "Duncan killed the wrong guy. Turns out Plantagenet Smith was the one driving and dialing. Ernie only brought the car down the hill for him."

"Shut up! Shut up all of you." Duncan said. "Nobody has to know. The police say a gang killed the Mexican kid and that's that." He stopped as he noticed the blood on Walker's hand. "Walker, your blood is dripping everywhere. Maybe we should get you to a doctor…"

Walker gave him a sneer and shoved Marva with his good arm.

"Get going, you three. Into the kitchen."

I marched ahead, my head pounding. After the dimly lit den, the kitchen light nearly blinded me. Light gleamed from polished granite and stainless steel.

"Walker, please?" Duncan dabbed at the blood on Walker's hand with a kitchen rag. "At least let the girls go? They haven't done anything. Donna's a little selfish, and Dr.

Manners isn't the sharpest fork in the place setting, but they don't deserve to die..."

"Everybody deserves to die. It's the price of being alive," Walker said. "It's either their time or ours, Duncan."

"But it would be such a waste." Duncan gave a let's-be-reasonable smile. "If you shoot them, we'd have to throw away another gun. Do you want to lose this fabulous Smith and Wesson 500? They're back-ordered at least two years..."

Walker gripped the smaller pistol with his good hand.

"I'll use Marvin's gun. Nobody can trace it to us."

"Unless somebody notices we left a few dead bodies lying around the kitchen. Walker, we've got to make it to LAX by 8 AM. The helicopter's fuelled and ready. Do you want to miss our flight because we're cleaning up a bunch of bodies?"

Walker looked at his watch and sighed.

"You're right. We don't want to leave rotting bodies in the house. We should keep them refrigerated." He gave us a grin. "Maybe it's time we showed these three trespassers our newest GE Monogram appliance."

Before I had time to picture what might be in store for us, I heard the sound of a car engine starting up outside.

"There's somebody out there," Donna screamed, yanking open the back door. "Help!" She waved her arms, then stopped.

"Oh, my God — the Mustang. It's moving!"

I ran to the window. The Mustang was accelerating down the dirt road. The trunk wasn't quite closed, and the person at the wheel — she looked a lot like Lucille Silverberg.

"That bitch! That bitch!" Walker screamed, pulling himself up to look out the window over the sink. "How the hell did she get out of the trunk?"

"You left Luci in the trunk of your car?" Duncan said. "How stupid was that?"

Chapter 55—The Manners Doctor Reverses her Position on Cell Phones

LUCI HAD ESCAPED WITH Walker's Mustang. That was something. Maybe she'd go to the Sheriff.

Or maybe not.

She'd have to admit her own guilt.

Walker pushed us on through the kitchen toward what looked like a big steel box.

"Ladies, you must admire Duncan's famous Monogram wine vault."

Duncan opened the big door. Walker motioned the three of us toward it. Now I could see it was a room-sized temperature-controlled, prefab wine cellar. The walls were honeycombed with wine racks and the floor stacked with cases with labels from local vineyards.

"Inside. Now," Walker said. "All three of you."

"I can't," Donna said with a smug smile. "It's all, like,

alcohol. I'm underage."

Walker grabbed her wrist and swung her against a case of Edna Valley Viognier. Donna whimpered and clutched her hobo bag like a security blanket.

"You too, Dr. Manners."

He pushed me into a corner, where I barely avoided falling on a couple of magnums of Laetitia sparkling wine.

Beside me, Donna's phone began to play its little tune.

"I have to get this," she said.

With a roar, Walker grabbed the bag and pulled out the phone. He didn't seem to be able to find the "off" button. The phone kept playing its tinny melody. Finally he threw it onto the slate floor and crunched it under the heel of his boot.

The crunched phone. So that was Walker's modus operandi. Rick probably hadn't destroyed Luci's phone after all. I felt better.

"I hate those phones," Walker said. "Duncan's right. Using one should be a capital offense."

"Will you be quiet about that!" Duncan picked up the remains of the phone with his good hand. "And could you please stop making a mess? You're leaving evidence everywhere."

His hands still gripping his gun, Walker started closing the door of the wine vault with his foot.

"Sorry there's no corkscrew in there, ladies. 'Wine, wine everywhere, but not a drop to drink'...Such an unfortunate accident. You shouldn't have been wandering around looking for booze in the middle of the night. But you were so drunk..."

He gave his terrible smile. "Too bad we're leaving for an extended vacation. They won't find your bodies for weeks."

"Wait a minute, Walker," Duncan said, his voice rising with hysteria. "Let's think this through. This is not a freezer. It's just a cooler. It won't preserve them for a whole month. Do you have any idea what decomposing bodies will do? I'll never get the smell out. I am not going to allow this, Walker."

"You're not going to allow it? What are you, now, my mother?"

Duncan started shrieking.

"I'm calling the police. This has gone far enough. I'm going to turn myself in."

He reached for the phone on the kitchen wall.

With a roar, Walker yanked the phone from its moorings, pulling plaster and hand-painted Italian tile with it.

"Duncan, so help me, if you do one more stupid thing..." He stomped the phone with his cowboy-booted heel and looked at Duncan with exasperation. "What, you can't even close the door?"

Duncan gave us an apologetic look as he pushed on the vault door. It thudded to a close, sealing us into the chilly dark.

Terrible, cold, black dark.

"You are not leaving us in here!" Donna threw her weight against the door of the wine cooler.

"Save your strength." Marva said with a sigh. "That door is steel. A hundred of us couldn't break out of here."

"Why should I listen to you, bitch?" Donna said. "You planned to leave us here with them."

"No, I planned to stop Walker from attacking Camilla with that letter opener. I saw him pocket that thing and start sidling over to her."

I didn't know whether to believe her or not, but that made sense. It would have been easier to attack me than the military-trained Marva.

I felt around for a sturdy wine carton. "Why don't we all calm down and think logically about how to get out of here." I put the folders I'd been clutching on the box and managed to sit.

Marva gave a yelp.

"What the hell is this? I've just been goosed by a giant

champagne bottle."

"Probably a magnum of Laetitia sparkling wine," I said. "I caught a glimpe of the labels before he shut the door. "

Donna moaned.

"Doesn't anybody have a phone? What century do you people live in?"

"The Manners Doctor does not approve of cell phones," Marva said. "So I never carry one when I'm being Dr. Manners."

"The Manners Doctor has changed her position on that." I shivered.

"You are both batshit-crazy," Donna said. "We're gonna die in here."

Chapter 56—Magnum Force

"DUNCAN HAS PEPOLE COME IN to tend his horses," Marva said. "They'll be here in the morning. I don't think we have any chance of being rescued until then, so we'd better keep warm. Alcohol is good for that."

"You heard him," Donna said. "There's no corkscrew. Not that we'd be able to find it in the dark anyway."

"You don't need a corkscrew for champagne," Marva said. "This should calm us right down, don't you think, ladies?"

I heard the sound of tearing metal foil as I felt around the door, wildly hoping there might be some way to open it from the inside. After a muffled pop, I was showered with bubbly foam.

"Elegant," Marva said after a moment. "A nice, lemony mousse. With a hint of vanilla and pear."

She handed me the big bottle.

Maybe her plan was the best one after all. I hefted the bottle to my lips. It was delicious.

I tried to pass it to Donna, but she shoved it back at me.

"I don't want to calm down. What makes you think any stable guys can hear us in here? We're going to die. Why do these Bozos want to kill us? We haven't done a damned thing! And Duncan used to be my boyfriend..."

I reminded her we'd just heard them confess to murder and kidnapping.

"Yeah. I guess." Donna accepted the bottle after all. "Can you believe Duncan killed Ernesto because he thought Ernie was Plantagenet Smith? Ernie died because of that stupid blond hairdo. It so totally did not work with his coloring."

"Actually, he died because Duncan Fowler is a heavily armed two-year old," Marva said. "Poor Duncan. He's always had anger management issues. Walker bullies him and then he takes his anger out on everybody else—especially other drivers. Who gives a gun to a guy with road rage?"

Talk of road rage made me think of Rick and I realized he'd be wondering what happened to us—and his car. He'd start looking...but, probably not here. The reality of our situation fell on me with its full weight. We really could die in here.

"Duncan always wanted a Ferrari," Marva said. "But Walker hates Italian cars. That's probably why Duncan was so jealous."

Donna sighed loudly.

"This totally sucks. Are you two just going to sit here and, like, have a chat fest while we're freezing to death?" She banged on the door again. "Duncan, you bastard! Get us out of here, now!"

Marva laughed. "Go ahead and jump around and warm yourself up, sweetie, but don't expect that man to save your life. Even if he has a modicum of affection for you, he has no mind of his own."

I had another cheering thought. Plantagenet and Silas knew I was here at Duncan's house. Once they missed me, they'd come looking.

Except they were on their way to the county jail and didn't intend to come back until Gaby was released — which probably wouldn't be until tomorrow.

"He was my boyfriend. We have history, Duncan and me." Donna said.

"You were his beard," Marva said. "Can't you see that the only thing that ever mattered to that man was Walker Montgomery?"

"I don't get it. Walker Montgomery is a geezer, and he treats Duncan like crap. Duncan is a pundit, for God's sake!" Donna seemed to be chugging the champagne now.

Marva gave a rough laugh.

"As a practicing dominatrix, I can tell you that most relationships are sado-masochistic in one way or another. Some of us are just more honest about it. Those two murderers out there have been locked in an S/M game for fifty years that makes everything I've done look totally vanilla."

"You're one of those...? You beat people for a living?" Donna said. "That is way too kinkizoid for me. Is that what Jonathan Kahn likes? He hired you to hurt him?"

"No. He hired me to spank him. Camilla here, she's the one who hurt him."

This was so completely uncalled for, I nearly choked on my mouthful of champagne.

"Me? I hurt Jonathan? In case you haven't been on this planet for the last year, Marva, he's the one who cheated — with cheap street hookers, for goodness sake. I never cheated. I adored him!" I did not want to re-live all that hurt and humiliation at this point. What was Marva's game?

"He loved you, too. Still does. Why do you think he hired me to impersonate you?"

"I — have no idea." I hadn't let my mind dwell on that. I wasn't sure I wanted to. "Where's that bottle?"

"Here you go," said Marva, thrusting the cold bottle neck

in my hand. "Jonathan married Camilla Randall and ended up with Dr. Manners. Kind of hard to live up to the good doctor's standards, you know. She's so perfect, she's scary."

"He was afraid of the Manners Doctor?" I took a big gulp of champagne. And another. But as I thought about it, a knot of anger in my belly started to dissolve. "Maybe you're right. Sometimes I'm afraid of the Doctor myself."

"How about a little champagne over here?" said Donna. "I was not a beard, you guys. I knew Duncan had something going on with Walker, but we hooked up, Duncan and me. Sort of. I mean oral stuff. That's what most old guys want anyway, isn't it?"

Donna and Marva giggled, but their giggles had a brittle, hysterical edge. I tried to remember exactly what I had said to Plant and Silas and if it was possible Rick might call them if we didn't show up soon.

"Okay," Donna said. "So Duncan killed Ernie out of road rage because he thought he was Plantagenet Smith. But which one of them killed Toby?" She let out a hiccup.

"Yeah, that's weird," Marva said. "Walker almost sounded like he was telling the truth about that. I can't figure out why Walker would have killed Toby before he got the letters back. Maybe Toby was killed by some gang after all."

"That's stupid," Donna said. "The Viboras would not do a guy with a frying pan. Besides—I probably shouldn't tell you this, but my cousin Miguel—he's in that gang, the Viboras—at least he used to be. With Ernie."

"Are you sure Miguel didn't kill Toby?"

That was the only scenario that made sense to me, if Walker really hadn't done it.

"No way. He was with me," Donna said. "He kept me with him in the kitchen like, two hours after I was supposed to meet Toby—until I promised I wouldn't go through with it. Later, like, after midnight, I got mad at how Miguel was being a control freak, and I got the bottle of champagne and the key out of the ice machine and went to see if Toby was still waiting for me. But... Well, you know what happened. I got in bed with your cop and poor old Toby was already dead."

That gave me a hopeful thought.

"If Miguel is that protective—do you think maybe he'll start looking for us?"

Donna let out a heavy sigh.

"I don't know. I tried to call the Hacienda earlier, when we were in the car, but the only person I could get on the phone was Santiago—you know that Guatemalan kid? He grew up in some jungle talking a weird Indian dialect. He speaks terrible Spanish and he didn't make sense. He kept talking about how he's burning. He thinks he's like, totally in love with me. Hey, is there another bottle of this champagne?"

"Your phone," I said, thinking out loud. "Somebody was trying to call you when Walker took your phone. Do you think that might have been Miguel? Maybe he tried the hospital and now he's worried..."

But Donna only screamed.

"Look!"

A sliver of light appeared in the darkness. Slowly, the sliver expanded as the door creaked open. In a blaze of kitchen light, we saw Duncan Fowler, blood gushing from his nose, a massive chef's knife gleaming at his throat.

The person wielding the knife was Santiago, the Guatemalan kitchen boy.

Chapter 57—The Manners Doctor Rides Again

"SANTIAGO!"

Donna let out a torrent of Spanish as she made a drunken lurch out of the vault toward our rescuer.

Santiago replied in his hesitant version of the language, still holding the big knife at Duncan's throat.

I ran out into the warm kitchen and gave Santiago a grateful smile.

"I don't know how you found us, Santiago, but thank you."

The boy looked confused and frightened as he looked from Marva to me and back again. He said something more to Donna.

"Mr. Fowler, what happened?" I said as my wine-fuddled brain tried to make sense of things. "Did Santiago do that to you?"

Duncan shook his head.

"No. It was Walker." His eyes were glazed and his face and hands sticky with blood.

"Where is Walker?" Marva said.

"Gone. But not before I got off a few rounds." Duncan gave a surreal chuckle. "I ought to be able to shoot out the lights of my own my car. He was stealing it. Let him try to avoid the cops driving with one headlight."

Marva grabbed a dishtowel and ran it under the kitchen tap.

"Duncan, how many times have I told you? That man has no conscience. He'd shoot your grandmother in her bed and call it upholding the Second Amendment."

She examined Duncan's face and turned to Donna.

"Could you ask your guy to drop the cutlery? Duncan's not going to hurt anybody now." She dabbed at Duncan's wound with the towel. "Camilla, why don't you look for a working phone to call the Sheriff?""

"No!" said Santiago, "No *policia*!"

Duncan groaned as Santiago tightened his grip on his arm.

"The land line is out. Walker cut the cable. Took my cell. He didn't want me calling for help."

Marva sighed.

"Donna, tell Pancho Villa here that the crisis is over, okay? He can let Duncan go, for goodness' sake. He's not going to hurt anybody else tonight. Look at him."

Duncan whimpered as Marva tried to clean his face.

"No!" Santiago threatened Marva with the knife.

"What the hell is wrong with this guy?" Marva said.

Santiago spoke to Donna in short, whispery bursts.

Her face went pale. "No, Santiago. No..."

The boy let go of Duncan, who ran to the sink to wash the blood from his hands.

But Donna looked as if she might cry as Santiago continued to brandish the knife and murmur to her. She answered him in hesitant Spanish, then turned to Duncan.

"I hope you can fly that helicopter. He wants us to go to Mexico."

"Mexico? Why does he want to go to Mexico?" Marva looked up from tending to Duncan's injury. "Is this a new trend? Reverse wetbacks?"

My elation at being rescued was fading fast.

Donna turned pale as she listened to the young man's broken Spanish.

"He doesn't want to go to prison," she said in a wavery, childish voice. "He...like, killed Toby. He thought Miguel would let him join the Viboras if he did."

Her face regained her jaded-teenager pose for a moment as she listened to Santiago's hesitant words.

"He thought that since Miguel was my cousin, Miguel would, like, make me hook up with him if he was in the gang."

She gave a sarcastic eye roll before a grunt from Santiago brought the fear back.

"Santiago killed Toby?" I tried to fit the puzzle pieces together. That must have been the news Silas heard before he left. The boy must have confessed to Rick—then escaped somehow.

Santiago spoke with Donna again, his tone agitated and intense. Whatever he was saying seemed to upset Donna even more.

Finally she looked at me, her voice shaky.

"I guess Rick figured out he did it. But obviously, he didn't want Rick to call the Sheriff, so he pulled out his knife and threatened to commit suicide if they didn't make me go to Mexico with him. He tried to get on Jonathan Kahn's show to—I don't know—propose to me or something."

Her eyes filled with horror as Santiago spoke some more.

"Oh my God, then I guess I totally messed everything up by calling the Rancho for help after Marva rescued me. Because then he knew where I was..."

She stopped and took a deep breath.

"Look, I'm drunk and his Spanish sucks, but I think maybe he, like, set the Hacienda on fire. He says he locked them all in something he calls a hole in the wall: Rick, Alberto and Miguel. And started a fire in the kitchen..."

The Hole in the Wall room was right across from the kitchen. I sure hoped she'd understood wrong.

Santiago grunted something at Donna and grabbed her wrist. He picked up the knife again and pointed it at Duncan.

Donna's voice was squeaky now.

"Come on, Duncan, we have to do what he says or he'll kill us, too. You do know how to fly that thing, don't you?"

Duncan nodded slowly.

"Walker's going to pay for this." He dabbed at his wound. "He just left me here alone with the mess. Just because I wanted to call the Sheriff. And we had reservations for *Tosca* at the Sydney Opera on Wednesday!"

Santiago waved the knife as he spoke to Donna again, pulling her toward the outside door.

"Don't call the Sheriff or he'll kill both of us!" Donna said. "He's all, 'if he can't have me, nobody can.' So stand where he can see you." I heard her whimper as Santiago shoved her on the path that led to the helipad.

Marva and I stood in silence at the open door, watching the three of them parade down the path.

"Do you smell smoke?" Marva said. "Damn. Maybe the kid did set the old place on fire. The Rancho Grande is only over on the next hill."

I smelled fire all right.

"We've got to figure out how to get help. If they're locked in the Hole in the Wall—nobody will find them! It has a hidden door." I couldn't bear to think of how helpless the men would be in there.

"I know where the key to that room is hidden." Marva said in a matter of fact voice. "I'm going to the Rancho."

"In your car? That will take forever with punctured tires, if it makes it at all. They'll be dead by then..." I stopped as my voice was drowned out by the roar of the helicopter engine starting up.

"Like I said, Duncan has horses," Marva shouted. "Cross-country is the fastest route, anyway." She reached in her bag and tossed me her car keys. "Here, good luck trying to get that car to move."

"A horse?" I stared at the grinning Marva with shock. "You're going to ride a strange horse over the mountains in the dark? Are you sure that's wise?"

"Wise? Of course it's not wise. Especially since the place is bound to be full of Sheriff's deputies, and I've got twenty thousand dollars in ill-gotten cash on me, but I'm pie-faced drunk, so I'm not likely to do anything wise, am I?"

I watched Marva run out into the night. I could see a plume of dark smoke coming from across the canyon.

On the helipad, the chopper began to rise, a dark shadow on the moonlit sky.

I said a little prayer for them all.

And for myself.

Chapter 58—The Good, the Bad, and the Dentally-Challenged

I MANAGED TO GET MARVA'S car's motor running after a few tries. It lurched a few feet and died again.

I realized I was going to have to walk all the way down the mountain.

In the dark.

In clown shoes.

I set out along the dirt road, flanked by scrub oak and chaparral. With every step, I prayed that Marva would make it to the Rancho Grande on time.

I couldn't read my watch in the dark, but I estimated I'd been walking more than two hours when I finally saw a beam of light through the gnarled old oaks. My feet felt as if they were encased in cement and my whole body ached, but I trudged toward it, praying I was seeing headlights shining from the main road.

The light quickly grew brighter, and I realized it was coming toward me: a vehicle with one light. My head started to pound. Walker Montgomery. In the Lexus with a shot-out headlight. Probably coming back to pick up Duncan after having punished him with temporary abandonment.

I ran back to a stand of oaks I'd just passed. Probably covered with poison oak, but it would be a place to hide. But as I ran, the toe of one of the huge Nikes caught on something: a big tree root. I almost regained my balance for a moment as the car roared closer.

Then I fell forward — into dusty, rocky dark.

◊ ◊ ◊

I have no idea how long I lay unconscious, face down in the dirt.

The first thing that made its way into my consciousness was an unpleasant smell coming from somewhere above my right cheek. My left cheek, pressing against the dust, felt raw and sore.

"She's breathing!" said a familiar voice.

I managed to get an eyelid open, and saw, out of the corner of my eye, a familiar, gap-toothed smile.

My dentally-challenged biker friend.

His face was illuminated by the blue light from the cell phone he held to his ear.

"How soon can you get an ambulance up here?" he said into the phone. "Looks like she took a bad fall."

My palms hurt. So did my head. I tried to roll over. Something covered me — heavy and smelling like leather.

"I'm okay," I tried to say. "The Rancho Grande. There are people locked in there. It's on fire."

"She's wasted or something," the biker said into the phone. "She don't remember nuthin'." He clicked off the phone and laughed. "County Fire has everything under control now. What did you do, fall off that horse?" He leaned down and peered into my eyes.

"I'm okay. I just tripped. These stupid shoes..."

I tried to turn over again.

"Hold it! My brother says you're not supposed to move. You got a head injury, so we gotta wait for the paramedics. Falling off a horse can mess you up bigtime. You gotta lay still."

There was dirt in my mouth. I felt like throwing up. I searched my brain for words.

"How did you find me here?"

"That crazy old lady, Mitzi—she called my brother Daryl earlier tonight from the Saloon, talking about how Walker Montgomery and some airhead took your car keys. Daryl found Mitzi, but not you, and he didn't have the manpower, so I volunteered to check out the Fowler ranch. It's kind of an open secret around here that Duncan Fowler and Walker Montgomery are a twosome."

He adjusted the leather jacket that covered me, and patted my back as if he were soothing an infant. My head felt wooly and his voice seemed to drift away. I almost could have gone to sleep if it weren't for the sound of that siren...

Chapter 59—A Hearty 'Hi-Yo Silver!'

I WOKE ON A HARD bed in a noisy room that smelled of medicine and flowers.

"Hello, darling." Plantagenet stood above me with a huge bouquet of roses. Silas loomed behind him.

"Our cowgirl is awake," said Silas.

I could see Gabriella Moore and Mitzi Boggs Bailey next to him. Mrs. Boggs Bailey was carrying a bouquet, too.

"Are you all right?" she said, giving me a big smile.

But I couldn't answer—or even smile back. My head felt unattached to my body and my mouth wouldn't move right.

"Don't try to talk. You're on some heavy-duty meds," said Plantagenet

"Daryl Sorengaard sent his brother Dirk to get you on his motorcycle, because I called 911," said Mrs. Boggs Bailey. "Daryl answers the phone when I push the button for 911. But only when I use my cell phone."

"A little system we worked out with Officer Sorengaard to keep the 911 line from getting jammed," Gabriella said with a grin. "I set up a button on her phone that goes to the sheriff's substation in Solvang instead of the County 911 dispatch number."

"Alberto—and the others? They're okay?" I tried to sit up.

"Don't." Plant put a gentle hand on my shoulder. "You've got a mild concussion. But they say you're in amazing shape considering you fell off that horse."

"I didn't fall off a horse. I tripped…"

Then I realized—Marva must have made it. She got to the ranch on her borrowed horse and saved people from the fire. They thought it was me.

"Nobody's upset you stole that mare," said Gabriella. "They found her in a pasture near Duncan's ranch—she's just fine."

"The Rancho. The fire…"

"Don't worry about my old place," Gabriella gave a resigned laugh. "The kitchen's in bad shape, and there's a lot of smoke damage in the rest of the service wing, but the Rancho has survived worse. The insurance will cover it. The important thing is that nobody got hurt."

"Nobody?"

Gabriella squeezed my hand.

"Don't worry hon. Your sweetie is just fine. Rick's quite the hero, you know—getting Santiago to confess to killing Toby, then keeping the kid from killing himself."

So if Rick escaped, where was he?

"I rode a horse, too," said Mrs. Boggs Bailey. "Jonathan Kahn and me got arrested by the Indians."

"Jonathan? Is he here? Don't let him take any pictures…"

I pushed through my semi-conscious fog and tried to reach up to my bandaged face. I felt something on my cheek, and something else on my forehead.

"Darling—" Plant looked pained. "I'm afraid Jonathan did

get some video. He was on his way back to the Rancho early this morning when you were riding off after rescuing everybody."

Marva. When Marva was rescuing everybody. She did it.

"It's brilliant footage, actually." Plant grinned. "You look fantastic against the background of the fire. We could practically hear the 'hearty hi-yo Silver.' It made all the morning news shows. You looked so fabulous in that black satin trench with all that décolletage, and those adorable jeweled flats. Dr. Manners is a national heroine. Should translate into a lot more readers for the column."

I tried to explain. "The Doctor was Marva."

Plant squeezed my hand. "Yes, marvelous, darling."

I'd have to explain when my mind was working better. Now it was jammed with images: Walker with his wounded arm, and all those guns. Duncan, Donna and Santiago on their way to Mexico in the helicopter.

"Donna," I managed to say. "She's in danger. Santiago took her…"

Chapter 60—A Cowgirl Hero

"SANTIAGO ISN'T A DANGER to anybody anymore," Gabriella said, giving my hand a squeeze.

"The boy is in custody. He did kidnap Donna—along with Duncan Fowler. Apparently Santiago tried to make Duncan fly the two of them to Mexico in his private helicopter. But Duncan kept circling this area until they ran out of fuel. He made an emergency landing in the parking lot of the Pea Soup Andersen's. Then he confessed Ernesto's murder to a whole busload of Japanese tourists. Real dramatic. Kahn and his crew got that on tape, too."

"A cowgirl hero, a kidnapping and a celebrity confessing to murder. That should put Kahn's ratings through the roof," someone said in a gravely voice.

The curtains that surrounded my bed parted and Rick appeared.

"You're all right!" I tried to reach for him with my

bandaged arms.

"Yes. Captain Rick's all right," Mrs. Boggs Bailey said. "Handsome, too."

Rick laughed. "I'm fine except for this sandpapery throat from breathing smoke. They're keeping Alberto for observation, but Miguel and me, we checked out okay."

He sat down on the edge of my hospital bed.

"I can't say the same for Walker Montgomery. He's being treated for a gunshot wound. And Fiscalini just told me Luci Silverberg has filed kidnapping charges against Montgomery. Seems he kidnapped her from her hotel room and kept her in the trunk of his car for hours, until she finally jimmied the lock open with one of her boot heels."

"I'm sure there's a great book in it for her." Gabriella said. "Now we've got to check on Donna. When she came in she seemed pretty delirious — talking about being locked in a wine vault with two Manners Doctors."

"We need to go, too, darling," Plant said. "Silas has a memorial service planned for Ernesto this afternoon."

Mrs. Boggs Bailey's phone rang from her tote bag.

"Sorry, I gotta get this," she said as she bustled out the door after Gabriella. "It might be Jonathan Kahn. He's gonna put me on his show."

Rick shook his head as Mrs. Boggs Bailey left, eagerly talking into her phone.

"I still hate those things," he said.

There was something I had to ask. I fought the drug fog and managed to make the words.

"Did you really stomp on that man's iPhone, the way it looked in that video?"

Rick shrugged.

"I admit to prying it out of his hand. The stomping was an accident."

He gave me an enigmatic look.

"Did you really let an outlaw biker think he was going to

get an evening of "discipline" from you as a reward for your rescue last night?"

"Not on purpose." I laughed. "He's a nice man, actually." I reached for Rick's hand. "You're not hurt? Really?"

"I'm fine." He squeezed my hand and leaned down to kiss my good cheek. "The docs say you will be, too. They're all amazed at how minor your injuries are after falling off a horse."

He looked into my eyes.

"But that wasn't you, was it? On that horse? The hallway at the Rancho was smoky, but I got a pretty good look at the person who unlocked the door for us. No way are your, um…feet that big."

I laughed, looking down at my chest.

"Right. That was… somebody else. Somebody very brave. But me, I just tripped. An ordinary fall. That's what I am. Ordinary. A wimp. Not some superhero cowperson."

"If cowboys were superheroes, Mexicans would rule the world." Rick gave me his goofy grin. "We kind of dominate the stoic, itinerant agricultural worker market these days."

I thought of poor Santiago, trying to be some kind of cowboy hero, but getting it so wrong.

"Well, it's good you could speak his dialect. They say you got Santiago to confess. How did you know it was him?"

"A bunch of little things he dropped in his conversation — like gang signals that he didn't get quite right — started me thinking he could have done that graffiti in the bar. It looked like the work of a wannabe. Then when he started asking if I had 'permission to court' you, and he told me about trying to get Miguel's permission to court Donna, I put together what might have been his motive. I didn't count on him pulling a knife and threatening suicide, though. Things got a little hairy."

He leaned down and kissed me again.

"But your mystery heroine saved the day, so it's all okay."

"Yes. I wish I could be half as brave as she is."
I wondered where Marva was now.
I hoped she was scheduling her operation.

About the Author

Anne R. Allen is a publishing industry blogger and the author of the hilarious Camilla Randall Mysteries as well as the comic novels *Food of Love*, *The Gatsby Game*, and *The Lady of the Lakewood Diner*. She's a graduate of Bryn Mawr College and now lives on the Central Coast of California near San Luis Obispo, the town Oprah called "the happiest town in America."

Anne has a blog for Camilla fans at "AnneRAllen'sBooks.blogspot.com" She loves to hear from her readers! You can also contact her at annerallen.allen@gmail.com.

Her writing blog, "Anne R. Allen's Blog...with Ruth Harris" was named one of the Best 101 Websites for Writers by *Writer's Digest* Visit her there, or on Twitter, Facebook, Goodreads, LinkedIn or Google Plus.

If you've enjoyed this book, we hope you will consider writing a brief review. It will help others find the book. Thanks!

Other Books by Anne R. Allen

THE CAMILLA RANDALL MYSTERIES: Chick Lit Noir—Smart, funny mysteries with a touch of romance. The first three Camilla books are available in a convenient e-book boxed set.

#1 GHOSTWRITERS IN THE SKY.
#2 SHERWOOD, LTD
#3 THE BEST REVENGE (the prequel)
#4 NO PLACE LIKE HOME
#5 SO MUCH FOR BUCKINGHAM

◊ ◊ ◊

FOOD OF LOVE (Romantic-comedy/thriller
THE GATSBY GAME (Romantic-comedy/mystery)
THE LADY OF THE LAKEWOOD DINER
WHY GRANDMA BOUGHT THAT CAR

◊ ◊ ◊

HOW TO BE A WRITER IN THE E-AGE: A SELF-HELP GUIDE
co-written with Catherine Ryan Hyde

Printed in Great Britain
by Amazon

20296491R00200